STEALTH

STEALTH

Margaret Duffy

This first world edition published 2012
in Great Britain and in the USA by
SEVERN HOUSE PUBLISHERS LTD of
9–15 High Street, Sutton, Surrey, England, SM1 1DF.

British Library Cataloguing in Publication Data

Duffy, Margaret.
    Stealth.
    1. Langley, Ingrid (Fictitious character)--Fiction.
    2. Gillard, Patrick (Fictitious character)--Fiction.
    3. Detective and mystery stories.
    I. Title
    823.9'14-dc23

ISBN-13: 978-0-7278-8210-3 (cased)

All Severn House titles are printed on acid-free paper.

Severn House Publishers support The Forest Stewardship Council [FSC],
the leading international forest certification organisation. All our titles that
are printed on Greenpeace-approved FSC-certified paper carry the FSC logo.

MIX
Paper from
responsible sources
FSC
www.fsc.org   FSC® C018575

Typeset by Palimpsest Book Production Ltd.,
Falkirk, Stirlingshire, Scotland.
Printed and bound in Great Britain by
MPG Books Ltd., Bodmin, Cornwall.

I wish to thank Police Constable Malcolm Webley and his colleagues at Manvers Street Police Station in Bath for their help and advice. Any errors I have made with regard to police matters are mine alone and show I wasn't listening.

AFTERMATH

Yesterday, seemingly, he had killed – murdered – three men. At least, it seemed like yesterday – the memory was still searing into his brain like acid, a drop at a time – but in truth it had happened five months and six days ago. If Patrick Gillard closed his eyes he could still see the barn, one of several semi-ruined buildings near the old Sussex farmhouse, the yard in front of it scattered with pieces of rusting farm machinery and rubbish; old plastic feed bags and filthy straw blowing from one corner to another and then back again as the strong breeze eddied around.

Night had come and, thirst tearing at his throat, he had waited for them in the darkness. Two – another two – were dead already in the house, and he knew that could be described as self-defence. Young, strong, stupid, carrying hand guns, their fingers heavily armoured with rings, they had been ordered to put their guns aside and help the gang leader's minder, Murphy, beat the interloper to death. No one had known about his knife, no one had known that knives could kill so quickly, easily and silently. The two had died.

After he had escaped outside to the barn they – the gang leader Northwood and Murphy – had left him alone to become hungry and thirsty before they began to wear him down. There was a water butt at the bottom of the ramshackled wooden stairs to the loft but it stank and he had not dared to drink from it, catching just a few drops of water as rain dripped through the roof. So he had waited up in the hayloft for the attacks to come. In all, he had reckoned, there were around thirty of the gang remaining.

For the next forty-eight hours the gang had taken it in turns to come in rushes of twos and threes and to begin with he had managed to beat them off. There had then been a pause, possibly while most of those indoors had slept off their main occupation: heavy drinking, during which lull reluctant 'volunteers' had been sent out, one at a time, to watch him, loitering nervously in the *yard, smoking, drinking, ordered to report any movement, signs of weakness or attempts to escape.*

He had killed them, three of them, when it had got dark again. Special Forces training had made it easy. Stealth. They had been slightly drunk, probably drug addicts, as helpless to a professional like himself as the cardboard cut-outs on the indoor firing range where he did some of his training. But he was a policeman now, no longer an undercover soldier. Perhaps he should not have tried to lessen the odds for this had not been a war and they had not been his enemies in the way he used to understand the term.

Murder?

ONE

Five months later

Cannes was cold. Not just cold, also grey, dreary and windy; I huddled deeper into my fleecy jacket and told myself it was stupid to expect anything different as the Mediterranean has winters too. Grumpily, I surveyed one of the marinas, La Panteiro, where expensive pleasure boats were moored, no doubt looked after by skeleton crews while their owners lounged in warmer climes. I had been down for a closer look and found myself profoundly unimpressed by vessels one could only describe as 'plastic', inhabited by bored, hostile-looking people with fake tans, no doubt miserable because they had to stay in this place as they were paid to do so.

Although working part-time as a consultant for SOCA, the Serious Organised Crime Agency, my husband Patrick being officially an adviser, my main activity is that of author. I write crime novels with a smattering of romance under my own name, Ingrid Langley – Langley is my maiden name – and was in the South of France to attend an international writers' festival.

Yes, he's *officially* an adviser. In truth, though, this retired lieutenant colonel was engaged because of his service in Special Forces, subsequent experience with national security and what someone once described as an ability to get the opposition shit-scared. Being a student of the human condition I am mostly a consultant to *him*, a little feminine insight sometimes being required, and he, mostly smilingly, refers to me as his oracle.

Our names are still on several terrorist hit lists and for this reason Patrick has clearance to be armed with a Glock 17, which he carries in a shoulder harness. When things get really difficult I act as back-up with the Smith and Wesson he was issued with when working for D12, a department of MI5. They either forgot about it, which seems highly unlikely, or its continuing presence is a result of what I can only call a little smoke and mirrors activity on the part of the one-time official holder.

The stiff breeze was increasing; even the water inside the harbour wall was spiky with small, choppy waves, and I moved to leave my vantage point. Then paused, my eye caught by a vessel I had not previously noticed, probably because it was moored between two larger ones. It was either dark grey or black in colour and had the kind of lines that reminded me of a stealth bomber or fighter aircraft that are designed to be virtually invisible to radar. Anything more in contrast to the other watercraft was hard to imagine.

I was staying at the hotel, *Les Fleurs*, on the Boulevard de la Croisette, right on the sea front, where the two-day festival was due to take place. This wedding cake-style edifice had recently undergone complete renovation to restore its rococo-style splendour and because it was off-season and workmen were finishing some of the rooms on the second floor the rates had been significantly reduced to lure the organizers of the festival. Otherwise, I gathered, it was a playground only for the very rich.

My room was on the fourth floor and had sea views. The only indication that building work was still being undertaken were the distant and muted sounds of drilling and banging during working hours, plus the presence of a couple of vans I had noticed parked in a small side street. I wandered over to the window, for some reason still thinking about the 'stealth' boat. It was impossible to see that particular marina from here as the view of it was blocked by the casino and adjacent buildings. I turned away and forgot about it.

The festival, small by the usual international standards – described cruelly by Patrick, but perhaps, if I am honest, more accurately, as 'a two-day drunken bash' – did not start until the following morning. The programme indicated that there would be an opening talk by a Norwegian author who had been showered with any number of literary prizes. There would then be a coffee break before the gathering split into groups, when panels of experts – publishers, agents and authors – would debate various subjects and then perhaps answer questions from the audience. This session lasted until lunch. I had volunteered for one of these.

There were also readings and presentations by authors, workshops and, on the last evening, what was described as a 'bookish banquet', whatever the hell that was. Oddly, from what I had seen and heard so far, not many of the French authors one might expect to attend seemed to have yet arrived.

Patrick and I, when not working for SOCA – although my contribution is very modest time-wise – cannot normally attend this kind of gathering as we have a family: three children of our own, Justin, Victoria and baby Mark, and two adopted, Patrick's late brother Larry's children, Matthew and Katie. Even with the essential help of a nanny and Patrick's parents, John and Elspeth, who live in an annex at the rectory we bought in Somerset when the diocese was going to sell it – John is rector of the village – everything non-essential that we might like to do has to be deferred or simply abandoned. The only long break we get is a three-week summer holiday when we usually go abroad for part of the time and take Matthew and Katie, who are quite a bit older than our own children, with us.

However, this four-day trip to France was mostly work of both kinds: a rare outing for the author with a little snooping for SOCA on the side. Not to mention the companionship of a very low-key minder.

The next day dawned wet and just as chilly and drear, the sea as grey as the English Channel, seagulls standing disconsolately on the branches of the trees in a small park near the beach with little prospect of crumbs from tourists' picnics. It was a good day to be indoors.

The previous evening I had set out to dine alone, ostensibly with a book but in fact keeping a watchful eye for anyone I recognized. I already knew that my agent, Berkley Morton, was not planning to attend: 'The South of France is *ghastly* in March, darling. Only oranges and lemons to look at'. As usual, he was right: trees were loaded with fruit in people's gardens. He must have forgotten about the mimosa in flower on all the hillsides which was gorgeous, its scent nostalgic, reminding me of the bunches my father used to bring home when I was a teenager. For me, that is – my mother hated the little fluffy pompoms, saying they made a mess.

The dining room had gradually filled. A few people I recognized: a couple of romantic suspense authors, a retired eminent professor of forensic pathology who now writes historical crime novels, Alan, my one-time agent, who I knew had been severely ill, and two or three fiction editors from library publishers who were huddled together, presumably comparing notes. Then, when I was having coffee there was the arrival of a man with greying, wavy black hair, who had more than a sniff of the dark side about him and who was still a hell of a lot thinner than he ought to be. I had not told him where I would be sitting on the very good grounds that I had not known in advance, but after looking around as if seeking a spare table – there were actually several – he had come over to mine.

'Ingrid Langley, by all that's holy,' he had said just loudly enough so that those at the nearby tables would be able to hear.

'That's right,' I had responded.

'May I join you?'

'Only if you don't have squid,' I hissed.

'Not even snails?' he replied in an anguished whisper.

'*Especially* snails.'

'OK.'

'Delighted,' I had cried.

Patrick had seated himself, still acting. After this first light-hearted exchange, he had become quiet and eaten, sparingly, with no appetite. For security reasons we had arranged that for these four days we would not be Mr and Mrs, and we were not even sharing a room. But by that time the dining room had been emptying and there was no need for over-caution. Nevertheless, he had carried on acting, playing a part, almost like a stranger to me right through the rest of the evening.

I turned from looking out of the window when there were taps on my door in a certain sequence. 'Who is it?' I called, just to make sure.

'Simple Simon.'

I let him in, commenting that it had been a name he had used when we worked for D12.

'It's as good as any,' Patrick said. 'And I know you have a good memory.' He flopped on to the bed, laid back and closed his eyes.

'Didn't you sleep well?'

'I hardly ever do now.'

'Still having the nightmares?

'Yes, but not quite so often. It helped – you writing it down like that for me.'

Then I had printed the reasons for his nightmares and handed the sheets of paper to him. He had read it through and, at my urging, had then screwed it up and, his face grim, thrown it into the flames of the log fire. Home-grown psychology.

'Is there any tea?' he wondered aloud.

'One tea bag, no pot, plastic milk.'

'In a hotel like this, too. Bloody France.'

'How about coffee? Instant, obviously.'

'That might be more drinkable.'

'Look, I thought we weren't supposed to be—'

'I know.'

I filled the little kettle in the en-suite bathroom and switched it on, making no comment.

'Mike rang me.'

Mike is his boss in London, Commander Michael Greenway.

'There have been developments.'

'Oh?'

'She's been found dead.'

'Who, Rosemary Smythe?'

Patrick sat up. 'Yes, yesterday afternoon. She was found at the bottom of the stairs in her house by her niece, Jane Grant. As you know, Miss Smythe was in her early eighties and to begin with it was assumed that she had fallen and it was an accident. But the PM revealed that she'd been strangled. There was bruising to the body – old people bruise easily – that suggested she'd been grabbed and pushed or thrown down the stairs either before or just after death.'

You suffer when you write and my imagination immediately presented me with the horrible scene.

Patrick continued: 'The house had been turned over as though it had been burgled but the Met sergeant who attended started to change his mind as he walked around – had a gut-feeling that something wasn't quite right – and called in his boss.'

The police forces are always receiving letters from members

of the public and SOCA is no exception. Many are from those who write at length on such subjects as imagined conspiracies, malicious gossip involving celebrities, and to report that their neighbours are aliens from Venus. Miss Smythe had had a lot to relate about one of her neighbours. According to her they, or at least, the man of the house, were criminals. She had watched them for months, she said, using binoculars from an attic room and also from a tree house in her garden. The latter had eventually fallen down, with her inside it, and she had broken her left leg and suffered cuts and bruises. Undeterred, she had carried on with her surveillance when out of plaster. The neighbours had noticed her activities and after the woman had taken to lurking in their back garden she had eventually been served with an ASBO, an Anti-Social Behaviour Order. Infuriated that no one believed her, Miss Smythe had started writing to SOCA, in impeccable English too: she was a retired schoolteacher from a highly-regarded girls' boarding school in Surrey.

One of the problems with the accusation was that her neighbour, Hereward Trent – this was leafy Richmond – of necessity a wealthy man to be able to reside in this area, was highly respected, chairman of various worthy committees and generously supported local charities. He had a beautiful wife and two beautiful children and initially had been very forbearing with regards to the cranky old lady next door. But everything had got out of hand and when, after being given several police warnings, she had been caught peering in through the kitchen window one night when someone had left the rear gates to the garden open, he announced that his patience had snapped – to one of his friends who was a very senior CID officer.

All this had somehow landed in Mike Greenway's in-tray, possibly because the senior policeman in question had recently been discovered to have quite the wrong sort of cronies and was now the subject of an urgent internal investigation. One of these associates, some kind of boxing promoter and also a director of a London football club, was known to the police on account of having connections with others involved in serious crime and was not thought to be squeaky clean himself. This web of various people, which Greenway was insisting on calling 'a rats' nest', was exceedingly complex.

My brief with SOCA lay with another of Miss Smythe's neighbour's associates, a successful crime writer, Clement Hamlyn, who was staying in this hotel for the festival. The name was, apparently, a pseudonym: his real identity I had not been able to discover and he had used several in the past, under one of which he had served three years for GBH – grievous bodily harm. I had not read any of his books but they were, I understood, very realistic, or 'gritty', as they say in the trade.

Patrick broke into my thoughts. 'There's absolutely nothing to connect her neighbour with the death.'

'Well, there wouldn't be, would there?' I snapped. 'He was probably in Bermuda at the time.'

'Skiing with the family at Klosters, actually.'

'You were feeling down last night?' I said after a short silence.

'Yes, sorry.'

'Patrick—'

'Yes, I know. I shall have to get over it soon or go and see a shrink.'

After a longish silence, I said, 'What does Greenway want you to do now?'

'About Miss Smythe? Nothing for the moment. The Met's on the case and we'll get the info when we return. We're to drop the travelling separately bit and I'm to move in with you. He doesn't like the look of this crime writer he's asked you to watch and wants me to keep a closer eye on you in view of what's happened. You do seem to have the knack of stirring up mobsters in general.'

I took that as a compliment.

Miss Smythe had mentioned Hamlyn, spotting him at dusk one summer's evening staggering drunk and urinating against a tree in her neighbours' garden during a party, which, judging by loud music and the sound of cars revving late at night, they gave quite often. She had recognized him only because she had seen him on TV the previous week taking part in a books programme talking about his latest publication, a crime novel set in wartime London that included a murder that had taken place in Richmond, not far from where she lived. It was soon to be dramatized for television. This, I thought, could have made an elderly lady feel uneasy, imagining him loping the streets near her house to get the feel of the location. Hamlyn was a giant of a man with a deep, booming voice, a mane of black hair and an eye that was half closed by a scar across his face as a result of a car crash some years previously. Someone, another author, had once said to me, waspishly, that his grim looks alone probably sold thousands of copies of his work and the man seemed to be aware of this and played on it.

His revolting social lapse had not been the sole reason for Rosemary Smythe bringing him to SOCA's attention, although she had seemed to know about his criminal record. She had already reported that he was a frequent visitor to the house next door and usually arrived with a woman, possibly his girlfriend, who she recognized from the television news as a councillor in another London borough who had been suspended during an investigation into allegations of expenses fraud and irregularities concerning council contracts. No, later that same day, after it had got quite dark and she was watching the house through binoculars from the tree house she had seen several men including, she was sure, Hamlyn, in what she had an idea was Hereward Trent's study, handling weapons: handguns, she thought. As if feeling an outsider's gaze on them, someone had wrenched the curtains across the window.

I said, 'I only know the main details of what Miss Smythe wrote as I read a heavily edited version. How many letters were there?'

'At least a dozen,' Patrick replied. 'We do need to look at them in detail. Have you spotted Hamlyn yet?'

'No. Perhaps he's having his meals in his room. Does Mike really think he's going to make contact with one of the Met's Most Wanted hiding here in the South of France?'

'He was linked with a gang when he did time when the boss was a bloke calling himself Cat Danny on account of his burglary days. Danny went on to specialize in the vice trade and drug dealing and eventually fled to Spain. He was sent on the run again by Operation Captura, which as you know we, SOCA, are working on together with Crimestoppers to arrest British criminals living on the Costas. Danny – the name he mostly uses is Daniel Coates – is now thought to be in this area – Cannes. Mike's theory is that he might owe Hamlyn money, his share of whichever scam he missed the pay-off due to having been inside.'

'Does Hamlyn need money?' I asked dubiously.

'You're normally good at criminal profiling. Think about it.'

OK, never open mouth before clutching in brain. 'He would want what he probably regarded as compensation for the time he spent behind bars.'

'Correct.'

'Are you going to search his room?'

'I am.'

'And follow him when he goes out?'

'That, too.'

'I take it he's arrived.'

'Late yesterday afternoon. I had to get the hotel manager on board. Luckily for me his son's in the local *gendarmerie* and he was delighted to cooperate once I'd produced my ID card. I just hope he doesn't gossip.'

'The man might have gone out already.'

Patrick looked pained. 'He hasn't. While you were stuffing your face last night I was watching him in the bar. He drank enough Bourbon to drown himself in and then reeled off to bed.'

'It's a wonder he has enough brain cells left to be able to write.'

'You could always ask him about that.'

TWO

Clement Hamlyn remained elusive, not appearing for breakfast that morning, for the short opening ceremony or the address by the Norwegian author. He may well have been forewarned as the latter was so stupifyingly dull I will not bother the special characters application of my computer in order to type his name. Afterwards, everyone seemed to be drinking coffee and chattering with huge relief. I glanced around but failed to spot the black-haired Hamlyn. Surely he would tower over just about everyone else? I had made sure that I was on the same panel as he was – we were both, after all, crime writers – and made my way to the room set aside for it.

The whole affair was still giving the impression that the visitors to the festivals of Cheltenham or Bath had been picked up, wholesale, and dumped down on the south coast of France. Most of the voices I heard were British, seemingly from every possible region, very few speaking English with foreign accents.

'Are you still giving a reading?' asked a woman suddenly appearing at my elbow.

I turned to see someone I knew to be one of the organizers: slightly out of breath, glasses awry, her long fair hair escaping from an untidy bun on the top of her head.

I told her that I was, at two thirty.

She frantically scrabbled at the papers attached to her clipboard. 'Oh, God, I've got you down for three.'

'No, it's definitely two thirty, with Ian MacBride and Stephanie Blackwood.'

'You are Barbara Somerville, aren't you?'

'No, Ingrid Langley.'

'Oh, oh, sorry. You won't be late, will you?'

'I'll try not to be,' I replied evenly.

'They're complaining already, you know.'

'Really?'

'People always complain. I really don't know why I do this year after year seeing as . . .'

Still talking she rushed off before I could ask her if Clement Hamlyn was still expected on the panel session. To my disappointment, as I had been hoping to find out something about him for the commander, he did not appear. His place was taken by a volunteer from the audience, a young writer who had had two crime novels published, modestly hoped to learn something and, not having thought of himself as sufficiently famous, had not put his name forward. As it happened he was very articulate and amusing and when it was over I congratulated him.

'Thanks – but what happened to the big man?' was the blushing response.

'Size isn't everything,' I told him and went off to look for Patrick, not expecting to find him and more than a little desperate to know what was going on. True enough, I failed to locate him, met Alan and we went in to lunch together.

He looked ghastly, the once tubby and frankly, sleek and self-satisfied man now gaunt and hollow-eyed. Despite his assurances – he has always been a very positive soul – that he was recovering after two major operations, radiotherapy and chemotherapy, I feared for him.

'You're with Berkley Morton now, aren't you?' he enquired after some general conversation, not really eating what was on the plate in front of him.

'That's right.'

'Never did like the man. A whole brass band of self-blown trumpets.'

'You have a point there,' I said, amused by this neat vignette. It was Alan who had helped me immensely when I had first started writing, taking me on when I had not had so much as a short story published. Our relationship had been a slightly stormy one – my fault, especially when Patrick had come back into my life and I was going through emotional turmoil – but Alan had always been able to make me laugh.

'Tell me, what do you know about Clement Hamlyn?' I requested.

'Nothing repeatable in the present company,' was his immediate response.

'Censorship isn't important to me.'

A glimmer of the old gossip-junkie appeared. 'May I ask why you want to know?'

'He was supposed to be on a panel with me and a couple of others this morning but didn't show up.'

'I'm not surprised. He drinks heavily. Probably sleeping off his breakfast.'

'And? Come on, I'm curious. What have you heard through the agents' grapevine?'

Alan took a deep breath and then said, 'That he served an apprenticeship for crime writing in London by hitting old ladies over the head to steal their pension money, acted as a paid thug for a couple of minor crime barons as well as having his own little gang on the side. One of his hobbies is rape, both sexes, isn't fussy. Uses it as a weapon to settle old grievances or as a threat to extort money out of one-time partners in crime. Or if he just happens to feel like it.'

'That last bit was in the present tense.'

Alan nodded. 'But for God's sake, don't quote me as it's rumoured he has admirers, even eyes and ears, in the world of crime *and* crime-writing. I have enough problems as it is without that bloody monster knocking on my door.'

I rather got the gist of that and changed the subject.

The afternoon passed. To a modest audience – true enough almost everyone seemed to be in the bars – I had given the reading from my latest novel, *Death Calls on Friday*, which seemed to be well received, and then attended a debate on the subject of: *Will Ebooks Mean the End of Libraries?* Still no sign of Patrick or Hamlyn. This was not what I had expected at all, the plan having been that I would monitor the author while he was attending various functions and inform Patrick accordingly via my mobile. I had been rather hoping that this would have allowed him some rest, sleep even, and thus go towards enabling him to draw a line under what had taken place at that farmhouse in Sussex. I found myself wondering what had happened to it: the Keys Estate that had belonged to the Woodleys, a long-established local family.

I was also finding it difficult to get the episode off my mind. Commander Greenway had commended Patrick, and he had been cleared by the subsequent inquiry of any wrongdoing. He had been engaged, as Greenway had emphasized, on account of his Special Forces experience for situations exactly like this. What he had done – and he was not to know at the time that the situation would be saved, bizarrely, by the arrival of a rival gang headed by a mobster referred to as Mick the Kick, now dead – had potentially prevented innocent people from being killed or wounded. Patrick knew all this; he had pointed this out at the inquiry.

I went to Reception to discover that Patrick had checked out of his room, not surprising as we had arranged that he should and I had told the hotel before breakfast that he would be moving in with me and asked for him to be given a key. Whatever anyone thought of this new arrangement I did not care: I had not bothered to mention that we were married. Going up to my room I found that his stuff had indeed been dumped on the floor but there was no sign of the owner.

After circulating generally in the large side lounge where various authors had copies of their books for sale – I had declined to load myself down with extra luggage, which had probably paid off as the bars were still heaving, the writers talking mainly to one another, and themselves – I showered, put my feet up for half an hour and then changed for dinner. We have a working agreement that I do not call Patrick's mobile when he is watching and following someone, which I imagined was the case, and was about to break that rule, my phone in my hand, when it rang.

'I'm down opposite the ferry terminal for the Lerins Islands,' Patrick reported. 'Hamlyn's aboard one of the boats on the nearby marina and has been for almost two hours. I don't intend to tail him closely when he leaves in case he sees me but my guess is he'll head back towards the hotel.'

'Did he walk there?' I asked.

'Yes, very fast, like a bull at a gate. See you later.'

I went down, the thought of a glass of wine, or two, before dinner appealing. I am not in the habit of drinking during the day.

Just inside the conservatory bar entrance someone tapped me on the shoulder, hard, and I spun round.

'That bloke who picked you up last night followed me this afternoon,' said, or rather shouted, Clement Hamlyn right in my face, a couple of drops of spittle hitting my cheek.

Heads turned.

'No one picked me up last night,' I told him icily. 'We're old friends and if he happened to go for a walk at the same time as you did then—'

'He's moved in with you though, hasn't he?' the man sneered. 'And as a matter of fact I spotted him, down by the harbour near where I was calling on someone.'

'Perhaps he's a fan of yours,' I said, backing away a little so as to be out of his spit range.

'Don't mess me around!' he yelled, advancing. 'Just tell him to stay away from me in future!'

'You're drunk and this isn't doing your reputation one bit of good,' I said quietly.

I got a few obscenities for this and then he stormed out, thrusting a woman to one side as he did so.

A little shakily – the man looked like something really nasty from *Pirates of the Caribbean* – I organized my drink, found a table in a corner and rang Patrick, needing his presence right now, his bird having definitely flown.

A short and dapper man dressed formally for evening with a black bow tie hurriedly approached.

'Mademoiselle Langley, I am the manager,' he said in an undertone in heavily accented English. 'I hear from Jules at the bar here that there was a little trouble for you . . .?'

'Hamlyn's been drinking,' I said. I had smelt whisky on his breath.

'You are all right?'

'Absolutely fine, thank you.'

'Please let me know if he offends you again. I will not tolerate such behaviour.'

A few minutes later Patrick turned up, quick march, slightly out of breath. 'What happened?'

'He was rather rude, that's all.' I had decided to play down what had occurred and delay telling him what Alan had said to me as my husband has been known to take drastic measures against men who have, to varying degrees, 'bothered' me. 'And he'd spotted you,' I continued. 'Down by the harbour.'

'He must have got off the boat without my seeing him.'

'How, though?'

'God knows. But I couldn't get that close as it wasn't moored by the jetty but towards the end of a pontoon at right angles to it and, obviously, I couldn't stand right out in the open. If he'd stepped over the rail on to the boat next to it I suppose it might have been possible to go from there up on to the outer harbour wall that the pontoon's fixed to at that far end. There are all kinds of huts and piles of stuff on it. But I still should have seen him.'

'The worst thing is that he knows you've moved into my room.'

Patrick's eyes narrowed. 'Then someone's watching *us*.' He got up, went to the bar and returned with a Scotch for himself, another glass of wine for me and for a while said nothing, staring pensively into space. Then he said, 'I've screwed up again, haven't I?'

'No, you have *not* screwed up,' I countered crossly. 'Whoever's watching us spotted you and called Hamlyn on his mobile. Did anything happen that distracted you?'

'Yes, a bloke fell in the water and I thought I might have to jump in and rescue him. But when I got to the edge of the harbour wall I saw that he could swim.'

I gave him my best Mona Lisa smile and sipped my wine.

'Yes, it could have been a ploy,' Patrick conceded.

'Are you getting changed for dinner?'

'I'm not really hungry.'

'Your oracle is about to lose her rag and resign,' I said slowly and through the teeth.

This seemed to shake him slightly. 'Eh?'

'Look, Mike asked you to keep an eye on me because Miss Smythe's been murdered. I *need* you with me and I think it's important to act normally. But if you keep starving yourself like this and get any thinner and carry on beating yourself up about what happened on the last job, you'll either go home in a strait-jacket or by ambulance. I've never seen you like this before and it's really upsetting me.'

He just looked at me, driving me to continue with: 'I know it doesn't make it all right but what you must remember is that one of the men you killed was the subject of a European Arrest Warrant, wanted in Germany for the triple murders of his ex-partner and her two children. The other two were Londoners on the Met's Most Wanted list, again in connection with the murders of women. How many lives did you save by what you did? How many women and children are alive now as a result of it?'

'Point taken,' he whispered.

'Can we find out to whom that boat Hamlyn went aboard belongs to?' I asked the following morning.

'I intend to ask the harbour master about it very shortly,' Patrick replied. 'I'm pretty sure my SOCA ID will do the trick as he must be aware of what's going on in Spain.'

After surreptitiously watching Hamlyn's second night of heavy drinking in the bar until the author had had to be assisted to his room, Patrick had slept fitfully and was now, under my stern gaze, consuming a modest breakfast. Added to my concerns was the thought that although Hamlyn had given us a wide berth at dinner the previous night he would, after what he might think of as yesterday's triumph, push his luck and go as far as to leer in our direction. He would be in grave danger of getting a fist in his crooked and discoloured teeth. Which would be dreadfully unprofessional.

'What would?' Patrick said.

I came down to earth. 'Sorry, I hadn't realized I'd spoken aloud.'

'So, what would?' he persisted with the ghost of a smile.

'You flooring Hamlyn.'

'Yes, of course it would.' Cold-bloodedly he added: 'And the man's far more valuable to us vertical right now.'

'I spoke to Alan yesterday.'

'Oh? How is he?'

'Dreadful. The poor man looks as though he's about to die.' I then related what he had said about Hamlyn.

'You used to know Alan quite well. Is he reliable?'

'Yes. He could be really theatrical and posing sometimes but I've never known him not to be right on the line when I asked for his advice or for information. But please don't quote him.'

'No, that snippet of info shall remain anonymous.'

Patrick's French is passable, the harbourmaster's English was not, and we discovered that the boat in question, *Ma Concubine*, was owned by a British consortium based in London, listed only as Jones Enterprises. Not surprisingly the name, according to Google, covered just about everything saleable, worldwide, from rugs for donkeys to cures for piles.

'I detect Mike's rat's nest,' Patrick muttered as we strolled along the *Allées de la Liberté Charles de Gaulle* on the waterfront.

'I take it you've abandoned following Hamlyn.'

'I haven't, just banking that after the state he was in last night he'll sleep it off until around midday. Then if he goes out or has a meal in the restaurant I'll have a look round his room. But right now I'm more interested in who's watching us.'

'He'd only have had to bribe a member of the hotel staff, someone like a chambermaid, to report our movements.'

'I agree. There might be someone else as well if the bloke falling in the water yesterday wasn't an accident.'

Patrick had been gazing about in casual fashion, playing the tourist, so I asked him if he thought anyone was tailing us this morning.

'There is one person I'm suspicious of. No, don't turn round.'

'OK. So which boat is it?'

'The large double-decked catamaran with the red hull over there.'

'It's right next to the sort of stealth boat I noticed the other day.'

'It is a stealth boat. There have been cases of them being sold for drug-running from Africa to Spain as they were powered to outrun everything else on the water.'

'It might have been Hamlyn's real destination.'

'Well, he definitely went below on the one to the right of it.'

'Shall we stroll down in that direction?'

The man in my life is not stupid. 'There are bound to be people on board,' he said thoughtfully.

'And Hamlyn might have given them your description.'

'Too right. Also, at this stage it would be *exceedingly* unprofessional to start a small war.'

'What did Mike actually want you to do about Hamlyn?'

'You're the one with the mission – I'm here to act mostly as your minder. What did he actually say?'

'He just told me to watch him in the hotel and share anything I discovered with you.'

'Having seen how he seems to drink himself into the ground for most of the time my every instinct tells me he's fairly small fry and to leave him alone and await developments when we get back to the UK.'

Nevertheless, we strolled.

The boats jostled against their fenders in the swell, the water gently slapping against the hulls. That and the gentle chinking of metal halyards against masts were the only sounds but for the seagulls and the distant hum of traffic along the seafront. When we got closer a man appeared on the deck of the catamaran, appeared not to notice us – there were other pedestrians around – and went towards the bow, lighting a cigarette.

'Whatever Hamlyn's come here for – and it doesn't seem to be the literary festival – it can't involve anything that requires a clear head and much intelligence,' I murmured. 'Perhaps he did just come here to get money from Daniel Coates. But just because he's a drunken oaf with a criminal record who can't tell the difference between a tree and a lavatory it doesn't mean he's doing anything other than that here – anything illegal, I mean.'

'No, but being in receipt of the proceeds of crime is illegal and Miss Smythe did spot him in that room where several men were handling guns. He got mighty upset about me following him, too. Talking of which . . .' He turned. 'Ah, it's the little shit who acted as his eyes and jumped in the water.' And louder, 'Are you bored with being dry, Monsieur? Shall we have an action replay?'

The thickset man, some ten yards behind us on the pontoon, every tensed muscle and the expression on his face indicating that he had been about to launch himself at us, hesitated for a moment then turned and hurried away, only pausing a couple of times in order to look over his shoulder.

'That was interesting,' Patrick said.

'D'you reckon that man on the boat is Coates?' I whispered as he watched him go.

'He could be. Coates is quite a small man, only about five foot four and that bloke isn't very tall.'

'Would you arrest him if he was on board?'

'Strictly speaking, I'm not involved in Operation Captura and for all I know he's being closely watched and given the softly-softly treatment, hoping he can lead the law to bigger fish. So, no. But I'd tell Mike where he is if I positively identified him.'

'I think we're likely to achieve more by searching Hamlyn's room than hanging around here. And if it is Coates and he feels he's being watched we might mess up someone else's investigation if he does a runner.'

'Thus speaketh the oracle?'

'If you like.'

'You're right – stick to the immediate brief.'

He took my arm and we walked back. We saw no more of the man who had followed us but I had filed his description in my memory: swarthy, dark-eyed, short dark brown hair, Spanish-looking.

THREE

Clement Hamlyn's room was on the third floor. Patrick had decided not to attempt to search it on the two previous evenings when the author had been in the hotel bar as he wanted to see who he might meet there. But no one had arrived and Hamlyn had sat alone, his dour and forbidding demeanor not inviting conversation. We decided, therefore, that after I had shown my face at various events for the rest of the day we would eat in the restaurant as usual and then I would go in the bar and, in the company of other people I had met for safety, keep an eye on the man, instantly phoning Patrick the moment he left.

Hamlyn, as he had done previously, stayed in the bar all evening and by the time Patrick came into my line of vision in an adjoining room, a small lounge off the restaurant, presumably having completed his investigation, my little group was having a ball, me included. I could not remember having laughed so much for a very long time but had not actually realized how late it was or how much wine I had drunk and only became aware of possible excess when I tried to stand and had to grab hold of the table. Problem was, Patrick would not want Hamlyn to see him in case it caused more trouble, thus drawing attention to himself. Finally, and concentrating deeply, I succeeded in bidding my friends goodnight and made my way, steadily or not, I did not know, from the room. Fortunately Patrick saw the state of affairs and hurried over to catch me as I staggered before I fell flat on my face.

'You're really gorgeous,' I can remember saying, clutching on to him.

'And you're really sozzled,' he remarked with some surprise.

'Only because he stayed right where he was,' I slurred.

He told me the next morning that he had ended up having to carry me up several flights of stairs to our room as all three lifts were not working due to a sudden power failure.

* * *

Solemnly, two Paracetamol tablets were handed over together with a mug of tea.

'Sorry,' I mumbled, setting my head pounding even more.

'I'm not complaining – well, only about lugging you up the stairs, getting a giggling idiot out of her clothes and the snoring.'

'I can't remember the last time I drank too much. I didn't honestly think I was.'

'I can't either. If you don't feel queasy I suggest some breakfast.'

Having something to eat and the painkillers did indeed repair most of the damage and I detected that my husband appeared to be quietly amused by my lapse. I was driven to question him about this.

Patrick chuckled.

'The bloody oracle fell off her golden perch, I suppose,' I said belligerently.

He turned a wide gaze on to me, eyes almost fizzing with laughter. 'That's a neat way of putting it.'

This had implications that I simply could not be bothered to think about right then. I said, 'And Clement Hamlyn's room?'

'The only thing of interest was a large amount of money in the safe, at a guess a couple of thousand euros and around five hundred pounds in sterling.'

'They even let you have the key to *that*?'

'The manager loathes him now. Shit, full stop.'

'It looks as though Greenway's hunch was right.'

'Mike's usually right about things like that.'

'There's no proof that he received the money from Coates, though.'

'No, none whatsoever.'

'Is there any point in staying longer?'

'You have the bookish banquet tonight. Don't you want to go to that?'

I thought about it and must still have looked a bit glassy-eyed because Patrick waved a hand in front of my face. 'Hello?'

'Sorry. I was thinking back to last night. We were taking pictures of one another with our phones. I think I took one of Hamlyn and a woman he started talking to quite late on.'

'You haven't mentioned him talking to anyone.'

'I've only just remembered, haven't I?' I said, finding my mobile and handing it over. 'You get them up. It might be the councillor girlfriend who's in trouble over her expenses claims.'

'Had you noticed her here before last night?'

'No.'

He pressed buttons and perused the pictures. 'All girls together then. Bloody hell, some of them actually appear to be more sloshed than you were. Did you just talk books?'

'That and about blokes, men in general and sex.'

An eyebrow quirked. 'Sex?'

'Quite a lot about that.'

'I see,' he murmured. Then, 'She might be just a tart hoping to be picked up as I know what Hamlyn's councillor girlfriend looks like. She's the woman sitting opposite you.'

I took the proferred phone. 'Surely not. No, that's Alice. She said she wrote travel books.'

'Her name's Claudia Barton-Jones. Did you discuss what your partners did for a living?'

'Some did. I didn't. I didn't even mention that there was a man seriously in my life. Oh, that's right, I did. I said he worked in a bank and was fantastic in bed. Not you, though.'

'Thanks.'

'You know what I mean!'

'Are you sure you didn't say we were married and what my job is?'

'Of course. Look, I'd hardly—'

'But you were canned,' he interrupted, police interrogator-style.

'I can distinctly remember what I said,' I countered. 'Ye gods, I've had enough time working with you for SOCA, plus MI5 before that, to know not to talk about anything like that. And, don't forget, as far as I'm concerned you're just here as an old friend and people can make of it what they will.'

Patrick made a 'peace be with you' gesture that I've seen his father utilize at the end of services. 'OK. Did this woman buy a lot of the alcohol?'

'Now you mention it, she did. She insisted on treating us all to drinks as she was celebrating getting a contract for several books.'

'Could she have spiked them, do you think? Bought shots of vodka and put it in the wine? I'm only asking because I've never seen you drunk like that before.'

'I suppose it's possible.'

'Did you like this woman?'

'Not really. She's rather a loudmouth.'

He went off into a reverie, concerned, I knew, that we had achieved little, having merely established that a best-selling, filthy-tempered and heavy-drinking author had gone to a literary festival, visited someone on a boat that could belong to one of several million people, had quite a lot of money in his room and that his current female friend had joined him.

'I think we should stick it out,' Patrick said. 'And stay until tomorrow morning as planned. If it makes the pair of them jittery and puts them off making contact with anyone else dodgy it's regrettable but can't be helped.' He shrugged.

'It would have been better if you hadn't been seen following him and we could have remained unnoticed,' I pointed out cruelly.

'He doesn't know for sure that I *was* following him. I wasn't the only one down by La Pantiero marina. The fact that he ranted and raved at you just demonstrates that he's twitched. That the woman pretended to be a writer and lied about her name also demonstrates that they're nervous and want to know about us. All we can do in the circumstances is bear in mind what evidence we have: the fairly large sum of money in the safe in his room. Who knows, it may have useful repercussions back in the UK.'

I would have preferred to go straight home to see if we could become involved with finding Miss Smythe's killer. I was also worried that getting the pair of them 'jittery' was counter-productive.

'Are you due to do anything literary-wise this morning?' Patrick asked.

'There's a talk I might listen to,' I said, without much interest.

'I don't need to stand guard on the door, do I?'

'I wouldn't have thought so.'

I went for a walk instead.

Drawn, I went in the direction of La Pantiero marina. But, aware of the need for caution, I headed round to the Quai St

Pierre on the far side and one of the small cafés from where, sitting beneath the awning outside, I could see nearly everything that went on some two hundred yards away across to the moored boats. I had already noticed that the stealth boat had gone, another vessel just nosing into the space next to *Ma Concubine*. Someone – Daniel Coates? – poked his head up from below to see what was going on and then went from sight again. Little else moved but for listlessly patrolling seagulls; the sky was a clear blue this morning but it was still cold.

My cappuccino arrived and I wrapped my hands around it gratefully. I kept thinking about Rosemary Smythe, that plucky lady obliterated perhaps on the whim of serious criminals. Proving that Hereward Trent had been involved would be difficult and I knew it would be just as difficult for me to remain even-handed as I found myself loathing him and his cronies already.

I daydreamed, for some reason recollecting something that had happened not long after Patrick and I were first married. Late for a party in the officers' mess because the car had refused to start, we had arrived when the gathering had reached the stage of playing forfeits. Patrick walked straight into having to kiss the tallest girl in the room. It was not his forfeit but Miranda's, the younger sister of the host's wife.

The forfeit was the wife's idea and I cannot remember her name, only that she was not famed for her charity and kind heart. So there was Miranda, standing bravely in the centre of the room, everyone looking at her, obviously hoping that the carpet would open and swallow her up. She *was* tall, around five foot ten, at a guess sixteen years of age, and was going through the stage of having braces on her teeth and a few spots. Her sister had almost certainly lined her up for the adjutant, who had arrived just before us but had lingered to talk to someone in the hall. He was short and fat, the sort of man Miranda would have found repulsive – no, on reflection, very repulsive.

Patrick and I had greeted our hosts and Patrick was told of his onerous task before he was allowed to have a drink. He told me afterwards that although she was smiling shyly at him her eyes were like those of a wounded deer. And deeply wounded she would have been if he had so much as turned to grin at his colleagues in 'let's get this over with' fashion.

Nothing like that happened. He went to the girl as though being offered the greatest gift on earth, tilted up her chin gently and kissed her. Although a perfectly proper kiss in the circumstances it went on for quite a long time and there were nuances, I felt, that made the enterprise one of beguiling illumination for Miranda. The kiss over, he took her away from her sister and brother-in-law and gave her a gin and tonic, which, come to think of it now, she might have needed. I followed the pair, smiling into the sister's annoyance. Only a few months later Miranda had shed her braces, lost her spots and developed quite a mature attitude to life.

The past. Another country.

'So sad,' said a sudden voice, startling me.

Looking down at me was, I was sure, the man we had seen on the boat. He did not wait for a reply, waved what looked like his wallet and went into the café. Half a minute later he returned with a packet of cigarettes and an Americano – I had still not really gathered my thoughts – drew out a chair at my table and sat down.

'May I?' he asked, feigning that it was an afterthought.

'You already have,' I told him.

'My name's Danny,' he went on. 'And yours?'

'Jezebel.'

'Is that your real name or a job description?'

'Neither.'

He frowned at me. He did not appear to be quite sober.

'I don't allow men to pick me up either,' I said. So this had to be Daniel Coates, wanted criminal.

'Oh, you're far too posh for me.'

'You have a posh boat, though.'

He glanced quickly down at the marina. 'You've seen me aboard? That's where all the money goes, darlin'.'

'Not on tarts?'

'Oh, yes, on *tarts*. But not on high-maintenance birds like you.' He eyed my solitaire diamond ring. It was actually my engagement ring which I was wearing on my other hand having left off my wedding ring in connection with the pretence of travelling alone. Seemingly unattached women tend to learn more when they talk to men, criminal suspects or not.

'So what do you do?' he wanted to know.

'I'm a writer.'

'Here for the festival?'

'That's right.'

'Wanna see the boat?'

'No, thank you.'

He spread his hands. 'I'm not after you, promise.'

'So why *are* you talking to me?'

'I like meeting people.'

Had Clement Hamlyn asked, or ordered, him to talk to me? Told him to get me on the boat and find out, one way or another, if Patrick had deliberately been tailing him? I was factoring in several things: the fact that I was bigger than he was and, when forced to, can run like crazy. OK, we would talk.

'It's been a bloody awful winter,' said Danny after a sip of his coffee, scalding himself.

'You've been here all the time then.'

He nodded and lit a cigarette. I supposed he was around fifty years of age but dressed younger in 'yachty' style: blue slacks, a heavy cotton blue-and-white-striped top worn under a navy gilet, the outfit completed by scruffy canvas deck shoes that had probably once been white. His fair hair, evidence of highlights at the ends, was still quite thick but greying at the roots. I was sure he thought he looked the part: I thought he looked, and sounded, exactly what he was: an east end London gangster.

'That bloke . . .' Danny began before taking another sip of coffee, more carefully this time.

'Which bloke?'

'The writer. Big, scarred face.'

'Clement Hamlyn?'

'That's right. Is he with you?'

'*Hardly!*' I exclaimed.

'No offence, darlin',' he said hastily. 'I thought you two might be friendly, that's all. You know, professionals together and all that.'

'Between you and me,' I said quietly, in conspiratorial fashion, 'he's bad news.'

The faded and slightly bloodshot blue eyes stared at me. 'Seriously? No, come to think of it . . . Go on.'

'He raved and swore at me, saying that my friend had followed him down here to the harbour just because he went for a walk at about the same time. He was really offensive.'

'Wait until you hear this then. He had the nerve to come down here, stepped on board without so much as a by-your-leave and told me I owed him money.'

'And did you?' I risked asking.

'No, of course not.'

'But why would he think such a thing? Marching down to someone's boat in a foreign place and demanding money sounds like the action of a man who's brain isn't quite right.'

'You've got it, darlin', bonkers. He'd been drinking too. And then he got on his mobile, hollerin' in French. God knows what he was saying – I've never learned it. Real bag of nerves he was, looking round as though someone was after him. Perhaps that's what it was, your bloke just strolling about. Perhaps he thought he was a cop. Is he?'

'No,' I said, smiling. 'I'll tell him, but I don't know whether he'll be pleased or not. He works in a bank.'

Danny gave me an empty smile in return and drank some more coffee.

'Being bonkers apart, did you get the impression that Hamlyn might be some kind of criminal then?' I enquired casually.

'What makes you think that?'

'You said he could have thought my friend was a cop.'

'*You* said he was bad news.'

'Yes, but I meant ill-mannered, foul-mouthed and generally rather revolting.'

Silence.

Then, slowly, Danny said, 'Yeah, now you mention it I reckon he *could* be dodgy.'

'Did he threaten you?'

'Yeah – in a way.'

'You ought to go to the police.'

The man did a sort of shimmy in his seat. 'No! No need for *that*! Besides, the French cops are useless. And the bastard's going home tomorrow. At – at – least, I should think he must be,' he amended, all in a rush. 'You know, when the festival ends.'

'Being an author I'm absolutely fascinated by this. It sounds just like the plot for a novel!' I gushed.

'Still don't want to see the boat? You'll get the feel of it then if you decide to use something like it in a book.'

'All right, I will. Thanks.'

He gulped down the rest of his coffee and jauntily led the way, saying with a grin over his shoulder, 'I'll expect a share of the dosh you get for it, mind.'

'Do you know who it was who fell in the water the day before yesterday?' I asked, making my tone light.

He turned. 'No. Did someone?'

'Some bloke or other. But apparently he could swim.'

'He was probably sozzled as well. Some of these boaties live on booze.'

On closer inspection *Ma Concubine*, which appeared to be around forty feet in length, had seen better days. The upper deck and a higher one, referred to, I believe, as the flydeck, were coated in salt spray, this not concealing the fact that some of the metalwork frames of the windows were pitted and corroding. The decking was very dirty and slippery in places with bits of seaweed, plastic and other wind- or sea-borne detritus in corners. At the top of a companionway a plastic bucket held empty wine and whisky bottles and what looked like rubbish from the galley. I got a whiff of bad fish as I went by.

'Not too good on the old housekeeping these days,' Danny said cheerily, heading down into a spacious saloon.

Swift impressions were of curving, upholstered bench seating with a central table. Open to this living area was a galley set high on the port side reached by a short staircase and, forward, two large cabins, or staterooms, as I think they are called. On the starboard side a ladder led up, presumably one of the ways to access the wheelhouse. There were clothes and other possessions dumped everywhere.

'Packing up?' I asked.

'Nah, just having a big turn out.'

I followed him around the boat, not getting too close. The staterooms had their own showers and toilets and could be closed off at night from the main saloon for privacy. They were fitted out practically rather than with extravagance, which rather gave the impression that, having had the thing built, Danny or the original owners had had to economize when it came to the rest. This state of affairs was echoed around the remainder of the vessel, including the wheelhouse, which had been finished in extremely nasty wood-effect brown Formica. I guessed that Danny would not care a toss about the decor.

'Take a pew,' he said when we returned to the saloon, throwing some stuff on the floor to make space for me.

I sat, trying to do the maths. Even if he had bought this vessel second hand and in the condition it was now in it must have cost in the region of a million pounds. The proceeds of serious crime?

And, thinking about money . . .

'You don't want that to go up the vacuum cleaner,' I said, handing him the fifty-euro note that had been revealed near where I was sitting.

'Oh – great! Thanks,' Coates chortled, stuffing it in his pocket.

'This all yours then?'

'Hell, no. I'm in it with some chums. But I've got the largest share and live on board for most of the time. They take it in turns to come out for hols with their girlfriends.'

I found that I could easily picture these people.

'Drink?' he enquired.

'No, I'm fine, thank you.'

'I was thinking of something stronger than coffee,' he added, going over to a wall cabinet.

'No, honestly.'

He opened it, grabbed a half-empty whisky bottle and sloshed some into a tumbler. 'Sure?'

'Quite sure. I over-indulged last night.'

He guffawed, took a swig of his drink and flopped into a seat. I said, 'So what did Hamlyn actually *say*?'

'It doesn't matter what he said for your book, does it?' Danny retorted.

'No, of course not. I'm only making conversation.'

'He thought I was some bod from his past, that's all.'

'On the other hand you might want to drop him right in it.'

He gave me a hard stare.

'It's a crime writer's imagination at work here,' I went on with a light laugh. 'An author, someone like Hamlyn, up to his neck in dodgy dealings or even criminal activity, visits an old buddy who, many years previously, had some kind of perfectly legal business dealings with him. Hamlyn, or whoever, is really short of cash right now and it goes through his mind that the old buddy, who now swans around in an expensive boat, might be a soft touch, or even give way under threats, to a request for funds. That's not a bad plot, is it?'

He carried on staring at me and I suddenly wished that Patrick was not too far away. Then Danny said, 'No, it's quite good. Are you going to do it?'

'I might.'

'No names, mind.'

'You can't, or people can sue you for libel. But a bit of background would help.'

He knew exactly what I was asking of him. 'You hate this bloke, don't you?'

'I don't like being sworn at.'

'What will you really do with the info if I tell it to you straight?'

'I'll write the book – a work of fiction but make sure people know exactly who I'm talking about.' I was beginning to sweat now. Would he swallow this?

'No names then. Especially mine.'

'No. I promise, all different names. Fiction. Straight out of my head, based on what you tell me.'

He got up to refill his glass, his hands a little shaky and then started to pace around. I kept him right in my field of view.

'He's a real bastard,' Danny burst out with. 'He's only been writing books for a few years, based on his time inside and when he knocked around rough in London, Leytonstone. I used to run a garage in East Ham and he worked for me for a while valeting the motors and stuff like that. At nights he used to act as a heavy for some gang boss or other and also used to do a bit for himself on the side.'

'Did he tell you this himself?' I asked, making my tone incredulous, when he paused for a gulp of his drink, and knowing it was not a good idea to enquire who that gang boss was.

'Bragged about it. How many rival mobsters he'd put in hospital. I got rid of him in the end. It wasn't good for business as he used to give the evil eye to the punters. And that was before he was in a car crash. Now he's posing around as a famous writer – well, I suppose he is in a way – but hasn't the money for the high life he's after and is hooked on booze and gambling so what dosh he has goes nowhere. And yeah, he thought I might like to help him out.'

'He could be posing around with high-life gangsters and that's why he can't make ends meet from writing,' I said thoughtfully.

'He is. He said he was big chums with some bod who knows how to make a penny or two the easy way and has a posh house in Richmond, bragging again – just the same as ever – about how he could ask him to send out a hit man to get me if I didn't give him the dosh – some dosh, rather.'

'Did you?'

'What the bloody hell would you have done with this ugly great bastard towering over you? Yes, I did – to get rid of him. But not as much as he wanted.'

I suddenly remembered what Alan had told me, how Hamlyn used the threat of rape, either sex, not fussy. I did not have the courage to ask, saying instead, 'You said he'd been drinking.'

'The man was always half canned.'

'Will you be safe now?'

'I might just head for St Tropez. You just have to stay one step ahead, don't you?'

For one nanosecond I actually felt sorry for him. 'Richmond, though!' I exclaimed. 'That's a very upmarket area of London.'

'Apparently this bloke's living a whiter than white lifestyle giving to charity and all that crap. But really he's involved in a mega-business with drug-running plus money laundering through other schemes.'

'Did you get this man's name?'

'Nah. Better not to know.'

Concerned that he might be seriously regretting telling me all this and try to stop me leaving in permanent fashion I got to my feet, saying, 'As far as the book goes I don't know you. I've never been here.' Then, on deck, I gestured towards the newly-arrived motor yacht. 'You have new neighbours.'

'Thank God,' the man said fervently. 'The stealth boat was all part of the threat. Just called in to breathe down my neck. Hamlyn said it's part of that Richmond geezer's empire.'

'Did you believe that?'

'At the time I did. But he was always a liar.'

My fears might have been realized then as he immediately turned and hurried below. My cursed writer's imagination presented me with a view of him getting a firearm of some kind from one of the wall cabinets with which to erase his indiscretions. I have never felt more defenceless than I did walking away from that boat.

As I hurried by the doorway of a nearby shop that had closed for lunch, a voice said, 'Learn anything?'

'Yes, and I'm freaking out right now that he might be about to shoot me in the back,' I replied, appalled to hear the sob of pure fright in my voice.

'Just carry on and I'll walk a short distance behind you, spoiling his aim,' Patrick said calmly.

FOUR

After being in receipt of a short but to the point husbandly lecture on the inadvisability of what I had done, I gave Patrick an account of what had been said on *Ma Concubine*, practically verbatim. As he himself had said, I have a good memory and intended to write it down for reference purposes.

'I'm staggered that he told you so much,' was Patrick's first comment.

'I don't think it was his first drink of the day – and of course he loathes Hamlyn even more now.'

'Mike'll give you a gong. But you took a hell of a risk.'

'Just stay right by my side for the rest of the time we're here, please.'

'I will. Some of the things he said: running a garage, Hamlyn working for him valeting cars and looking him up in a casual way because he needed money have to be discounted. I rather admire the guy for thinking on his feet like that. But why did he start talking to you in the first place?'

'Loneliness? Full of grievance after having had to part with so much money, possibly a large chunk of available funds and unconsciously wanting to tell someone about it? Needing female company? There didn't seem to be any evidence of another person on board. He admitted spending money on tarts.'

'I have to confess that I don't know whether to get the police on to him or not.'

'Phone Greenway.'

This he did. The commander responded by saying that he would relay the information to those SOCA personnel involved with Operation Captura and would mention to them that if Coates left Cannes he could well head for St Tropez. We were to forget about him, although, in view of what he had told me, exercise all due caution as he had a record for committing firearms offences. Greenway then went on to say that he would like us to attend the banquet that night in order to observe Clement Hamlyn, assuming that he would attend, and then return to the UK, as planned, early the following morning.

Still not happy about being in a position to openly watch this man I urged caution, whereupon Patrick said he would think of something.

We duly presented ourselves – slightly pretentiously it was black tie – at the appointed hour, seven thirty, my companion succeeding, I thought, in not looking like a minder. There appeared to be far more people in the large, quaintly old-fashioned but sumptuous dining room than had attended the conference during the past couple of days, but I then remembered that we had been promised the presence of various *glitterati literati* for this final evening. I recognized no one and it made me feel out of touch and hopelessly provincial.

'Why should you know who they are? They probably all run bookshops or write very bad poetry for the local rag,' Patrick declared robustly when I had voiced my gloom. All the ex-choirboys I have ever known possessed a carrying sort of voice and this one is no exception.

'There's Hamlyn,' I said, spotting the man on the far side of the room.

Patrick took a couple of glasses of orange juice from a

waitress's tray and handed one to me. 'So it is. Heading straight for the bar too, so there's a surprise. Keep close.'

We set off through the throng that was packed into the space surrounding the long table laden with flowers, glassware and silver cutlery – plated, I had a surreptitious look – in the centre of the room, this particular author wondering how closely he intended to 'observe' his quarry. Fairly snuggly, by the look of it. There was also the possibility that the foray was nothing at all to do with work but merely the action of a man furious with someone who had hurled obscenities at his wife. I felt a regrettable *frisson* of girlish excitement.

The bar was extensive, a curving affair taking up one whole corner of the room with a small section at one end reserved for serving coffee. It was furnished with several small tables and dinky little chairs, at one of which Hamlyn was sitting, uncomfortably, a large whisky in front of him, accompanied by the woman who had introduced herself to me as Alice but Patrick was convinced was Claudia Barton-Jones. He leaned on the nearby bar, drank half his juice, dumped it down on the counter and subjected the writer to a steady stare. There is a good repertoire of these, ranging from amused curiosity at one end of the scale through open derision to penetrating malevolence at the other. I was standing next to him, but on the leeward side, so could only guess which particular one had been selected. At a guess it was the second most likely to hit the mark.

But I was wrong, completely, utterly and absolutely wrong.

'Do I know you?' the author enquired heavily.

Patrick cleared his throat and when he spoke it was hesitantly with a mid-West American accent. 'I just wanted to apologize to you, Mr Hamlyn. I mean, for the other day. When you – you thought I was tailing you, kinda lurking around. But I wasn't. I don't do things like that. Folks from where I come from know how important privacy is to important people like yourself.'

Hamlyn's face sort of cracked into an expression that had every possibility of being a smile. 'That's all right. I have to say though that when I first saw you I did imagine you might be after my wallet. That was before I learned that you were Miss Langley's – er – friend.' Here he looked right through me. 'Is that all you wanted to say?'

'Gee, y-y-yes,' Patrick stammered. He turned and hurried away. I had no choice but to follow.

'Remind me to lift his wallet before he goes,' Patrick said under his breath, handing me a glass of wine.

'Well, you already have in a way and that was quite the right thing to do,' I soothed, giving him one from the same tray while really, really needing to give Alice's/Claudia's smirking face a good smack.

'Damn the man – but I was hoping he'd come out of his shell a bit. We might have learned something.'

'I don't think we would have done. Just call it damage control.'

'But did he swallow it?' Patrick persisted. 'Be honest.'

I gave it thought. 'No, possibly not.'

We spent a fruitless evening. Hamlyn and the female went from sight so either ate at a nearby restaurant or in their room. Patrick slipped back into his role of escort to medium famous novelist, chatted to all and sundry, applauded the speeches, even a closing one from the interminable and impenetrable Norwegian author and we finally got to bed at just after one a.m.

'Look, I don't expect every moment of your time working for me to be loaded with incredible breakthroughs and mass arrests,' Commander Michael Greenway said after Patrick had voiced his general disappointment in the results of our mission.

Greenway is head of the small team of which we are peripheral members. As we work directly for him and are not part of day-to-day enquiries we rely on him, or his assistant, Andrew Bayley, to give us the latest findings and it is vital that nothing we do interferes with the team's investigations. This means that we are on first-name friendly terms with them but hardly ever confer unless it is during a general meeting. This is just as well and I am sure a deliberate move on SOCA's hierarchy's part, who are no doubt worried that some of Patrick's MI5-style methods of working might prove dangerously catching.

'I'm actually very interested in what you did discover,' the commander continued. 'To re-cap, you saw Hamlyn going on board a boat belonging to Daniel Coates, a wanted mobster – he's left Cannes, by the way, and they're watching out for him in St Tropez – who gave him money, or at least said he did, a large amount of which was in Hamlyn's room safe. I think we can gold plate that even though it might not stick in court. Coates also revealed that Hamlyn bragged to him that he was associated with a man who lives a whiter-than-white life in Richmond. That has to be Hereward Trent. Hamlyn's been seen at his house. That's real evidence. The woman, Barton-Jones . . . are you sure it was her?'

'Around ninety-nine per cent sure,' Patrick answered.

'But as she called herself Alice when talking to Ingrid, and others, she must have been travelling incognito. Why?'

'Perhaps because she has a husband. I seem to remember reading it in a newspaper article in connection with her being investigated for expenses irregularities. He's something in the City.' Then, to me: 'Did she mention him that evening?'

I shook my head, loving him to bits for not adding: 'You got stoned.'

Greenway said, 'Coates came up with quite a lot, didn't he? Even if we factor in the possibility of Hamlyn being all mouth and not much substance he did tell him that Trent, or rather someone we must assume is him, has a drug-running business and associated money laundering schemes, which I'm inclined to believe.'

'I think we still have to treat any information from Coates as potentially iffy,' I cautioned.

This Greenway acknowledged.

'What does Trent do legally for a living? Do we know that?' I asked.

Patrick said, 'He's boss of a small chain of car dealers, mostly located in the wealthy London boroughs. Top-of-the-range stuff.'

'I find it a bit of a tall story that the stealth boat was all part of the Trent empire and had been sent into port to put the fright-eners on Coates,' Greenway commented. 'And Coates did say that he didn't think Hamlyn was sober.'

'Well, the boat was there,' Patrick said. 'And left, shortly before Ingrid went on his catamaran. But, as you say, Hamlyn could have made that up in order to put extra pressure on Coates to give him the money.'

'Or *some* money, as he corrected himself,' I added. 'A rather obvious lie. It must have been, as was first suggested by you, Mike, a debt for services rendered sometime in the past.'

'And Miss Smythe appears to have paid the price for her public spiritedness,' Greenway mused. 'God, how I hate these bloody mobsters.'

London was warm with bright sunshine, a contrast to central France which, when we had flown over the country very early that morning, had been white with overnight frost. The commander had met us at a little bistro around the corner from SOCA's HQ, saying that he was desperate to get out of the office.

He went on: 'The Met were delighted to hand over everything in connection with the Rosemary Smythe case and let us handle it as now there's a strong link to organized crime. They've absolutely nothing on Hereward Trent, not even points on his licence for driving offences, but of course Records is much more useful when it comes to Hamlyn and Coates. The pair of you need to acclimatize yourselves with all that info and then read the letters that Miss Smythe wrote to us over a period of several months before you do anything else. Then we'll have another get-together. But keep me right in the picture.'

We decided to work from home. Other than a hard copy of the Met's file – the case had been handled by a DI Branscombe – which Greenway had arranged to be printed off for us, plus handing over the keys to Miss Smythe's house, all the information and things we needed could be gleaned from various password-protected police websites. Patrick also has access to most MI5 files, hardly any of which, needless to say, were relevant or, for that matter, available on the Internet. Provided one has clearance they may be viewed at appropriate establishments. This being likely to take far too long – he was keen to discover what, if anything, was known about Trent by the security services – Patrick suggested, before we headed west, we pay a visit to a man who, with regard to what can loosely be described as national security is known by insiders as the keeper of all grapevines. That was if he was free to see us.

Colonel Richard Daws, 14th Earl of Hartwood – although he does not use his title for everyday matters – at one time Patrick's boss at D12, the department we used to work for in MI5, had been one of the chief advisers when SOCA was first set up. He still works one or two days a week in this capacity and when in London stays at a small apartment he has retained in Whitehall. As it happened he was neither there nor in his office on the top floor of the SOCA building but on his way to give evidence at a parliamentary committee meeting. If we cared to meet him at his club afterwards . . .

'If he's successfully chewed up the committee he might treat us to lunch,' Patrick said, having also relayed to me Daws's rather open-ended final remark.

As I am married to one I did not need to be told that senior army officers, both serving and retired, tend to loathe politicians of all hues. I also knew that the club in question was quite close to the Houses of Parliament, being situated just off Smith Square, and was glad the pair of us had decided to dress fairly formally for travelling as we were reporting to HQ.

We had a fifteen-minute wait for Daws in a tiny visitors' lounge at the club before he breezed in. I could not say that I had ever seen him breeze before and could only assume that he had had a very satisfactory morning. He looked hardly any older, his once-fair hair now grey but still with a tendency to flop over his forehead so he had to scoop it back with one hand – a lifetime's gesture.

'Good, you made it,' was all he said to begin with, giving us a swift appraising glance while shaking our hands.

We followed him up a wide, deeply-carpeted staircase to a broad landing where he buttonholed one of the stewards.

'Anywhere quiet where we can talk, Edwards?'

'There's no one in the Lord Nelson Bar at the moment, sir.'

We went in and sat down. Daws ordered drinks from the same steward who was discreetly hovering and there was a little silence. I reminded myself that this man, who emerged from early retirement at his family seat, Hartwood Castle, to take up his part-time post, has in the past treated Patrick very harshly, even to the extent of having had him 'tested' by a group of Royal Marines to see if he was fit, both mentally and physically, for the job being offered to him by D12. Strictly speaking he had not been but as the Marines caught up with him at my cottage on Dartmoor he had had very minor rein-forcements: a poker and me. After a short but bloody war in the barn we had sent them on their way with one broken wrist, a couple of broken noses and several split lips.

Patrick and I have been married twice, the newly published author finally ridding herself of the insufferably superior and arrogant man her husband had become after one last, huge row. The divorce papers had come through when he was serving with Special Forces just before an accident with a hand grenade had resulted in him sustaining severe injuries. Eventually, the lower part of his right leg had had to be amputated and he is now active thanks to a man-made substitute with a tiny internal computer and lithium batteries that cost roughly the same as a medium-sized family car.

I have never been able to walk past an abandoned kitten or a dog with a thorn in its paw and when this man I had divorced not all that long ago had turned up on my doorstep, limping badly and still very weak in those early days before the pins in his right leg had failed, I had found the situation quite unbearable. He told me that he had been ordered to find a female working partner as, initially, much of the job would involve watching people at social occasions and official thinking was that lone men were conspicuous. With that in mind he admitted he had turned to the only woman with whom he could guarantee to get on well with in public – we always had. Far more importantly, I discovered later, was the need to find someone who would not want to sleep with him, all confidence regarding that having been lost due to his injuries.

Still dizzy with excitement from the set-to in the barn I had hardly hesitated and accepted his offer, telling myself I would probably scoop a lot of material for my next novel – and hey, who the hell wants to write romance when crime and spying now grew on trees?

After my rose-tinted glasses had fallen off it had been very difficult: Patrick frosty, in a lot of pain, even more so after the battering the Marines had given him and wondering if I could be trusted for, after all, this was the person who had thrown his classical guitar down the stairs during that last row, smashing it. I had subsequently felt very guilty about that, apologized the following morning and offered to buy him a new one. Not necessary, he had informed me, he had already done so and the original had only been a cheap one he had bought in a charity shop to learn on. Slowly, the magic that had been in our early relationship returned and, not long afterwards, we threw the sleeping together problem out of the window.

But for some of this trauma, especially causing Patrick extra suffering, I still blamed Daws.

There was some polite conversation about our family – seemingly he had kept abreast of everything about us, even the birth of Mark – and I reciprocated with questions about the castle garden as I know growing roses is practically an all-consuming hobby of his. He then invited us to have lunch with him, which we accepted.

'Quite soon you'll be working for the National Crime Agency,' Daws went on to say. 'As you probably know, SOCA's being swept up in its creation. There'll be a lot more power for you.'

'And as a result of that a lot more aggro from cops in the Forces,' Patrick commented.

'Shouldn't be. Tact, that's all it takes.'

Using commendable tact, Patrick said, 'And you, sir? What do you think?'

'It'll probably work. That's if they don't mess around with it again in another four or five years. Working on anything interesting? Is that what you wanted to see me about?'

'Hereward Trent,' Patrick said quietly.

When engaged in socializing and working undercover, the latter of which I understand he still does sometimes, Daws utilizes the persona of a genial old duffer and that was what we had mostly seen up until now. Underneath, the real man, that part of him that I distrust, if not dislike, is like polished steel. We got a glimpse of this now.

'Never heard of him.'

Patrick merely smiled politely.

'No,' Daws said with an air of finality. 'What do you have on him?'

'His neighbour's been murdered. She wrote to us several times to tell us that she'd been watching him and visitors to his house and in her opinion he was a criminal. I don't yet have the full details of what she said as we've only just come back from France and it happened while we were away.'

'And?'

'Ingrid spoke to a wanted man in Cannes, Daniel Coates, who said that someone who lives in a big house in Richmond living an outwardly respectable life is heavily involved in serious crime. That's almost certainly Trent.'

'Evidence?'

'Information courtesy of Clement Hamlyn, a crime writer.'

'I think I've heard of him. Yes, suspect kind of fellow, been to prison – a fact he seems to think warrants admiration.'

'That's him. Hamlyn went to France under cover of attending a literary festival that finished last night. There's very strong evidence to suggest that the real reason for his trip was to get money that he reckoned Coates owed him. Ingrid spoke to Coates, who said Hamlyn shot his mouth off. There was a stealth boat moored next to Coates' catamaran that Hamlyn said was part of the mobster's empire and there to intimidate him into paying up. That may or may not be true but as you must be aware, these craft have been used for drug-running.'

Daws nodded slowly. 'This is now your case?'

'As of an hour or so ago but we were already monitoring Hamlyn. The Met's given everything they have on the neighbour's murder to Commander Greenway.'

'I told Greenway it would take fifteen years off his life, employing you two.'

'I do believe he mentioned that to us, sir.'

'I'll see what I can find out about this Trent character.'

We lunched, talking of past cases, the protagonists – some of which Daws was keen to update us on – and more general matters.

As we were parting Daws spoke softly. 'You sailed a bit close to the wind with that last job.'

'I know,' was all Patrick said.

'It was them or you.'

'Yes.'

'If you'd left to get help and the police had arrived shortly afterwards, before those other mobsters turned up, there would have been a bloodbath – theirs.'

'Yes.'

'If the gang had succeeded in killing you there would have been the same result.'

'That's right.'

'I happen to know you're feeling guilty about it.' When he got no response Daws continued: 'A gurkha has recently been awarded the Conspicuous Gallantry Cross for taking on thirty Taliban single-handed in Afghanistan and killing or wounding the lot. You're hard-wired to be a soldier, nothing's going to change that, and you took on over thirty mobsters, who in my view were drugs- and drink-soaked vermin, single-handed, most of whom were arrested shortly afterwards and a few killed or wounded. I wanted you for the job for that very reason. Get over it, Patrick!'

When we were outside on the pavement Patrick said pensively, 'Leopard, non-changing spots, for the use of?'

I gave him a hug. 'Some leopard.'

Obviously, we could not arrive at home after an absence, unpack work-related impedimenta and just get on with it. For one thing there was a deluge of delighted young people demanding our attention, parents to hear all the latest news and gossip from, a nanny to give one of the presents – perfume – to, baby Mark to cuddle, not to mention checking that George, Patrick's horse and Fudge, Katie's pony, kept at livery, were well. The two kittens: Pirate, called after her predecessor, and Patch, her brother, had put themselves right at the head of the queue by having to be lifted down from the lower branch of a tree growing over the drive where they had been precariously teetering.

Finally, and of course reluctantly, we started work shortly after breakfast the following day. Patrick hates sitting reading files and I knew he would much rather be parked somewhere in the vicinity of Clement Hamlyn's house, watching him, but that was not an option until we had more information.

We started with the letters to SOCA from Miss Smythe. The first dated back almost a year. At first, she related in her neat hand, there had been events that although in her opinion were serious they were not the kind of thing with which she would normally bother a national crime organization. Her neighbours' visitors had been firing an air pistol in their garden, supposedly at a target but also at birds and someone's cat which had been hit and seriously injured.

Everything had taken a more serious turn one summer's evening when she had been reading in her tree house, which she admitted was the only way *anyone* could see into the neighbouring garden as it was otherwise very secluded. She had happened to lift her eyes from her book to glance across to the house next door. Several men were on the patio just outside the French doors and, although her view was partly obscured by foliage, she could see that they were unpacking what looked like rifles and handguns from a wooden case. There were also small boxes that she guessed contained ammunition. One man had paraded across the lawn, playing soldiers with one of the weapons over his shoulder. That was not the only time she had witnessed men handling guns on her neighbour's property, the second occasion being that with which I was already familiar, occurring in Hereward Trent's study.

The rest of the information was slightly repetitive, especially concerning nocturnal comings and goings and more than one visit by Clement Hamlyn, whose girlfriend, Claudia Barton-Jones, had once gestured to Miss Smythe with two fingers when the two women had happened to see one another at the front of the two houses. Barton-Jones had been with Hamlyn, who had roared with laughter. After this, I could not help but feel that the elderly lady had become obsessed about these people and could hardly blame her, especially after she had been hurt when the tree house collapsed. It was after this, when she had recovered, that she had taken to watching them through binoculars, venturing into their back garden.

Highly relevant I felt was Rosemary Smythe being convinced one night – before the tree house collapsed – that someone was in her own garden and being deeply afraid that they were out to silence her. This was in the third letter from the last. The very last was a résumé of all that had happened so far, ending with her regret that nothing seemed to have been done about it and that she hoped to be able to provide more proof.

'But surely there would have been official replies,' I said. 'These wouldn't just have been ignored.'

'Just acknowledgements, I expect,' Patrick said quietly. 'The usual "Thank you, your comments have been noted", kind of crap.'

'Patrick, I really get the impression that, towards the end, after she thought someone was lurking outside just before the tree house collapsed, this woman became terrified. She doesn't actually say so but, somehow, it's there.'

'OK, I suggest you write a précis, buff up on the police case notes and this pathologist's report when I've finished with it. I'll read the letters and when we've really done all our homework by also going through Clement Hamlyn's and Daniel Coates' criminal records we'll head back to London and take a look at Miss Smythe's house.'

'And she was still working on it, wasn't she?' I persevered.

Patrick nodded soberly. 'Looks like it.'

The work – altogether there was a lot of it – and in between necessary family matters, never mind eating and sleeping, took another thirty-six hours. But I was content for I had written not just a précis of the letters but also clarified the Met's report on the murder inquiry so far, it being thorough but the English lumpy in places, the kind of thing that I knew irritated Greenway. I appended my version to the original because of course it could not replace it, having been endorsed by senior officers.

DI Branscombe had noted that although the killer had apparently endeavoured to make it look like a break-in, he, or she, had not found the two hundred and fifty pounds or so concealed in one of a pair of Chinese vases in the living room, which would have been one of the first places a professional burglar would have looked. Drawers under the murder victim's bed had been pulled out, the contents scattered but more money hidden between the pages of an old photograph album had not been discovered. Branscombe thought whoever had killed Miss Smythe had then hurried around the house knocking a few things over, opened most drawers and cupboards, pulled out the clothes and other possessions within on to the floor, ransacked a jewellery box, scattering the contents, and then made their escape through the back door, which had been forced to gain entry and left open. The niece was fairly convinced that a few of the best pieces of jewellery were missing but had pointed out that her aunt may have given them away or put them in a bank. The DI emphasized that one of his priorities had been to try to discover the truth behind this but, so far, he had got nowhere. If SOCA had no objection, and he himself had the time, he would continue working on this aspect of the case as he had a contact who knew the whereabouts of several fences.

As was routine, the murder victim's clothing and various samples taken by scenes of crime personnel in the house had been sent to a forensic laboratory, but it would be a while yet before any findings were known. The murder victim had apparently employed a cleaning lady, who must have been dedicated in her work as early results showed that the only clear fingerprints found, so far, were hers, those of her employer, Miss Smythe's niece and those of a friend, another elderly lady, who had all been eliminated from the investigation. But work was still underway as the house was quite large and there were signs of disturbance in every room but the attics. No doubt delighted to be able to give away the greater part of one of his cases, Branscombe had attached a note to the file assuring Commander Greenway that all outstanding forensic reports would be sent directly to him.

FIVE

The view from Richmond Hill along the River Thames to distant Windsor is preserved by an Act of Parliament and regarded as an icon of beautiful English scenery. This might have been the attraction when she retired for Rosemary Smythe who, we were shortly to discover from her niece, Mrs Jane Grant, had taught English and art. She had been a Londoner by birth having been brought up in nearby Mortlake, an only child who had inherited more than modest wealth on the slightly premature death of her parents. She had not taken early retirement on the strength of this and I could imagine her, having begun to understand her character from reading the letters, feeling that it would be selfish to abandon her young charges for this reason.

The house, one of a terrace in a quiet side street, was obviously still a crime scene, traffic cones preventing the general public from parking their cars across the entrance, incident tape around railings and lamp posts creating a cordoned-off area. This meant that our movements would probably be limited within the house whether people were working in the rooms or not. We discovered that they were, with a constable standing outside, the DI having undertaken to carry on providing that kind of backup while scenes of crime personnel were still on the premises.

It was a Victorian house on three floors if one counted the attics, and as one might expect from the late owner's neat hand-writing, the windows sparkled and the dark blue paintwork of the front door was immaculately clean. There were beds of pink and pale blue and white striped pansies bordered by a Lilliputian-height box hedge on each side of the short path to the front door.

We showed our IDs and went in. The hall was light, bright and quite lofty, the staircase wide and carpeted in a shade of deep cream. I did not really want to look at the area at the bottom of the stairs as I knew that was where the body had been found. But I did, and stood there for a moment, very sad.

A man in a white anti-contamination suit bustled forward to tell us that we could only look into the rooms from the hallways on the ground and first floors, and grudgingly added that work in the loft rooms had been completed and also outside in the back garden. Oh, and the kitchen. He actually finished by saying that he would rather we were not there at all.

'When are you likely to finish?' Patrick asked him.

'I've absolutely no idea,' was the cold response before he turned on his heel and went from sight.

Patrick raised a meaningful eyebrow in my direction and we commenced our now curtailed tour of the house by immediately ascending the stairs as, if Miss Smythe had indeed been thrown down them, that was where she and the killer had been just prior to that.

'OK,' Patrick said, pausing. 'What happened here?'

There was nothing to see, and despite the Met's findings that there were signs of disturbance in almost every room there was none on this spacious landing, no damage to anything, not even to some delicate small bone china figures of animals on a nearby half-moon table. I made no comment but jotted down details in my notebook.

Patrick said, 'We know from the Met's report that he – I'm

sure it was a he – broke in through the back door, which we can take a look at in a moment. Was Miss Smythe hard of hearing? Do we know?'

'We don't,' I said.

'Please make a note and remind me to ask the niece if I forget. We must talk to her today if possible. At what time, roughly, was she killed?' Answering the question himself, he went on: 'The pathologist reckoned she had been dead for between twelve and eighteen hours when the niece found her at three thirty that afternoon. One doesn't have to be very clever to arrive at the conclusion that she had been killed late the previous evening and before she went to bed as the body was fully clothed. I don't reckon he could have been in the house for more than ten minutes, almost certainly a pro.'

Slowly, trying to take in as much detail as possible, we moved on. The report indicated that the murder victim's bedroom was at the back of the house, a detail we already knew from her letters. Incident tape was secured across the doorway. The room was plainer than I would have expected: the walls ivory white, just two or three small pictures that appeared to be reproductions of religious paintings and a larger one of birds, a cornflower-blue carpet with toning curtains and bedspread in a muted floral pattern. The bedcovers had been neatly turned down at one corner but that was where what must have been normality ended, for all the drawers under the bed and those of a nearby chest had been pulled open, the clothing inside them scattered over the carpet, as were the contents of a fitted wardrobe.

'Obviously, she had been about to get ready for bed,' Patrick said under his breath. 'We must find out from her niece at what time that might have been.'

The two other bedrooms on this floor had been similarly dealt with but the general impression was of someone who had run from room to room flinging things around but not pausing to search for something to steal. In the bathroom, all the towels were on the floor. Why do this other than to try to give the general impression that the house had been ransacked by a burglar?

Almost listlessly, I gazed into the rooms, unable even to start answering any of the myriad questions in my mind. Then we went up the slightly narrower staircase to the attic. This consisted of three smallish rooms, once presumably servants quarters, which were jam-packed with furniture, packing cases, and every kind of lumber imaginable.

'This must be all her parents' stuff,' I said. 'And she couldn't bear to dispose of it or throw any of it away.'

'I'm not surprised chummy downstairs said they'd finished up here,' Patrick commented wryly. 'They just took one look at it and bolted. But to be fair, everything's covered in dust and it doesn't look as though it's been disturbed for years.' He went into the room nearest to us which contained an ancient brass bedstead stacked high with cardboard and wooden boxes. A very dusty teddy bear gazed down sadly from the top of the pile and I longed to take it home to be loved by the children.

'He didn't come up here,' Patrick was muttering. 'And if he did, he took one look and realized it was not much more than a load of second-hand furniture.'

I went into the adjacent room and made my way, gingerly, through lots of cobwebs, between several old bicycles and a hallstand and looked out of the tiny window. The rear garden was fairly narrow, as was to be expected, and charming, the oak tree about two thirds of the way down dominating it. Either Miss Smythe or a previous resident had used it to full advantage, creating a woodland garden with a couple of paths meandering between shade-loving shrubs and groundcover plants. At the bottom of the garden there was obviously access to a rear lane as I could glimpse a gravel parking area through the emerging foliage of the oak.

'The remains of the tree house are still there,' I called. 'Perhaps she intended to have it repaired or rebuilt.'

We returned to the ground floor. The kitchen was large, very clean and sparsely fitted out with basic and surprisingly cheap equipment but for a top-of-the-range microwave cooker.

Patrick was looking at the broken lock on the rear door, situated in a little lobby off the kitchen, examining it minutely with a magnifying glass. It was old fashioned with a fairly large key and still in the locked position, the screws on the striking plate, the section fixed to the doorframe, having been forced out by what one could only imagine as someone having put their shoulder to the door from outside. This plate, with its screws, which looked rusty, was now on the floor. Bolts top and bottom on the door for added security had not been put across and I could imagine Miss Smythe leaving those until just before she went to bed.

I went into the garden where an almost overwhelming sadness came over me as I wandered along the winding paths. It had been designed with great skill so that you could never see all of it from anywhere. This made it seem much larger than it was and there were almost concealed, and delightful, surprises: a wrought-iron table and two chairs by a tiny pool, a miniature statue, another corner to go around and explore, little mysteries. Rosemary Smythe would never see it again.

The oak tree stood in the only large open space, the lawn, some of which was taken up with the planks and smashed larger sections of the fallen tree house. It had been a much more substantial structure than my limited view of it from upstairs had led me to believe and I tried to piece together what it must have looked like. Some, if not most, of the fixing struts were still in the tree.

'I think you should take a look at this,' I told Patrick when he joined me moments later. 'This was a solid, well-built thing and it doesn't appear to be rotten.'

He waded in among the shattered woodwork. Grass was growing through it and I wondered why it had not been cleared away.

'No, there is a certain amount of rotten wood,' he concluded a few minutes later after I had explored the end of the garden. 'Do you think you could climb up and take a look at what's left up there?' He pointed skywards.

'Patrick, I've *never* been any good at climbing trees,' I protested.

'You can stand on my shoulders whereas I can't stand on yours,' he reasoned winningly. 'Then it's easy to get on that lower branch. After that it's a piece of cake.'

He is quite good at catching me, drunk or sober, after all.

'They might see me from next door – it isn't in full leaf yet.'

'We'll have to risk it.'

'My life is in your hands,' I told him grimly. 'Literally.'

He cupped his hands and I stepped into them, finding myself elevated – I always forget how strong he is – so I could put my other foot on to one shoulder and was then steadied so I could sit sideways on and then astride the branch. I was at least wearing the right kind of flat shoes but would still have to be careful on the mossy bark. Luckily there were plenty of upper branches to hang on to.

'That's fine,' I was encouraged. 'Now make your way to the centre where the tree house was secured around the main trunk. Mind your head.'

He had not mentioned the bit about having to climb at least another ten feet higher. But the tree was old and there were holes and fissures and the stumps of sawn-off branches so it was easy to use these almost like a ladder. I only clouted my head the once. Then I arrived in an area which, from up here, looked like the arms of a candelabra, a perfect place upon which to put a platform for a tree house. Except that . . .

'But why did the platform fall down?' I called, but quietly.

'Quite.'

I could see into the garden next door through the partly opened leaves and wondered if the tree's natural growth might now obscure what Miss Smythe had been able to observe without hindrance when it was not in full leaf. Moving carefully and keeping low I examined the remaining struts that were fastened to the tree. They were very substantial, the job done properly, not just nailed on, and with regard to the health of the tree, but all those I could easily reach had been sawn almost all the way through. Still speaking quietly I passed on this information to Patrick below.

'They would almost certainly marry up with some of the fairly heavy chunks of wood down here that are partly buried by the other stuff so I can't see the ends,' Patrick said. 'But some of the other timbers must have also been cut before they finally broke, including what were probably the horizontal supports of the platform. It must all have come down like a pack of cards.' He began to walk away. 'You can come down now.'

I maintained a dignified silence and he chuckled and came back to help me. My descent was a lot less dignified but finally, and accompanied by rather a lot of moss and dead twigs, I landed. And, yes, he steadied me when I tripped on something and almost fell.

There was a thoughtful silence as we went back towards the house. We had moved some of the wood to have a look at the corresponding partly sawn-through ends and then gone down to the end of the garden where there were parking spaces for two cars on a gravel area. There were double gates, locked, that must lead out into an access road of some kind. We would have to look at that as well.

'Do we have a key for these?' I asked, indicating the gates.

There were four on the ring, a couple of modern-looking ones, presumably for the front door, a large old-fashioned one that we already knew fitted the lock on the back door and another that was smaller. It fitted and turned, answering my question.

Quietly Patrick slid across the bolts top and bottom and opened the gate. We went out and found ourselves in a lane, a picturesque little by-way to the rear of the terrace. Like Miss Smythe's, some of the houses had gates, others no barrier at all, giving views down the gardens, used in some cases as car and wheelie-bin parks and little else. We, of course, were really interested in Hereward Trent's property next door and had been careful not to openly stare at the house from the front.

High wrought-iron gates, fitted with electronic locks, and railings with spikes on top fenced off his car parking space and just beyond it was an equally high wooden fence. We could see nothing of the house beyond except the roof and chimney pots. Then I caught sight of a security camera fixed to the trunk of a tree.

'This is the kind of place that brings out the worst in me,' Patrick said in a low voice.

'You mean you yearn to fashion a man-sized cat-flap in the fence, break in and leave the greasy remains of a takeaway on the dining-room table.'

'Something like that.'

'They'd tried to kill her before, hadn't they?'

'Well, someone did. I'm staggered that the poor old lady only broke her leg.'

He went back and gave the exterior of the gates to Miss Smythe's garden, which were over six feet in height, the same careful scrutiny as he had the back door.

'There are no scrape marks, which one might expect if someone climbed over here quite recently,' I said.

'No. But if he was fit, and careful, he might not have made any. Or access was gained from the garden next door.' He locked the gate again. 'It won't hurt to leave it unbolted. We might need to pay a quiet visit one night.'

The address of the niece, Mrs Grant, had been in the case file and we found ourselves outside a tiny cottage, one of a row, very close to the parish church. The woman who answered the door looked at us as though she had been expecting someone else and was now extremely disappointed. We showed her our IDs and Patrick introduced us, adding to her depression.

'May we come in for a few moments?' he went on to ask.

'Well, I suppose I can hardly refuse . . .' she replied wearily, opening the door wide.

Patrick had to duck to go through the low doorway.

'I have been interviewed twice already, you know,' she said. Then, seeing that we were not about to now change our minds and go away, added: 'You'd better sit down.'

The front door opened into a small hallway dominated utterly by a long case clock. The beamed living room accessed through an open archway was furnished in the kind of chintzy fabrics that were just right. The chairs and one small sofa were antiques and of different styles but had all been re-covered in matching fabric. I settled myself on the sofa and found my notebook and a pen in my bag.

I supposed Jane Grant to be around forty-five years of age but she might have been younger, the strain of recent events evident on her face. Slim and of medium height she was smartly dressed in a plum-coloured loose-fitting trouser suit worn with a white silk blouse and low-heeled black shoes. Her hair was shoulder-length, skilfully highlighted blonde and she gazed at us, slightly apprehensively, with large hazel eyes.

'This won't take long,' Patrick was assuring her. 'And please accept our condolences.'

'Thank you. It was awful finding her like that, you know.'

'I'm sure it was,' Patrick replied sympathetically. Then he said, 'Tell me about the time your aunt broke her leg when the tree house collapsed.'

'Oh! No one's asked me about that. Well, it was dreadful.

Auntie was in a terrible state. She managed to get herself back to the house so she could phone me – I could never persuade her to have a mobile – but it would have been far better if she'd dialled nine-nine-nine there and then. So I did and that meant another delay. I tried to stop the bleeding from the cuts and scratches on her arms and legs with clean tea towels and there was a huge graze on her forehead. We had no idea then that her leg was broken even though she said it was very painful. Dreadful, Mr Gillard, dreadful.'

'I get the impression she was an indomitable lady.'

'Absolutely. Some elderly women would have lain out there in the garden and died. But Auntie wasn't like that; she'd always said she'd tried never to rely on anyone for anything.'

'But I take it you saw quite a lot of her and gave her a hand with the shopping. There was no car parked at the house.'

'Oh, you've been there. Yes, Auntie sold her car about eighteen months ago after she'd had a couple of minor bumps with it and I either took her shopping to Sainsbury's or picked up a few things for her in Tesco's down in the town on my way by. But she didn't bother me – preferred her own company and a good book. She even used to play Scrabble against herself in French. And now she's gone. I can't get over it really. Why should a burglar pick on her house?'

'If indeed it was a burglar,' Patrick said. 'Presumably you're aware of her opinions concerning the people next door.'

'It was a fixation with her,' Jane Grant lamented. 'It started in quite a small way – I mean, everyone sometimes gets a bit annoyed with the neighbours, don't they? – but then it began to take over her mind. I have to say I got impatient with her until I realized that she might be showing early signs of dementia. And then when she was given an ASBO . . .' She broke off and threw up her hands in despair.

'Embarrassing for you,' Patrick said with a smile.

'Of course. All I could tell my friends was that she was losing the plot. And she didn't care! I thought she'd be so upset with the disgrace of it but she just kept saying that she'd be proved right eventually. And the Trents are such *nice* people.'

'You've met them?' I queried.

Not for the first time during my involvement with SOCA the

one being interviewed expressed surprise that the note-taker was asking questions.

'Er, yes, at a fund-raising event in the park for a local children's charity. Hereward Trent was there with his wife and I was given to understand that they'd made a *most* generous donation.'

'So you shook his hand kind of thing.'

'Yes, exactly that.'

'But you've never been to the house.'

'No. I don't know anyone who has and get the impression they're quiet sort of people normally but do occasionally have parties. But everyone does, don't they?'

'From whom do you get the impression they're normally quiet?' Patrick said.

'Well, I suppose from general local opinion.'

'But not your aunt.'

'No, she said their parties could be really noisy. I have to say I thought she was confusing the Trents with the house on the far side of them where all the bins are in the garden. They must have been the noisy ones.' She added, slightly sharply: 'Is it really important?'

'Only to a policeman,' he answered. 'Are you aware of the latest findings? That your aunt was murdered?'

'Someone phoned me and said it was now a murder inquiry. I assume the burglar threw her down the stairs but how anyone can tell—'

'She'd been strangled either just before or just after she fell,' Patrick interrupted.

'I see,' she said stiffly. 'This is very distressing.'

'What time did your aunt normally go to bed?'

The woman collected herself for a few moments and then said, 'It varied. If there was a concert she wanted to listen to on Radio Three she'd stay up a bit later but was probably in bed by ten on most nights.'

'In the report prepared by the Metropolitan Police it's noted that you'd said that a few of the best pieces of your aunt's jewellery might be missing. Have you had any subsequent thoughts about that?'

'I've thought about it quite a lot actually but I don't know if she gave them away or perhaps put them in a bank. I simply can't say. I know there was a thick gold chain with a locket on it that was her mother's. That definitely isn't there. I can remember seeing her grandfather's gold watch chain too, and a diamond ring. They don't seem to be there either.'

'I'm afraid I shall have to ask you a few personal questions. You haven't mentioned your husband. Does he live here with you?'

'No, Clive and I are separated. He's a civil engineer and working on a project somewhere in Luton. I don't have his address there.'

'He went off with someone else?' I asked, not about to go all soft on her.

She glowered at me. 'No. We just decided to part. There was nothing acrimonious about it.'

'Then why don't you have his address?'

'It's a temporary one and I just don't, that's all,' she answered, her voice rising. 'And really, I don't see what it—'

Smoothly, Patrick interrupted with, 'Are you a beneficiary in your aunt's will?'

'I can't see what that has to—'

'Please answer the question.'

After a flustered few seconds Mrs Grant said, 'I – I suppose I must be. I know she's named me as executor as other than a cousin on her father's side who lives in Canada I am – was – her only living relative. My mother, who died when I was in my late twenties, was her sister.' After a little pause she added: 'It was one of the reasons Auntie came to live here, to be near me.'

'Might the jewellery have come to you too?'

'I think that's perfectly possible.'

'Perhaps you'd be good enough to run through what happened the afternoon you found her body.'

Visibly, the woman fought her irritation. 'As I've already explained, *several times*, Auntie had rung and asked me to fetch a few bits of shopping. She knew I was going to take the car and do my own.'

'She didn't want to go with you?' I said.

'No, not this time. And I have to say I didn't mind as it took for ever when she did come with me as she liked to dawdle and look at things.'

'So she didn't answer the door when you called with the shopping,' Patrick said.

'I have a key. It saved startling her with the doorbell if she was having a little nap.'

'Was she at all hard of hearing?'

'Very slightly, but not enough to be a real handicap.'

'And she was lying at the bottom of the stairs.'

'Yes. It was a horrible shock. I – I thought she might just have knocked herself out falling but . . .'

'Does anyone else have a key?'

'No.'

'You're quite sure about that?'

'No, I can't be absolutely sure but Auntie never mentioned anyone else having one.'

'I get the impression from that that your aunt could be a little reticent on some matters.'

'She was a very private person. Her generation often are. I never pried.'

'She never discussed in detail her suspicions about next door with you at all, the reasons behind them?'

'Er – she did at one time but . . .'

'Soon got to realize that you weren't sympathetic?'

Shoulders drooping, Jane Grant said, 'I became so wearied by it all I'm afraid that I just didn't want to hear about it any more. In fact, I warned her that she was only making trouble for herself. Do you have many more questions? Only I'm expecting a friend very shortly.'

'Did she have the tree house built?' Patrick continued as though she had not asked the question.

'Oh, no. That was put up by the previous people for their children. Auntie did love it though.'

'How long ago might that have been?'

'Less than ten years, I should imagine, as it was quite new-looking. Auntie had only been living there for five. She'd had a flat in the same road until that house came on the market. She found she couldn't live without a garden.'

Her gardener, a local man, Peter Blackmore, had been

interviewed by the Met. Originally Royal Horticultural Society trained he had had positions at several National Trust properties, finishing his career at Stourhead. Now semi-retired, he helped the elderly and infirm by cutting their lawns, trimming hedges and similar tasks, charging, one gathered, 'very reasonable rates'. A widower, he had been staying with his daughter in Woodford Green at the time of Miss Smythe's death and was not a suspect.

'Did you ever wonder why the tree house collapsed?' Patrick wanted to know.

She turned a frank gaze on to him. 'No, why should I? Perhaps it hadn't been very well built.'

'Did she question what had happened?'

'Yes, she said she thought someone next door might have damaged it in some way. Which is nonsense, of course.'

'And yet it's been left where it fell.'

'She wouldn't have it cleared away for some reason.'

Patrick asked a couple more questions about her aunt's past and her teaching career and then we left.

'Miss Smythe didn't mention suspecting the tree house had been deliberately damaged in the letters,' I said, thinking aloud as we crossed the nearby main road.

'She may well have thought she had no evidence.'

'Which rather points to her only having written about things that she saw with her own eyes and wasn't totally paranoid about everything.'

Patrick made for one of several small tables outside a nearby café, or more correctly, an establishment devoted to the serving and sale of fine teas. He chose to sit where a small cypress tree in a pot partially concealed us from being seen from Jane Grant's cottage away over to the right on the other side of the road.

'You want to see if she was telling the truth about expecting a visitor,' I said, perusing the menu.

'And if so who they are.'

Some fifteen minutes later, when we had ordered our tea, Patrick keeping careful watch around the tree and the traffic, he suddenly swore under his breath. 'Keep your back turned,' he whispered. 'He's looking around before he rings the doorbell.'

'*Who?*'

'Clement Hamlyn.'

SIX

'Do you think Jane Grant could be a willing partner in anything that's going on or might Hamlyn have some kind of hold over her?' Michael Greenway said later that day.

'Difficult to tell,' Patrick replied. 'Although the person she was expecting was described as a friend.'

The commander turned to me. 'Ingrid?'

'She was apprehensive, but I think most women would be if SOCA turned up on their doorstep. My problem with it is that I simply can't imagine the two of them being friends. I'm worried that Hamlyn's been asked to get to know her in an effort to find out what her aunt told her about things she had seen next door and, if that is the case, she's in danger.'

'Gut feelings though?' Greenway persisted. 'This bloke can hardly be described as love's young dream, so don't you think she would have confided in you if she was nervous about him?'

'It might be early days. And he is a famous writer. Perhaps he's a good actor as well and concocted some story using a false name about being a friend of her aunt's. Did Miss Smythe tell her niece the name of the man she'd seen urinating in the garden next door? Whatever, Jane Grant may well be in it up to her ears. Sorry, but that's the best I can do at the moment.'

'Did you inform Mrs Grant that her aunt had written to us?' Greenway went on to ask.

'No,' Patrick answered, 'but she may well have known already if her aunt told her. They appear to have been quite close. And *she* could have mentioned it to Hamlyn.'

Absent-mindedly, Greenway made patterns with paper clips on his desk for a quarter of a minute or so. He had recently acquired quite a collection of these, all colours. A bit like worry beads, perhaps. Then he said, 'The Met have already interviewed this Trent character which, as he's the immediate neighbour, is normal of course following a death thought to be connected with a suspected burglary, which was what it was to begin with. He said neither he nor his family had heard anything that night and, quote, "the old woman had recently kept herself to herself, thank God". I would like you to go and interview him again, and the wife if possible. But I must stress this – *don't* play it as though he's under even the faintest suspicion. You're merely carrying on with the investigation now it's murder and SOCA's got the job.'

'And the reason SOCA's got the job?' Patrick enquired, a very reasonable query, I thought.

The commander gazed at him steadily. 'I thought you used to work for MI5. Anything you like. Lie, man, lie.'

If Patrick was offended by this he showed no sign of it. I was more concerned by Greenway's apparent lapse of memory concerning us having already noisily bumped into Trent's afore-mentioned dodgy associate in France. I voiced this worry, adding that surely Clement Hamlyn would have related to Trent what had occurred and given him our descriptions, thereby causing him to conclude immediately that he could, by association, be under suspicion.

'It's worth taking into consideration,' Greenway said. 'But I think it's also worth the risk. I'm of the opinion that Hamlyn went to France strictly on his own business – which Trent prob-ably isn't interested in – and his threat to Coates about the stealth boat being there to make sure he paid up was nothing to do with Trent and a lie. No, as I said, play it cool.'

I had reservations about this as well but kept quiet. Just because you stir a murky pond it does not necessarily follow than anything stinking floats to the surface. This train of thought was soon to be oddly coincidental.

Patrick was not happy with his orders either. He said, 'Before I do anything – and frankly, sending the pair of us in to talk to him in view of what happened at the literary festival is, to my mind, folly – I would like you to—'

His face grim, the commander interrupted with: 'You don't think I've thought this through properly?'

'With respect, no.'

There was a tense silence broken when Greenway said, 'First you would like me to do *what*?'

'Consider investigating the possibility that this man is involved in what appears to be a protection racket involving, for once, gang bosses and their head honchos as victims.'

'I'm aware of something like that being noised around,' Greenway conceded. 'Go on.'

'As you know, there have been several murders of gang leaders and what might be described as their second-in-commands in the London area fairly recently, including Tom Berry, or Jerry, another surname he sometimes used, a self-styled crime lord in Enfield. He had petrol thrown over him and his car, the whole caboodle then torched. Another, a small-time mobster thought to be in league with him, Fred Duggan, had a nasty little accident down a flight of steps one night on the Embankment and ended up in the Thames, his body, head bashed in, fished out somewhere off Canvey Island by the coastguards. That was three weeks ago. A third, an illegal immigrant, referred to only as Rapla, who had imported himself into the UK together with a few next of kin from Estonia, and carried on his business as a drug dealer, only in Camden this time, had a lot of fresh air put into his brains by two bullets about a month ago. It's thought that his brethren took the hint and rapidly found their way home – either that or they've gone to ground. My point is that the criminal underworld thinks money and power is behind it all, surprise, surprise, but doesn't know who's responsible for the killings.'

'But the Met's line is that they'd clam up about that side of it anyway,' Greenway observed.

'That's exactly the kind of thing an overworked and glad-to-be-rid-of-mobsters bunch of cops would trot out.'

'You could be right,' Greenway acknowledged grudgingly. 'If someone from outside, someone living an outwardly law-abiding life, had chanced upon this novel method of making money . . .'

'And there's the business of the cop crony of Trent's being investigated on account of some of *his* friends.'

Greenway, originally from the Met himself and with the News International scandal and criticism following the London riots still fairly recent history, sighed.

'I'm not trying to be awkward here,' Patrick murmured with a smile.

'God help us if you were,' retorted his boss and then laughed tiredly.

'As we know already he has a crony involved with a London football club and boxing club,' Patrick went on, 'who knocks around with people known to have serious crime connections. They were the folk you described as "the rats' nest". Trent might be one of them. And, don't forget, someone had tried to kill Rosemary Smythe before by sabotaging the tree house.'

'I'm liking this theory more and more. Hamlyn might be some kind of Trent's Mr Fix It on account of past experience in the criminal workplace.'

'It's perfectly possible.'

I said, 'I forgot to ask Alan who acts for him.'

I had mentioned speaking to my one-time agent in France to Greenway but, as far as he and other law-enforcers were concerned, had credited what Alan had told me to 'reliable festival gossip'.

'Useful to know,' Patrick said.

I rang and spoke to his secretary. And then put my phone away.

'No luck?' Greenway said, watching my face.

I cleared my throat. 'He collapsed and died yesterday afternoon.'

I apologized, having to leave the room, tears ready and waiting.

I understood later that there had been further discussion between the two and Patrick finally agreed that he would interview Hereward Trent, going down with all guns blazing by saying that he would play safe by adopting a squint and a fairly impenetrable Irish accent. For once I was happy not to accompany him as Greenway had changed his mind and now deemed that I was 'too famous', as Hamlyn could well have given Trent an outline of his trip to France, mentioning my name.

Whether Patrick's threat would have been carried out or not, knowing him, probably, his call came to nothing. The Trents had all gone away, destination unknown, the au pair, conspicuously nervous, having been ordered either to tell no one or genuinely in the dark as to where they had gone, or even when they were returning.

Another point mentioned after my departure was the Met's 'advice' that morning on the inadvisability of SOCA getting involved with any independent enquiries into the policeman under investigation who was being watched, as they were already working, with Complaints, in connection with it.

'Greenway doesn't want me to get tangled up in that,' Patrick commented after he had related all this to me when he had come back from his abortive mission. 'His words.'

'You don't tend to tangle readily,' I murmured.

He smiled thinly. 'But I can remember getting really annoyed when people, cops usually, crashed into my scenarios when we were with D12.'

'So?' I prompted, having to laugh at the understatement.

'So?'

'Where do we go from here?'

'Mike still wants me to talk to Trent when he finally comes back from wherever he is. Meanwhile, he's going to get some kind of timber expert to write a formal report that the tree house was sabotaged, something that'll stand up in court. Sorry about Alan, by the way.'

'He helped me a lot when I had a writing crisis after a certain man came back into my life.'

'Was it that bad?'

I gave him a straight look. 'Yes – turbulent, for a while.' Not to mention having the living daylights scared out of me during the MI5 training sessions.

'No regrets though?'

'No, not at all.'

'Not even now? Now I'm a bit . . .'

'Tangled?'

'If you like.'

'Do you remember what you said when you proposed to me for the second time?'

'Be fair: blokes don't tend to remember things like that.'

'You said, "One day, if I'm alive and in honest employment, will you consider me for general tidying up and emptying your wastepaper basket?" And I replied, "Yes, I'll have you to grace my heart and my hearth even if you're broken and old and just out of prison". What I said still applies.'

We were in one corner of the open-plan office we work in when at HQ but he nevertheless leaned over and gently kissed me.

As far as the Miss Smythe case was concerned there followed a few days of almost complete inertia while we waited for forensic reports. They finally arrived when I had taken the opportunity to return home for a short while. The one concerning the murder victim's house contained nothing positive, Patrick told me when he rang one evening, the only item of possible interest being very small amounts of fairly fresh grass cuttings that had been found on the hall carpet which could have come in on the killer's shoes. These had minute traces of oil on them – used motor oil. From the appearance of Miss Smythe's lawn – her gardener had to mow around the fallen tree house – it was clear that it had not been cut in the few days before the crime was committed and we already knew that the gardener had been away visiting his daughter. There were no patches of liquid motor oil in the garden, not even where the car had been parked before it was sold, and the conclusion had been that both grass and oil had come in from outside. There were no signs of spillages in the lane to the rear of the property either.

'If he'd walked very far those oily traces, not to mention the bits of grass, would have come off,' Patrick told me Greenway had commented on giving him the report to read. 'So he either drove and parked nearby or lived nearby.'

'I'd put a lot of money on him having climbed over the wall from next door,' Patrick had said to him, relating the whole conversation to me just about word for word.

'Just get me the evidence.'

'I shall need a search warrant.'

'You won't – and we haven't discussed it.'

'I will, there are security cameras and you don't want SOCA brought into disrepute.'

Greenway had sworn vividly and slammed out of the office.

The other report had been the results of tests on samples taken from the woman's body. There was quite a list including those conducted on stomach contents, toxicology tests of the blood and urine, but all could be summarized very simply. Miss Smythe had been healthy for her age, had not been poisoned or under the influence of alcohol when she died. Heavy bruising to her upper arms had resulted from her having been gripped, probably to manoeuvre her into a position to be pushed or thrown down the stairs, other bruising a result of knocks she had received as she fell. The writer of the report felt that she had been strangled afterwards when the killer had realized she was still alive.

Early in the morning, after I had been apprised of this, Greenway rang me.

'There's been a development,' he began by saying. 'Are you free to come up?'

I was, very much so, between novels and in a kind of limbo of my own.

'I – er – don't know whether he's mentioned it to you but I've apologized to Patrick for my thoroughly unprofessional behaviour yesterday,' he went on diffidently. 'It's just as well he kept me on the straight and narrow.'

'A role-reversal, I would have thought,' I said.

There seemed to be no lingering reverberations of this when I entered the commander's office late that morning, having caught the train. Patrick was already seated, drinking coffee as he read what looked like a report of some kind.

Greenway handed me a photograph, a printout on A4 paper from his computer. 'Patrick gave the Cannes *gendarmerie* his card when he was there and they've sent this through. You've seen him before.'

I gazed into the dead face: swarthy, dark-eyed, dark brown hair, Spanish-looking. Horribly battered. 'Of course, it's the man who changed his mind about attacking us in the marina in Cannes. The one Patrick had previously witnessed falling into the water and who we had an idea had been snooping on us for Clement Hamlyn.'

'His body was fished out of the sea off Cannes yesterday morning having been spotted from an anchored dredger,' Patrick told me. 'Alonso Morella, Spanish citizen, did odd jobs around the marina and hotels and lived in a small basement flat that he shared with a railway station cleaner. Any spare money he had, which wasn't much, he spent on booze and cigarettes. Hadn't actually crossed swords with the law but suspected of being likely to do anything iffy for a few euros. Hamlyn wouldn't have had any trouble hiring him.'

'To snoop on us at the hotel too then,' I said. 'I presume that he drowned after being beaten up and his body was washed out to sea.'

'Not necessarily. Some or even all of the facial injuries were almost certainly caused by the corpse being buffeted against the bottom of the harbour, moving with the tide and battering against rocks and sunken detritus. As you know, bodies always lie face down in water with the head hanging. There were other quite deep, parallel cuts to the back caused by the body having been hit by a boat's propeller. That might have happened when it was rising to the surface as decomposition set in and was floating just below the surface.'

'How long had he been dead?'

'Three to four days, perhaps five.'

'And was it likely that the currents would have washed the body out to sea if he'd fallen, or been pushed, off the harbour wall?'

'Dunno. The email is in English – well, sort of – but the attached report is in French and that's as far as I've got with the translation.'

Greenway said, 'Apparently he'd been drinking, heavily. Even after that length of time significant concentrations of alcohol were found in the blood and urine. I don't know about France but in Britain two thirds of adult males found drowning or drowned had consumed alcohol. The vital detail as far as this man's concerned is that there was foam in the airways, indicating that he was alive when he went into the water. And yet you say, Patrick, that the man was a good swimmer.'

'Well, certainly good enough to swim the short distance to a flight of steps. But if he was totally sloshed and had ingested a huge amount of water as he fell in . . .'

'What else does the pathologist say?' Greenway went on to ask.

'My conversation French is much better than the written word and a lot of this is in medical language,' Patrick said. 'You'll have to get an interpreter to look at it to get the full story. But in his conclusion there's something along the lines of investigators having to determine the circumstances preceding death before final conclusions are reached. Finally, I *think* he says he cannot possibly be expected to explain the cause of all the lacerations and bruising to the body and, in his view, there is unexplained bruising to the back of the neck and head.' Patrick looked up. 'That's interesting if I've got it correctly. He could have been chopped across the nape of the neck or hit a couple of times with some kind of blunt weapon like a pickaxe handle. There's nothing in the police email about any witnesses, is there?'

Greenway shook his head. 'No, and it could have happened after dark. There wasn't anything in the email about police intentions to determine the circumstances before death before they reach any conclusions either. End of foreign immigrant nobody cared about. Sad, but it's not our problem and I can't see that anything would be gained by going over there and trying to throw our weight about.'

'The motive if he was murdered, though?' I queried. 'Clement Hamlyn or someone else working for him tying up a few loose ends? That seems a bit far-fetched unless Morella had threatened to go to the police, blackmailing him, perhaps.'

'Yes, I can't see Hamlyn having any strong connections with the South of France. Why would he?'

'Is Daniel Coates still on the loose?'

'Er, yes,' Greenway answered. 'Didn't turn up in St Tropez. If the truth were known the cops there missed him if he only stopped overnight. But I'm hoping he's still in the sights of Operation Captura.'

'He told me he didn't know the man who had fallen in the water. He could have been lying.'

'And went back to Cannes and had some kind of drunken altercation with him,' Patrick ventured. 'Or shoved him in the water just because he felt like it. It would figure.'

We then turned to the subject of Miss Smythe's murder and I forgot to raise the matter of tides and currents again and the likelihood of Alonso Morella's body finishing up in the sea off Cannes if he had fallen, or been pushed, off the harbour wall into the water.

Greenway reiterated that the Met had carried out comprehensive house-to-house enquiries in the immediate area of Miss

Smythe's house and nobody had reported seeing anyone loitering or behaving suspiciously. Local known villains, those not detained at Her Majesty's pleasure, had been questioned with no useful findings there either and police informers had been silent on the matter.

'This case cannot be allowed to go cold!' he finished by almost shouting.

I was beginning to see why the Met had been so delighted to hand everything over to us and afterwards had been so helpful.

'I have a suggestion,' Patrick said.

'Go ahead,' Greenway invited, calming down.

'We want to get hold of Hereward Trent right now but can't. Clement Hamlyn probably has to be put on the back burner – for now. With regards to other iffy associates the Met has *advised* us not to stick our noses into the suspect cop investigation as he's under surveillance. Does that apply to his chum the football and boxing Johnny who it would appear also has dodgy connections?'

The commander consulted the relevant email. 'No,' he said slowly. 'Not in so many words. But anyone with a modicum of intelligence would read that meaning into it.'

'But it doesn't actually say that he's under surveillance as well.'

'No.'

'I've always been a bit thick.'

Greenway frowned in the general direction of the window. 'Can't say I've ever been that bright myself.'

'Ingrid and I could go and take a look at him. What's his name?'

Burrowing into a wire tray on his desk, Greenway hauled out a thin file and opened it. 'Some years ago he was a Russian film star by the name of Anatoli Tomskaya. It may not have been his real name, just a professional one. These days he calls himself Anthony Thomas, which is an Anglicization of sorts, and to confuse matters even more I gather he's known as both Tommy and Tony, depending on who's doing the talking. That's those close to him, you understand. To everyone else he's Mr Thomas. What name appears on his council tax demands is anyone's guess.'

I said, 'And your file's on him because of the dodgy associates?'

'Oh, no, in my view he's *über* dodgy as well. The problem is that nothing evidence-wise has stuck to him yet, not even a genuine identity, mainly because he's a slimy bastard.'

'He's not likely to be on the Mystery Mobster Murderer's list then if we're right about his connection with Trent, Hamlyn and the policeman under investigation. He could even be the hit man responsible for the killings.'

'That could easily be the case if the money's right as the football club's doing very badly right now. He's not been known to carry weapons but my guess is he'd subcontract that out anyway to avoid getting his hands dirty. By all means go and take a look at him.' Greenway continued, turning to Patrick: 'Get a good photograph of him if you can. He's succeeded in keeping his face off television and out of the papers, God knows how. Records only have a couple of blurred shots of him taken at matches plus one good clear one where he's on a horse in some costume B-movie shot around twenty years ago on the outskirts of Moscow. I suggest you look at those first so you have some idea of his appearance.'

'I know hardly anything about the football world,' said the one-time rugby-playing man of mine, planning how he was going to get close to Anthony Thomas without tripping over the Met, if they were there. Not to take his photograph, that was unnecessary with telephoto lenses, but to try to find out how the man *ticked*.

'But you boxed at school,' I reminded him. As head boy he had taken real bullies – male – into the ring with him for a couple of rounds, thoughtfully providing gloves. With the head master's blessing too. It would not be permitted now, of course.

'Um, but that's a bit irrelevant these days,' Patrick muttered and went into a reverie, in his mental ops room.

I had begun noting down a few ideas for a new novel but having turned on my laptop to do a little more work on them I looked up Anthony Thomas on the Internet instead. Understandably, or not, he did not have a website but as was usual the football club did. As well as lists of other officials there was one of the directors with his name included, each with a short profile. It stated that he had moved from Russia, where he had retired from acting four years previously, to promote boxing. He had come to London 'to further his interests in sport', and no doubt, I thought, to better line his pockets. There was no mention of a family. Other interests were listed as classical music, the theatre and going for long country walks.

Did I believe a word of that hogwash? No. Did I think he had left Russia with the police in hot pursuit? Yes. In my heart of hearts was I sure that most of his earnings still came from crime? Natch.

Greenway had already told us that the man 'only' had several convictions for speeding and non-payment of fines for the same offences. Frustratingly, as far as the police were concerned, was that his name had been mentioned by witnesses and suspects in several serious cases involving murder, extortion and drug-dealing. By the time these cases – which was where there was a link to the policeman under scrutiny – had come to court people had either changed their evidence, saying they had been mistaken, or failed to appear, two witnesses due to testify against men known to be in Thomas's circle, including a couple of boxers, having gone missing. The body of one of these had been found floating in the Thames in similar fashion to that of Fred Duggan, the small-time mobster recently murdered.

The commander had updated us on the investigations into the murders of the other two gang leaders and their 'second-in-commands': Tom Berry, or Jerry, thought to be in league with Duggan, and the illegal immigrant, known only as Rapla, who appeared to have had no dealings with them. There was not a lot to tell: the Met was cautiously treating the killings as one case and were already finding links between them, mostly in the shape of thugs for hire. So far there were no links to Anthony Thomas.

Greenway had also given us the information that the investigation into Claudia Barton-Jones's, Hamlyn's girlfriend, expenses irregularities was now a police matter as larger sums of money than had first been realized were involved. She had been questioned but had been uncooperative and enquiries were continuing.

SEVEN

Fortunately, SOCA had Anthony Thomas's Barnes address on file. We decided to go house-hunting, taking a camera. 'How much are you looking to spend?' drawled the toothy young woman in the estate agents.

Patrick looked at me: he knows next to nothing about house prices.

'Around a million,' I told her. 'And preferably near the common. Not too far from the railway station either.'

'It helps, you know, if people have already spotted something they like online.'

'We prefer to see places as they really are without funny lenses effects and artificial lighting,' I retorted. Such superciliousness really does bring out the worst in me.

This, obviously, was heresy but she bore with us more or less politely and delved into the drawer of a filing cabinet, finally handing over the particulars of five properties. 'You can phone us if you want to have a look round any of them and we might be able to arrange it for this afternoon,' she said in a manner that suggested such technology could well be beyond us.

'Perhaps I should have worn my crown,' Patrick said when we were outside. 'Anything in the locality of Thomas's place?'

I had my London A–Z open at the page. 'There's one in the next road.'

'Good, we can go and make sure there's no other riff-raff living in the area.' Patrick chuckled and walked off.

'It's the other way.'

He paused to say over his shoulder, 'I know, I had a look at the map before we came. But there's a nice little baker's shop over there with a board outside advertising sandwiches and coffee; it's almost two thirty and we haven't had any lunch.'

Later, the property details prominently in my hand, we wandered along the road next to the one where Anthony Thomas's house was situated. We then turned the corner at the end of the road, feigned interest in another house that had a For Sale notice outside with a different estate agent and then slowly wandered on until we approached the property in which we were really interested, also semi-detached. Patrick, I knew, was scanning the area with professional interest but there were no cars with anyone sitting in them parked nearby and, to me at least, nobody appeared to be watching from any of the houses opposite which were smaller and older, built in the thirties, I thought.

'Perhaps no one's here because *he's* not here,' I suggested.

'I'm not sure about that yet. Put your street map away and we'll call next door.'

A man was in the front garden which was very, very tidy, the kind of place where every stray leaf, twig and creature that moved has been eradicated by the regular, and ruthless, use of a garden vac. There were no plants growing up the walls of the house and no spring flowers in the borders around the lawn, just bare, neatly-dug earth.

'Good afternoon!' Patrick said breezily in a plummy voice. 'Sorry to bother you, old man, but can you tell us where Cavendish Road is? We're looking to buy a house round here.'

The man, who had been peering with distaste for any sign of misbehaviour at a tightly-clipped holly, shook his head. 'Never heard of it, sorry.'

Crestfallen, Patrick made a play of consulting the details. 'Oh, stupid of me. That place is in Roehampton. Sorry to have bothered you.' Then: 'Perhaps I can pick your brains for a moment. We've been looking for a detached place. But are these semis solidly built? Do you hear your neighbours much through the party walls?'

'They're not very often there and I haven't been aware of anyone for weeks, if not months, just the bloke who tidies the garden,' said the man. 'So that's not much help to you. But all the property in this immediate area is good quality so I can't see it being a problem – unless people start having loud parties, of course. But everyone's very quiet and law-abiding. These gardens back on to the common too so it's open ground behind with nice views.'

'Are there rear gates to these properties with access to the common?'

'Yes. Very handy for taking the dog for a walk.'

We thanked him and left and I knew exactly where we were heading.

'Not very often there, eh?' Patrick said softly. 'My guess is that he doesn't live there at all except perhaps once in a blue moon and is more likely to be found not a stone's throw from Wanstead Flats because that's where all his hirelings hang out, so he can keep them all well screwed down.'

His mobile rang. It was a very short call, from Greenway I guessed, during which Patrick mostly listened and said little.

'Change of plan,' he announced. 'Hereward Trent has returned home – he was spotted by whoever it was from the Met who removed the crime scene tape from outside Miss Smythe's house and checked that the back door had been repaired – and I'm to interview him immediately. Greenway doesn't want us here any longer, especially as Thomas appears to be somewhere else. Not only that, he's been in contact with someone he described as his mole at the Yard who told him Thomas's place is being watched from a loft room in a house opposite. They must be rather bored so I think I'll wave to them on the way back.'

Which he did. Big smile too. I could almost hear the motorized camera shutters whirring.

'Further anarchy?' I suggested.

'Splendid. What have you in mind?'

'I'll come with you when you talk to Trent.'

'It was Mike who thought it a risk.'

'Don't you?'

'Yes, but your presence is always a plus.'

Yes, whether I am sober or not, he is a truly gorgeous man.

'Any significant reasons why you want to be there?' Patrick went on to ask.

'I've a funny feeling about him, that's all.'

In the past these have paid off and he did not enquire further.

'Mr Trent?'

The man who had answered the door nodded brusquely without speaking.

Patrick produced his warrant card and introduced us, just referring to me as his assistant. This is routine practice to avoid any possible repercussions or revenge against me personally should he happen to really upset a suspect, for example by threatening to screw their head off.

'The police have already questioned us.'

'There have been developments, sir. May we come in?'

'Well, if you must . . .'

Sumptuous was the word that immediately sprang into my mind as we walked on deep carpeting through the house to a large living room at the rear. Adjacent to it, through a wide archway, was a conservatory that appeared to be of almost equal proportions that contained ferns and palms in pots, a small fountain tinkling against a backdrop of orchids and more ferns in a raised pool in the right-hand corner.

'You'd better sit down,' said Trent, dropping into a four-seater sofa and frowning at us, one each. He was in his late forties, I guessed, smooth complexioned and had fair, thinning hair. Everything about him was as expensive and well-groomed as his house.

'My assistant will take notes, if you don't mind,' Patrick murmured.

The assistant had removed all her make-up, assumed a gormless expression and scragged her shoulder-length hair back into an untidy ponytail.

Another curt nod.

'I can tell you absolutely nothing about the death of my neighbour,' Trent said tautly. 'I've repeated this until I'm blue in the face.'

'It would appear,' Patrick said slowly, 'that her killer might have taken a short cut through your back garden.'

'Her *killer*?'

'Yes, this is now a murder inquiry. Miss Smythe was strangled just before or after, most likely after, her fall down the stairs.'

'That's appalling – but I still can't help you.'

'There are security cameras out there. Did anything show up on those?'

'I've already been asked that. They're not working.'

'Cast your mind back. Had your lawn been mown that day?'

'We were on a skiing holiday in Klosters. Besides, I can't possibly be expected to know things like that,' the man protested.

A crack appeared in Patrick's urbane and cultured manner –
actually his normal manner. 'There must be a record kept so you
know how much to pay whoever does it for you. Think.'

Trent dropped his gaze and shrugged helplessly. Then he said,
'Oh, that's right, my wife, Sonya, notes down when the gardener's
due on the kitchen calendar. I'll go and have a look.'

'Thank you.'

'It would appear that it was,' Trent said when he returned very
shortly afterwards.

'It it a petrol or electric machine?'

'Petrol.'

'Do you happen to know if any oil leaked from it?'

'I believe he phoned when we got back a couple of days later
and my wife spoke to him about it not being quite right, but
didn't take much notice. That's what you employ people for.
Why?'

'I'm not in a position to explain. I assume that your gardener
would have mentioned it if oil had leaked from the machine on
to your grass and he also would have had to obtain your permission before taking it away for attention.'

'No, he brings his own tools and machinery. I hate being
cluttered up with stuff like that.'

'Perhaps you'd be good enough to give me his name and phone
number.'

This was done, but with ill grace, Trent again having had to
leave the room.

'Is your wife at home?' I asked.

'No, she's – er – with friends.'

'And your daughters are with her?'

'Yes, that's right.'

'They'll have to go back to school on Monday, presumably,
as it'll be the end of the half-term holiday.'

'Is it? I'm afraid I leave remembering that kind of thing to
Sonya.'

'Were you living here when the previous owners of Miss
Smythe's house were there?'

'The Cuthbertsons. Yes, but they moved quite shortly afterwards. He was in the diplomatic service and was posted abroad
or something like that.'

'How disappointing for the children when he'd just had the tree house built for them.'

Trent's impatience was growing. 'Yes, I suppose it must have been,' he responded heavily.

'Did your children play with them?'

'I believe they did.'

'But they weren't allowed to go and see Miss Smythe.'

'No, of course not. She did initially make it clear that they were welcome to play over there but you simply can't be too careful these days.'

'But she was a retired *teacher*.'

'I really don't see what this has to do with anything,' Trent snapped.

'And it's just as well seeing the tree house collapsed when Miss Smythe was in it,' I persevered. 'They might have been seriously injured.'

I caught Patrick's eye and he said, 'May we have a look at the garden?'

'Carry on. The conservatory door's not locked and you can let yourselves out afterwards. I won't accompany you – I've work to do.'

He left the room and an interior door slammed.

'Other than indicating that he's on edge and a lousy father what did that achieve?' Patrick said when we out in the garden.

'Greenway did tell you to tread lightly,' I reminded him. 'But I think Trent knew the tree house had been tampered with and that's why the girls weren't permitted to go over there. I reckon it was sabotaged shortly after Miss Smythe moved in and was spotted sitting up there reading and, anything dodgy going on then or not, he didn't like being overlooked.'

'Surely, all he'd had to do was ask her to put up a blind or curtain.'

'You're right, these are supposed to be intelligent people. It does rather point to him being really nervous about what was going on here. And then when nothing happened to the tree house after a while he, or someone else, might have gone over there one night and done a bit more sawing. Didn't she say in one of her letters that she thought she'd heard someone in the garden one night and was scared Trent was out to silence her?'

'She did.'

'He was a bit hesitant as to where his wife was too, wasn't he?'

'I noticed that. Does any of what was said reinforce your funny feeling about him?'

'Sort of.'

'Care to elaborate?'

'No, not yet, as if I'm wrong I might completely throw the investigation.'

We sauntered around generally, not sure if Trent was watching us. Then, when it might be assumed that he had become bored, Patrick walked the length of the boundary wall on the right-hand side, branches of the oak tree next door leaning over it. The wall was brick built and probably as old as the house. Various kinds of creepers were growing on it together with a couple of rambling roses of large proportions, a thornless one near the house, the second farther down.

'Oil!' I hissed when we were working our way towards the bottom of the garden.

Patrick was a few yards away examining the wall as well as he could for the vegetation. 'Where?'

'Here, on the gravel path.'

'Enough to take a sample of?'

'There might be. But surely, mower oil's mower oil.'

'You never know with forensics these days. Do your best. And grab some blades of grass as well. We can go and get some samples off the machine afterwards to clinch it.'

Thinking that grass was grass too I nevertheless did as requested. We always carry small sample bags and gloves in our pockets when we are working.

'Eureka,' I heard Patrick say quietly. 'Someone got caught up on thorns and holed their sweater. Near the top of the wall too, when they were climbing over it. Does your bag have a pair of tweezers in it?'

'I've used them on my eyebrows – they'll contaminate the sample.'

'I'll try and use them through the bag.'

A couple of minutes of reaching up and muted swearing later he had what he wanted: several strands of navy-blue wool.

'A scenes of crime team should have looked at neighbouring gardens,' I remarked as we were finding our way out.

'Resources, resources, resources,' Patrick said, grimacing. 'Yes, in an ideal world. And first of all, don't forget, it was thought to be aggravated burglary. Who's to say how long it's been there? It might have happened when the tree house was sabotaged or be nothing to do with anything at all.'

A little later we spoke to the gardener, by phone, who was working elsewhere in Richmond but with no useful results. He had taken the mower he had used on the Trent's lawn to be repaired and they had drained out all the oil and stripped down the engine.

'I shall just have to go and talk to a few leading mobsters and ask them if they're paying protection money,' Patrick said.

'Would it be risky to ask Jane Grant first about her tall friend? I'm concerned that she's in danger.'

'I think I'd prefer to put that on hold at present. But, I agree, it is worrying.'

'You are far too valuable to me to go off alone raking over the London underworld for info,' Greenway said grimly.

The argument had gone on for some time, Patrick laying out his reasons for the proposal, concisely and politely, just as he would have done in his military days. Rarely then would he had received such a completely negative reaction from a superior. But this was the police, not an army intelligence unit.

'Look, we can't just sit around waiting for someone else to be firebombed or clubbed to death,' Patrick continued. 'Sorry, but I don't think you realize how this could escalate. If whoever's behind these murders either kills or gets a real hold over crime barons you're going to end up with a criminal empire to end all criminal empires as he'll control everyone left standing and be anonymous and untouchable.'

'You're assuming they know who's behind it – the threats might be delivered over the phone.'

'I can't believe the grapevine doesn't have a few ideas.'

'Apparently none of the snouts has the first clue.'

'They're probably looking after their own hides as well.'

'No, I don't want you going in.'

I cleared my throat and said to Greenway, 'What we must have is evidence. Can't Clement Hamlyn be pulled in and confronted with what Daniel Coates said to me in Cannes?'

'He'd deny everything saying it was the word of a convicted criminal against his.'

'We don't have to mention that Coates is a crook. If Hamlyn knows that, how does he?'

'I did see him boarding the boat too,' Patrick put in.

Greenway frowned thunderously at his paper clips which he had formed into a complicated pattern on his desk. 'I think we need more ammo to use against him before we do anything like that,' he said finally. 'And as we know, he writes crime novels. With an imagination like that he'd be able to cook up all kinds of fantasies. Miss Smythe's letters aren't enough either. Any brief worth his salt would tear those to shreds as the work of a silly old woman spitting mad because she'd been given an ASBO for being a local nuisance.' He looked me right in the eye. 'D'you reckon he killed her?'

'There's every chance he did,' I replied. 'Once a hit man . . .'

Patrick jerked to his feet. 'I loathe working in a vacuum.'

'Nevertheless, *don't* go off and talk to crime bosses,' Greenway told him.

True to his orders Patrick went off and shot one instead.

No one but the two of us knows the truth behind this and there was no question of the victim being able to identify his attacker. He did not even see him and nor did his two minders. The shot, at night, neatly taking him in the right leg as he left a nightclub in Stratford, caused a flesh wound that kept him in hospital for just over a week, under arrest and with an armed guard. The Met had been trying to locate him for a while to help with a murder inquiry so, hopefully, there would soon be a short but meaningful queue of people waiting to talk to him when the doctors announced him well enough.

Angelo da Rosta – right on trend insofar as it was not thought to be his real name – was known to be a drug dealer and also rumoured to be running a prostitution business employing various illegal immigrants and attendant heavies. He had recently, according to low-life gossip and having been released from prison only a few months previously, organized the 'removal' of another dealer who had tried to take over his 'patch', his body having been discovered in the boot of a stolen and abandoned car. There was some evidence to suggest that da Rosta was involved.

Officially, we were at home for a long weekend and now, at six fifteen on the Sunday morning Patrick had been in the house just long enough to tell me all this having raided my purse to pay off the taxi as he was broke. You do not carry credit cards or chequebooks when working undercover.

'Was selecting da Rosta just a shot in the dark, if you don't mind the pun?' I asked him.

'Not really. Someone said he was as jumpy as a cat and had disappeared for a while. Now he was back and on the lookout for a couple more lads as bodyguards. It sort of figured.'

'And that someone was?'

'One of James Carrick's old snouts. It took me twenty-four hours to find *him*.'

Detective Chief Inspector James Carrick of Bath CID is a close friend of ours and used to be in the Met's Vice Squad.

'I hope you didn't tell James what you were going to do.'

'Of course not.'

'And, obviously, you didn't use your Glock as you'd stowed it in the safe in the car.'

'Very easy to buy a gun in London these days. It's somewhere deep and watery right now.'

'You won't be able to claim for *that* on your expenses.'

He went off to make himself presentable before any other family members saw him, having been away for the best part of three days without a wash or shave and sleeping rough, by the look of him.

Patrick had the Monday off and stayed quietly at home, catching up on sleep and enjoying spending the rest of the time being a family man, wandering around in a tracksuit and generally relaxing. Early feedback courtesy of secure Met and SOCA websites indicated that da Rosta was actually grateful for police protection and had been almost beside himself with terror when admitted to hospital. His minders had bolted at the first sign of trouble, something I could quite understand as he had kept saying that the invisible gunman had called to him from an alleyway across the road, 'like something from the dead'.

'What did you say to him?' I asked.

'Payback time. Just that.'

'Voice-from-the-grave style.'

'Um. I'm good at those.' He demonstrated.

Horrible.

EIGHT

I f Commander Greenway had any suspicions regarding the shooting he gave no sign of it, the notion that SOCA undertook in-house mobster reduction simply not to be countenanced. Therefore I am sure he did not want to know, no doubt in my mind, if indeed he did harbour a little iffyness, that modest suffering caused to da Rosta now was better than possible death. Also, as the Met had their man for questioning and possible conviction for murder, it prevented more criminal activity on the suspect's part and also removed him from further danger with regard to the threats that it now really looked had been made to him. Patrick told me he had factored all this into his thinking. To expect any remorse from him – echoes of the Sussex affair notwithstanding – was unreasonable for when you have survived being blown up by a grenade and consequently have a right leg partly of man-made construction, a flesh wound is peanuts.

'We just need to interview him,' I said.

'The Met has first bite. That's happening the day after tomorrow unless he suffers a setback.'

'And meanwhile?

'Back to work to take a look at the area where da Rosta was shot, as would be expected of any good investigator. Coming?'

It was one of those areas of London that would look better at night – that is, when you could not see most of it. The shops that were not boarded up in this seemingly forgotten corner of Stratford had heavy shutters to be rolled down at closing time, the only one that I saw without them having heavy grilles across the windows instead. Outside a greengrocer's, sad-looking boxes of fruit and vegetables had gone well past the stage of being revived by the thin drizzle that fell from a wall-to-wall grey sky.

'The club's housed in the basement of that defunct church,' Patrick said. 'I understand the whole thing's due for demolition soon.'

'It's not exactly advertised,' I said. The building itself was hideous, a brick-built Victorian monstrosity.

'There is a neon sign but you can't see it from here as it's over the entrance, down the steps.'

'What time did all this happen?'

'Oh one five three. Da Rosta emerged with his two minders bringing up the rear. That was their first mistake. Then—'

'Patrick, how the hell did you know it was the right man at night?' I broke in, but speaking very quietly.

'Not difficult. He's six foot four and almost as wide. It's one of the reasons I chose him. And according to James's snout he nearly always comes here after he's eaten at the Bull's Head just down the road and sometimes pops in, or rather rolls in, for a quick one, or six, at another club on the way here as well.'

'OK. Go on.'

'There's not a lot more to it.' He turned aside into an alleyway and I followed, squeezing passed some boxes of rubbish and several dustbins.

Two men were in the alley – somehow one just knew they were CID – kicking the litter to one side to enable them to examine the ground. 'This is a crime scene,' one of them called. 'Bugger off.'

'If you're searching for evidence you should have it taped off,' Patrick said. 'SOCA. What have you got?' He waved his ID in their general direction.

There was an exchange of stares and he won. 'Nothing,' the same man muttered.

'Pity. No sign of the weapon?'

'No, it's probably in the Waterworks River by now.'

'No witnesses?'

'Not one. There never is after shootings like this.'

'Have you questioned the management of the club?'

'Just after it happened. Waste of time. They've no idea who it could have been, know of no disgruntled members. But he must have been a bloody good shot. Or lucky.'

'Unlucky if he meant to kill him. And, for God's sake, the man's the size of a barn door. So I reckon you're actually looking for a lousy shot.'

'It happens all the time. Turf wars.'

'Perhaps he hadn't paid up.'

'Oh, you lot know about that theory then. But it is only a theory. Personally I don't go for it. Too many mobsters and not enough potential loot to go round's the real reason for these attacks.' He turned his back on us and carried on with his search. 'Turf wars, mate,' he finished by grunting.

Thus dismissed, we made a play of examining the entrance to the alley.

I gazed around and, deliberately quite loudly, said, 'Normally there might have been a light over that side door but the bulb's broken and bits of glass are on the ground which leads me to think that the gunman smashed it.'

'Highly likely,' Patrick agreed. 'It would have made it very dark.'

'And then he would have made his escape down the alley to get rid of the weapon.'

'That figures too.'

We headed in that direction.

The two detectives were looking at something one of them had just picked up.

'Anything interesting?' Patrick enquired as we went by.

'A West Ham ticket for last Saturday's match,' replied the previously silent one.

'That narrows it down a bit then.'

We completed our little piece of theatre and made our way back to the club via a side street. The sign over the basement door, not lit and half grown over with ivy, could have been *Mo's, Joe's* or even *Flo's*. I found myself not caring all that much.

As we might have expected the door was locked but someone soon opened it after Patrick had removed a bit more of the peeling paint by battering on it with half a brick he had found nearby on a small pile of rubble that appeared to have fallen from the building.

'Serious Organised Crime Agency,' he said, pushing aside the man who had done the unlocking. 'Where's the boss?'

'He don't live 'ere,' said the man.

'Who's in charge right *now*?'

''is bruvver.'

'I'd like to talk to him.'

The lighting in what must have once been some kind of crypt, complete with deep-arched alcoves with tables in them, was harsh from large unshaded overhead bulbs, no doubt switched on to assist two middle-aged cleaning women, one with a vacuum cleaner, the second half-heartedly dusting the bottles behind the bar. The vacuum cleaner stopped.

'This effin' thing's packed up *again*!' the woman shrieked, mostly at Patrick.

'It's no good shouting at me,' he said. 'If you always yank it along like that you've probably snatched at the cable and broken a wire in the plug.'

She mouthed something at him and stumped off.

'Who wants me?' said a man, approaching from somewhere at the rear.

'Gillard,' said Patrick, producing his ID. 'And you are?'

'Hutton, John Hutton.'

'Thank you. The man, da Rosta, who was shot and injured outside here in the early hours of this morning is a regular customer, I understand.'

'He came in here several times a week,' the man answered with an uninterested shrug. Possibly in his fifties, overweight and pallid, he appeared to have only just woken up having slept in his clothes. He waved us over to one of the tables and after putting the chairs back on the floor we sat down.

'Were you a friend of his?'

'I try never to make friends with customers, especially men I know to be criminals.'

'So you didn't have conversations with him.'

'We . . . spoke, that's all. Look, I've been asked questions like this already by the police – at half past two this morning.'

'Sorry, but please bear with me. I've been told that he was afraid for his own safety, something that might have a bearing on what happened last night. Did he say anything to you about having received threats?'

'No, but I could tell he was nervous by the way he bit his nails. He'd hired the two boys – that's all they are really, boys, teenagers from a sink estate – and I knew he was on the lookout for a couple more as he asked me if I knew anyone who wanted a job. I didn't – I don't want to get involved with anything like that. But they never gave me any trouble so I put up with them. You might think this place a den of thieves but it isn't. Most of the folk who come in here are as good as gold. It's all coming down soon to make way for a supermarket and I shall retire.'

'And your brother?'

'He's younger than me and plans to open up somewhere else. But he's bone idle, hasn't bothered to learn the business and is hardly ever here so God knows how he's going to get on.'

'Did da Rosta meet others here – people who might have been working with, or for him?'

The man sighed wearily. 'What you must understand is that people drift in and out of this place all the time, from the moment we open at six p.m. until around two a.m. It gets packed, they drink like there's no tomorrow and then they go away.' A wan smile. 'That's why I'm able to retire soon.'

'Please think. Can you remember anyone coming here and talking to da Rosta who might have been connected in some way with his fear?'

A deep frown creased the man's forehead. Then he said, 'I did notice, a while back, a man at his table. If he can he always sits . . . He's not dead, is he?'

Patrick shook his head. 'No.'

'. . . sits at that table over there in the corner.' He pointed to one of the alcoves. 'The boys had been sent away, which was most unusual, seeing that their role was to protect him. The man didn't stay long, just perched on the edge of a chair and I only noticed him because he was so tall. But we were very busy and when I next looked in that direction and could see for all the customers he'd gone.'

'He didn't stay for a drink?'

'Just helped himself to da Rosta's, tossed down his single malt in one.'

'Exactly how long ago was this?'

The man drummed his fingers on the bar, staring into space. Then he said, 'Around two months, as far as I can remember. But, you must understand, one day in here is very much like another.'

'Can you remember anything else about this man?'

'Only his height, a bit taller than you. It was pouring with rain and he wore a long mac with the collar turned up and a hat, a fedora kind of thing.'

'You didn't see his face?'

'No.' Hutton then smiled again, broadly this time. 'Perhaps it was the ghost. Some local people say this place is haunted as there are graves under the floor, but I've never seen it.'

'Thank you, you've been most helpful.'

The drizzle had turned to heavy rain and we postponed a debriefing until we got back to the car. I felt that I had contributed nothing to the interview other than to take notes but had to admit that Patrick had asked all the important questions.

'Clement Hamlyn?' Patrick said, grabbing the windscreen wiping cloth to rub some of the wet off his hair and then handing it to me to do likewise.

'It could easily have been him. But it's still not evidence.'

'OK, we'll jump to conclusions to try to get results. Clement Hamlyn killed Rosemary Smythe. He turned over the house to make it look like a burglary but couldn't resist stealing the best bits of her jewellery because he's like that. Therefore he either still has it or has sold it on, probably the latter. Where does this bloody man live?'

'He has a website. It just says the Shepherd's Bush area.'

'I might just hang out around there for a couple of days, low-key – starting with the pubs and bars.'

'He *has* seen you before,' I reminded him.

'He won't know me.' Patrick brooded, back in his mental ops room.

'D'you reckon that man at the club is doing his brother out of most of the takings?' I said a minute or so later.

Sometimes you really can see the effect of men's brains

recalibrating when you bounce them from deep thought on to another track. Patrick started slightly as though I'd stuck a pin in him and said, 'I did note that he's retiring soon and bruvver is carrying on working. Good luck to him and serve the lazy little sod right.'

'I'm also wondering if DI Branscombe has had any luck tracing Miss Smythe's jewellery.'

'Good thinking. Let's ask him.'

The task – and I was really admiring Branscombe for not just forgetting about it – had been handed over to a DC Jameson, who regretted that he had had no material success at all. The only certainties were that Miss Smythe had not placed any items of jewellery for safe keeping at her bank, nor were there any fairly large deposits in her bank account within the past few years to suggest that she had sold them. Patrick had then gone on to ask him about fences but all the man could do was refer him to Metropolitan Police files where there were very, very long lists of known offenders connected with this particular offence.

'Shepherd's Bush,' Patrick decided after finishing the call and relating what had been said. 'Tomorrow. D'you want to tag along?'

No, but thank you, dearest heart. Slumming it around pubs playing darts and poker with the locals for money isn't my thing at all. It is definitely Patrick's and always has been, nothing what-soever these days to do with making a good job of roughing it undercover. It had not gone down too well with his superior officers in the Devon and Dorset Regiment either.

Da Rosta did suffer a setback to his recovery, not in connection with his actual wound but an unspecified complication thought to be brought on by obesity and high blood pressure. His inter-view with the Met, and anyone else wanting him to help with enquiries, was postponed for at least two days. As I had been wondering if Mike Greenway would allow me to have second bite at the mobster while Patrick was lurking in Shepherd's Bush, this was disappointing. I stayed on in London working at SOCA HQ and, the commander having been impressed by my clarifica-tion of the Rosemary Smythe case notes, asked me to rewrite a few more for him, in-house ones this time.

I had heard nothing from Patrick during the first twenty-four hours but did not expect to. As already indicated, he does not carry credit cards, his SOCA ID or even his own mobile phone when engaged in this kind of activity, using instead an 'anonymous' one with no phone numbers stored in the memory. This caution stems partly from our inclusion on terrorist hit lists and also the knowledge that it can be extremely hazardous to be identifiable as a policeman in some of the places he goes.

Then, when almost another day had gone by and I was still deeply involved with clanking syntax, my mobile rang for the fifth time that afternoon just as I was about to call it a day and go back to the hotel.

'Hi,' said a voice I recognized. 'I'm at Shepherd's Bush nick and have been trying to get hold of Greenway.'

'He's at the dentist's for an emergency appointment,' I told him. 'Broken crown. Perhaps his phone's switched off.'

'Can you come over and bring my ID?'

'What's going on?'

'I've been arrested for public disorder and they don't believe I'm one of them.'

I *almost* laughed.

The need to preserve your cover can land you in trouble, especially if you have mistakenly decked a plain-clothes copper. Bundled unceremoniously with the other brawlers into a police van, Patrick had preferred to keep quiet. OK, he had yelled 'drunken' abuse and thumped on the sides of the vehicle along with everyone else and this was the reason for official, added, chagrin.

'Serious Organised Crime Agency?' said the custody suite officer slowly and disbelievingly, staring at the warrant card as though I had just fashioned it in the garden shed. He then transferred his gaze – he had dark, beady eyes – to me and I thrust my own ID under his nose for good measure.

Finally, after a lot of heavy breathing, they dug Patrick out from where he had been incarcerated and returned to him what personal possessions he had, including rather a lot of money – notes.

'So, if you don't mind my asking, why carry all this cash if you're pretending to be as rough as rats?' enquired the man on the desk.

'I won it at cards,' Patrick answered with a sunny smile. 'Do apologize to the chap with red hair for me and tell him to sharpen up a bit if he doesn't want to be gone over by yobbos on a regular basis.'

'Apologize to him yourself – he's in the canteen.'

The speaker then registered surprise when Patrick did exactly that, returning, I felt, with less of his winnings.

'So, was that a fiasco or was it a fiasco?' I felt I had to ask when we were outside and having spotted a bruise under the stubble on the side of his chin.

Unconsciously perhaps, he touched his face. 'No, by no means. Most of those arrested were Anthony Thomas's lot.'

'*Really?* You saw him?'

'Yup, an older version of the bloke on the horse in the movie. He wasn't far from what's supposed to be home either as Barnes is just across the river over Hammersmith Bridge.'

'He can't have known who you were.'

'No, but he and another bloke were getting out of a car driven by Clement Hamlyn so I made sure *he* didn't see me.'

'I take it Thomas wasn't among those arrested.'

'Predictably he did a runner with the bloke, presumably his minder. I could have done with cutting myself in half right then and following them.'

'D'you reckon this was some kind of committee meeting?'

'Could have been, but later perhaps, when they'd done some drinking.'

Another few hundred yards down the road, I said, 'I have an idea you started the fight.' Which, I had been told at the nick, deep frowns all round, had spilled out from the public bar into an alleyway at the rear, three men having been found in a wheeled refuse bin marked General Waste Only.

'It's always a good idea to lessen the criminal odds against you.' Patrick then suddenly stopped speaking and I knew why.

'The leopard, non-changing spots for the use of,' I observed gently.

He shrugged sadly. 'I suppose so.' Then remained silent for a few moments before saying, 'I wasn't expecting the cops to turn up so quickly but with a bit of luck some of those nabbed are wanted for questioning in connection with other inquiries.'

'Was that the only reason you decided on a free-for-all?'

'It wasn't the reason at all. One of the men I'd been playing poker with suddenly decided he wanted his money back and produced a knife. People don't get away with doing that to me.'

I did not have to be told that this individual had been one of those in the bin.

'*And . . .*' Patrick began with a hint of triumph.

'And?' I queried obediently.

'Just before he disappeared I took Thomas's photo with my phone. Shall we put the cash towards the children's Christmas presents?'

'That can't be ethical. I mean, poker winnings from sleazy pubs, you having fought like a tomcat in an alley to keep hold of it?'

'Would you care to launder it for me then?' he enquired, straight-faced.

'OK, I'll pay it into *my* bank account.'

We had a very good meal out that night instead.

NINE

Angelo da Rosta scowled at us. 'Not more bloody filth. Sod off, I'm not talking to you.'

Patrick blithely introduced us, as usual just referring to me as his assistant, no name, drew up two chairs and we seated ourselves. The man in the hospital bed – a specially reinforced one for the seriously overweight, I felt – was the most unhealthy-looking human being I had ever seen in my life. His complexion was putty-coloured and he was sweating heavily, the overall impression, this deathly sheen, being that he was made of some kind of rancid tallow. This echoed a remark that had just been made to us by the doctor heading the team caring for him, a no-nonsense man who had said that if someone plaited what was left of his hair up into a point to make a wick he could be lit and used as a candle. This had staggered me coming from a medic and actually made me feel a bit sick.

'They've got their hands on me now, haven't they?' da Rosta bellowed. 'Effin' quacks. This test, that test, no proper food, shoving needles in me, pills, pills and more bloody pills. If I could get my hands on the bastard who—'

'You'd do what?' Patrick butted in with. 'Unintentionally, he's saved your life.'

'Balls.'

'That's what we've just been told. Apparently you've been living what was described as a suicidal lifestyle. Another six months, or less, and you would have been a dead man.'

'Someone did say that. I don't believe it.'

'Sad waste of a perfectly good bullet then.' Into the ensuing silence Patrick added: 'Why didn't you pay up?'

'Eh?'

'You heard.'

'I thought you were going to ask questions about my . . . er . . . well – business dealings, like the last lot.'

'No, this is me from the Serious Organised Crime Agency asking who's been threatening you.'

'No one threatens me. I can take care of myself.'

'We *know* people have been threatened and when they didn't pay they ended up fried in their cars or floating down the river with important bits of their heads missing. So, up till now, you've been lucky.'

Again, the man remained silent, albeit, I guessed, working on it.

'The thing to remember,' Patrick went on in a conspiratorial undertone, 'is that I'm not like other cops, I don't work like a cop and if you refuse to talk I shall simply walk away and hope that whoever's after you makes a much better job of it next time, whether you're inside prison or strutting around Shepherd's Bush.'

'I might take my chance then,' said the man with a big but wobbly smile.

'This is a very well organized and murderous outfit, clever mobsters preying on mobsters.'

No reply seemed to be forthcoming.

Patrick rose from his chair. 'With a bit of luck they'll clean up London and do the Met, and us, a favour.' He glanced at me. 'Shall we go?'

'No!' da Rosta bawled as I also got to my feet, making me glad he was in a side ward.

'No?' Patrick queried.

'I didn't say I wouldn't say nothing, did I? And you'll have to give me police protection from now on whether I talk to you or not.'

'Only if I'm feeling generous.'

As we already knew, there was an armed officer on duty out in the corridor.

'All right, some bloke . . .'

'Go on.'

The man flapped his podgy hands around. 'For God's sake, sit down.'

We sat. We had been asked not to risk raising his blood pressure to even more dangerous levels.

'Some bloke?' Patrick prompted.

'Promise you'll give me protection if I tell you everything I know.'

After a fairly long silence, Patrick nodded. 'I might, but only if I think you've been straight with me.'

'Some bloke phoned me. Said—'

'When was this?'

'Around two months ago. He said people in certain lines of business had to pay their dues – a membership subscription, he called it. Said mine was owing and had been for a while. Said I had to give him ten grand. I told him he'd be lucky and cut him off. He kept on phoning – got really nasty, finally said that if I didn't pay – and it was twenty grand now – I'd soon be . . . soon be . . .' Here da Rosta showed real signs of distress, tears in his eyes.

'Take your time,' Patrick murmured.

It all came out in a rush. 'The bastard said that if I didn't cooperate I'd soon be just a pile of pork scratchings. You probably think that's funny.'

'How did he know your number?' I asked, not finding it funny. Well, not right then, anyway.

'I run a launderette. It's in the phone book.'

'As a legal front to your other activities?'

No response came from this.

'Is da Rosta your real name?'

'It's the one I use,' the man growled. 'My grandmother on my mother's side was Italian. It's her name.'

'You often visit the nightclub that you were leaving when you were shot,' Patrick resumed. 'Incidentally, it's crazy to have a regular routine when you're in that kind of situation. Someone I spoke to there a few days ago remembered an occasion when he'd seen you talking to a very tall man. Was that in connection with the threats?'

Da Rosta quickly shook his head. 'No.'

'D'you remember him?'

'Yes, but—'

'I think it was. You see, we already have a suspect. A very tall man.'

'He wasn't anything to do with it.'

'So what did he want?'

'Nothing important.'

'But you sent your minders away so it must have been something you didn't want them to know about.'

Da Rosta shrugged. 'It was probably about the launderette. I've been thinking of selling it.'

I said, 'Did he want you to buy some jewellery?'

'No.' A flat denial.

I flipped back a few pages in my notebook. 'A gold watch chain, another thick gold chain with a locket and a diamond ring. Items stolen from a murder victim.'

The man's mouth shut into a tight pout that reminded me irresistibly of a chicken's backside.

'A harmless elderly lady,' I continued. 'Her killer, and he almost certainly did intend to kill her, tried to make it look like a burglary and does indeed seemed to have made off with some of her jewellery. I have an idea that, among other things, you're a fence and this man offered you these items. Did you agree to buy them?'

'No.'

'Why not?'

'Why not? Well . . . because . . . er . . . he didn't try to sell them to me.'

'You're a very bad liar,' Patrick said. 'Did you buy them or refuse to because you thought they were hot?'

'N-n-neither,' da Rosta stuttered.

Patrick flung himself back in his chair, turned to me and said, 'God, if he wasn't in hospital already and not so bloody fat I'd take him apart right now.'

'*Please* don't lose your temper,' I begged in an agonized whisper, playing along. 'You know how much trouble it causes.'

No lies there then.

Patrick merely regarded the man in the bed with what I can only call extreme malice.

'He – he said he'd let me have five grand off what I owed them if I took the stuff off his hands and paid up right then – fifteen grand,' Da Rosta finally said, tearing his gaze with difficulty from promised demolition, present or future, writ large.

'And did you?' I asked.

'No. I had an idea it was as hot as hell and planned to hire another couple of lads to watch my back.'

'Was what he offered you as I've described?'

'Just two gold chains, one with a locket. No ring.'

'Did you recognize his voice as the man who had contacted you by phone?'

'Might have been; hard to tell as he sort of muttered in a strange way on the phone. Might have been drinking.'

'The tall man drank your whisky in the club.'

'Yes, that's right, he did.'

'D'you know his name?'

'No, and I didn't ask. I didn't want to know.'

'What did he look like?'

'Ugly bastard. Scar on his face. Big mouth, horrible teeth. Scary. I don't really know how I had the bottle to tell him to sod off really. Sometimes, if I shut my eyes I can still see him, staring at me.'

I wrote Hamlyn in my notebook, underlined it and said, 'Is there anything else you can remember?'

'There might have been another bloke with him, sort of hanging around by the door.'

'Can you describe him?'

'Nah, the place was heaving. I only caught a glimpse of him.'

'Did you see the man who spoke to you just that once?'

'Yes, but the woman who runs the launderette for me said a tall bloke had been asking for me.'

'Are you sure you've never seen him before? Not even in the past, years ago?' Patrick asked.

'No.'

'Think.'

Da Rosta thought for quite a long time. Then he said, 'It can't have been the same bloke because he didn't have a scar and had his hair in dreadlocks but he reminded me of someone who used to work for a bloke who used to be a chum of mine, Danny, who had a second-hand car place in East Ham. This character used to clean the cars and things like that, little more than an errand boy really. Now Danny knew his way around but this bloke made him really twitched and apparently used to work as a heavy for local mobsters in his spare time. I think Danny gave him the heave-ho in the end because he was putting the buyers off.'

'Was this Daniel Coates?'

The man's eyes widened. 'Yes. But—'

'How did you meet him?'

'Inside,' da Rosta snapped. He switched on a sickly smile. 'Do I get my police protection now?'

'Not yet. You said Coates used to be a chum of yours. Is he not now?'

'Nah, we fell out over a bird.' He sighed. 'I was a bit thinner in those days.'

'Tell me, this man in the bar wanted fifteen grand just like that. Did he imagine you'd have that kind of cash on you? I can't believe he'd have accepted a cheque.'

'No, he said I could pay the next day by leaving the money in a place we'd arrange in the launderette. But, as I said, I told him to get stuffed.'

'We were told this happened around two months ago. I would have thought he'd have carried out his threats before now. Did he contact you again?'

'Er – yes.'

'When?'

'About ten days ago. Said I'd soon be in hell with all the others if I still didn't pay up.'

'Same arrangement as last time – money left in the launderette?'

'Yes, in a little cupboard at the back that has a pile of magazines on it for the punters to read while they're waiting for their stuff to wash.'

'In view of what's happened I presume you didn't agree to do what he wanted.'

'I did say I'd pay him but said he'd have to give me a couple more weeks to get the cash together. I thought it would buy me a bit more time. He gave me two days but in the end I didn't do it.'

One did tend to admire the man's courage.

'Did the woman who works for you notice anyone come in and look for a package?' Patrick went on to ask.

'No, but I didn't tell her. She got a bit twitched about the tall bloke first time round and I thought she'd up and leave if she knew someone like that was coming back.'

'I take it this man always rings you – you can't contact him.'

'No, I can't.'

'Did you know the other mobsters who were murdered?'

'I knew Fred, Fred Duggan. But didn't he have a genuine accident? The silly sod was never sober and could have fallen, hit his head and gone in the river as easy as getting out of bed in the morning.'

'He was murdered,' Patrick told him. 'Head seriously bashed in by several blows. And Tom Berry, or Jerry? Did you know him?'

Da Rosta shook his head. 'No. He was Fred's sort of boss and didn't chum up with no one. Right off the wall, according to Fred.'

'What about the man from Estonia known only as Rapla who was shot about a month ago?'

'Never knew him.'

'Who's next then?'

'God above knows.'

'You must have an ear to the ground. Who else is in the firing line?'

'Dunno. Everyone's clammed up.' Another phony smile. 'Do I get my protection now?'

'If you'll agree to testify against this man when we finally catch up with him.'

'OK – I promise.'

'You already have protection,' he was informed.

I asked myself what a mobster's promises were worth.

'It looks as though what Coates told you on the boat about his car business and Hamlyn working for him was the truth,' Patrick said as we made our way towards the hospital exit. Although we had no real leads he was cheerful. Was it because it appeared he really had saved the man's life by his actions? A little less guilt rolling around in his mind?

'There was no real reason for him to lie about that though, was there?' I pointed out.

'And da Rosta used to be a chum of his. This is where the list of those being targeted starts to make sense. I suggest we try to find out if there's a connection between them and any of the previous mobsters who've ended up dead. Perhaps Hamlyn knew them all. By the way, you're a genius for asking da Rosta about Miss Smythe's jewellery.'

'Thank you, but I'm sure Hamlyn will have got rid of it by now. It was interesting what da Rosta said about another man hanging around by the door of the club. I wonder if that was Anthony Thomas.'

'Could have been – or a hired bruiser. Mike may want Hamlyn picked up now.'

'I think you'll find he's much more interested in getting hard evidence against Hereward Trent first so he can arrest them both.'

'That connection is going to be very difficult to prove. Unless Hamlyn drops him in it.'

'Which he would, fast.'

Patrick laid a hand on my arm. 'Honeybunch, I think it's only fair that you share your theory about Trent with me.'

'Greenway might go off at a tangent and if I'm wrong . . .'

'Fine, we don't tell Greenway until we're really sure.'

I did not speak again until we were in the car. 'I think it's possible they're using Trent. Hamlyn might have something on him from his past – he seems to go in for that kind of thing. Trent has the respectability, outward or genuine, that Hamlyn can hide behind: a big house in a respectable district where he can conceal loot and weapons and hold meetings with his hired thugs without any fear of police interference. Rosemary Smythe witnessed things like that. And, as you yourself noticed, Trent was a bit hesitant about his wife and children's actual whereabouts. They might be being held as insurance.'

'It should be easy to find out whether the kids are at school or not.'

In this Patrick was wrong for these days schools are very reluctant to reveal anything about their charges, especially over the phone, and I cautioned against going down that route. Finally, and not wishing to risk a head teacher telling Trent that the police had been making enquiries about his offspring, Patrick requested that a short-term watch be put on the house at a time when children might reasonably be expected to come home from school. True enough, a plain-clothes woman PC having been despatched to do the job that same day, the au pair departed in the car and arrived back shortly afterwards with two young girls, both wearing the uniform of the local primary school.

'She saw no sign of the wife,' Patrick reported, putting his mobile back in his pocket. 'She's probably staying with a friend, or visiting her parents.'

'Does she work?' I wondered.

'I wouldn't have thought so. They're loaded, aren't they?'

'Women with wealthy husbands often have paying interests,' I reflected. 'Some are into interior or garden design or even carry on with their professional careers as doctors, dentists, judges, civil engineers, television presenters, chefs, you name it. Some have been known to write books.'

My husband performed an abject grovel on the table before him, hands over his head.

'You can come out now,' I said, when I could speak for laughing.

When enlarged and digitally tweaked, the photograph of Anthony Thomas that Patrick had taken with his phone proved to be good enough to be used for general identification purposes and was duly placed in relevant files. Otherwise, routine work went on. Findings on the strands of wool that had been removed from the rose thorns in Hereward Trent's garden were quite detailed but not a lot of use. The wool was from Scottish sheep and likely to have been machine, rather than hand, knitted due to technical characteristics that I could not make head nor tail of. I gathered that the lab had had expert opinion on this. This person had gone on to report that the dye was not of vegetable origin but of a commercial type not commonly used by the main manufacturers, such as Pringle. He, or she, had tentatively suggested that the garment, probably a man's due to the weight of the wool, had been made in Scotland at a small mill, and possibly bought there. The lab reported that there was no definable human DNA on the sample.

My next contribution to the investigation, there not being a lot else I could do right now – we still had no real leads – was to grit my teeth, go out, buy and begin to read Clement Hamlyn's books to try to find out more about him. There were five: four best sellers, the fifth published only a week previously and rapidly heading in that direction. In order of publication they were: *Chill, Heat, Blood, Burn* and *Rage*. It was *Burn* that had been dramatized for television; the others, I knew, were to follow, and as it was set in wartime London I was assuming that the title referred to the Blitz. No, wrong, it was hatred that burned, I would discover, not buildings.

Patrick walked into Greenway's 'snug', the room adjoining his office that I was being permitted to use, where, on rare occasions, the commander relaxes, just in time to have *Chill* whistle passed his nose and thud into a far corner. *Heat* and *Blood* rapidly followed. 'Not quite your thing?' he hazarded, an eyebrow raised.

'They're unreadable,' I raged. 'Sorry, but it's beyond the call of duty.'

'It was your idea.'

'I know, but the violence is sickening, the language revolting and it's making me feel like a middle-aged ninny for being disgusted by them.'

'Good plots?'

'Yes, not bad – as far as I can tell.'

He gathered up the paperbacks and tucked them under one arm. 'Lunch?'

After refreshment I tackled *Burn*. I had more interest in this one due to the Richmond connection. The storyline involved a detective sergeant in the Met whose house in Islington was bombed, killing his wife and baby son. At this time he was working on a murder case, a bank manager in Richmond having been found stabbed to death in Richmond Park. It was left to the reader to work out for themselves whether at this point the DS loses his sanity and blames the killer for the death of his family, but he commences an obsessive and almost frenzied hunt for him. This takes him deeply into the London criminal underworld.

I skipped most of this, unable to stomach the way this crazed cop rapes, batters and even murders his way to get to the man he hunts – finally, having narrowly failed to find his target and been badly injured in a fight with a gang boss and his honchos, he becomes delirious and wanders the streets of Richmond close to the house where the murder victim lived, hoping for inspiration. He meets an old woman who tells him that on the night he was killed she saw the banker with a man she knew had 'business dealings' in the area but refuses to tell him his name, panics and runs back into her house, slamming the door. He breaks in through the back.

I read on, not even aware for a little while that I was no longer alone in the room.

'Time to knock off for the day?' Patrick suggested quietly.

I laid the book aside, realized that it was getting dark outside and took a deep breath before saying, 'It would appear that Hamlyn acts out his plots.'

'Before or afterwards?'

'As far as this one's concerned, afterwards. His main character, a cop, loses his temper and throws an elderly woman down the stairs when she refuses to tell him the name of a potential murder suspect, discovers she's still alive and strangles her when she still won't, or can't, speak. Great detection work. I think the man's as mad as this character he writes about.'

Patrick's mobile rang and I guessed it was Daws as Patrick called him 'sir'. Greenway put a stop to the courtesy as far as he himself was concerned a while ago, adding: 'You used to be a lieutenant colonel, for God's sake.'

'Interesting,' Patrick commented after the call ended. 'Although

Hereward Trent has never officially been in trouble with the police there was a hushed-up scandal at a golf club he used to belong to when they lived in Essex – funds going missing when he was club treasurer. I say "hushed up" but Daws has discovered that because the club practically went bankrupt because of it, it made the local papers, only Trent's name wasn't actually mentioned. Everyone in the district knew who was responsible. It put an end to his position on the town council as well and he and his wife moved away – to Richmond.'

'How on earth did Daws find all that out?'

'I never ask. But he does know more people than Moses.'

'That could be the skeleton Trent has in the cupboard that Hamlyn's found out about.'

That night I finished reading, at speed, the book but found no further parallels to the murder case. It was with some trepidation the next morning that I began *Rage*. Having already discovered that if I skipped most of the dialogue, which Hamlyn was very bad at writing as it was stilted and a large proportion of the adjectives and nouns represented by profanities, never mind all his characters sounding the same, and concentrated on the descriptive passages, vividly portrayed, a real picture began to emerge.

This novel was set in present-day London, written in the first person and concerned a crime boss endeavouring to enact revenge on other mobsters with whom he had had quarrels in the past, owed him money and, in his view, had 'done the dirty on him'. Again, the theme was revenge. I became very bored very quickly with the ambushes in back alleys, car chases, general sexual abuse of prostitutes, drunkenness and finally the showdown when our hero slowly and messily tortures the last subject of his ire to death, finally slinging the blooded remains into a stolen car and tidying everything up with a well-aimed petrol bomb. The book ends with our 'hero' setting out to drink himself into oblivion.

Hamlyn, then, still seemed to be living the storylines of his books.

'What I simply don't understand is how he has the nerve to make threats in public,' I said, later that day. 'I mean, the man's appeared on television. Is he super-confident that he can frighten people into silence should they recognize him?'

'Da Rosta seemed pretty scared,' said Patrick. 'Or perhaps Hamlyn kills those who guess who he is anyway, no bother.'

'I want to know what he's doing right now,' I said.

'Writing-wise, you mean.'

'Yes.'

'All we have to do then is break into his place, work out the passwords on his computer and have a read.'

I ignored the slight sarcasm – no, the full-blown sarcasm – and said, 'I had another go at the first three novels and they were either just pure imagination or based on his past; the fourth, if one gives credence to the Miss Smythe connection, is about his immediate past, the fifth, if our hunches about him are correct, concerns the present. He's completely hooked on what he's doing, living the dream and making money out of it; it's an addiction, like alcohol. So what's next?'

I had a terrible feeling that Hamlyn would create the future and then make it happen.

TEN

As far as Patrick and I were concerned the next three days were about to be as good as wasted as he had to attend a residential course at another hotel, the subject matter of which was the new National Crime Agency. Initially, I saw little point in remaining in London – the commander had said he did not want me 'going off into the blue' working on the case on my own – as it would then be the weekend and, depressed and frustrated because Greenway's fears of the case going cold seemed about to be realized, I'd told Patrick that I would go straight home.

Then, disastrously, I changed my mind.

The keys to Rosemary Smythe's house were still in the drawer of the desk we use, together with the case file and my task would be to place everything in the safe before we left or hand the items to another member of the team if they needed them. I asked around and no one did so into the safe it went, but minus the keys.

Patrick had asked me to take the car home and put some of his belongings in it in order to travel light. He was not looking forward to being stuck in a hotel although they had been promised some kind of relief in the shape of a morning's 'leadership training, team bonding and outdoor activities'. Ye gods, my imagination ran wild. Scampering around Hyde Park frightening the horses? Crossing the Serpentine in boats fashioned from empty oil drums and bits of fallen trees? Had they known what they were doing when they ordered Patrick along? Would he pop the instructors into a sack and take everyone else off to the nearest pub?

My mood instantly sobered as I approached the rear of Miss Smythe's house. On foot, that is: I had left the Range Rover several streets away. I had used the time, waiting for it to get dark, by first walking down into Richmond to have something to eat. It was drizzling with rain, again and, afterwards, with the hood up on my dark anorak I had made a short detour to walk by Jane Grant's cottage. The place had been in darkness but whether the windows had really thick curtains, I could not remember, or she was out was impossible to judge.

OK, this did sort of come under the heading of 'going off into the blue' and I was slightly breaking the rules as far as my working partner was concerned as well but there could be no harm in a little quiet observation of Hereward Trent. I had no intention of climbing the oak tree again and had spotted on our previous visit a set of aluminium steps in an outhouse where gardening tools and so forth were kept.

No one had re-bolted the gate and it opened smoothly, no squeaking hinges, after I had unlocked it. I left it unlocked, switched on my tiny torch, shielding the light with a hand so I did not inadvertently shine it up in the air, and made my way down the garden. It was not yet absolutely dark and there is always a glow in the sky in large cities anyway from street lights and others so I only needed the torch to prevent me from tripping over something. Beneath the oak, and careful not to walk into the remains of the tree house, I paused to look and listen, switching it off.

There were lights on in the house, one downstairs and another on the first floor. As I watched, the latter went out and the one in the next room was switched on.

This was something I had not expected but there was no reason why, the place no longer being a crime scene, that someone like Jane Grant should not be there, perhaps checking that all was well or sorting through her aunt's papers as she was executor to the will.

I muttered something regrettable. All I had wanted to do was fetch the step ladders from the outhouse and have a look over the garden wall into next door, staying no longer than half an hour or so. Now, to struggle with an awkward aluminium contrivance likely to clatter noisily into anything and everything it encountered in the dark seemed a bit pathetic and, if heard by whoever was indoors, I would have some difficult questions to answer. And as my mentor has been known to warn, always stay on the right side of *bloody stupid.*

I remembered that there was a little garden seat in an arbour quite close by, found it and sat down, needing to think things through. There were aspects of this set of cases, which we were assuming made up one complex whole, that were puzzling from the point of view of the suspects involved.

First there was Hereward Trent, a man known to have embezzled money from a golf club, and reputed, no proof forthcoming whatsoever, to be some kind of crime boss. Patrick and I had interviewed him and what had been before us was someone nervous to the point of rudeness, alone in the house with no staff or anyone who might act as his bodyguard, a vital necessity for someone involved in serious crime. I had already come to the conclusion that there was every possibility he was being blackmailed to provide his home as a safe house, a place to stash weapons and stolen property.

Then, Anthony Thomas – an actor probably with criminal connections in his native country – requests for details to Moscow police had, so far, gone unanswered – who now lived a shady but no doubt more financially rewarding life in London. The photograph of him showed a man with quite heavily Slavic features – he had probably been quite good looking once – but it was not an intelligent face. Did he provide the 'personnel' for what we were assuming were well-organized criminal activities?

Third in the mix was the bent cop. I could not remember his

name and SOCA was not involved, although being kept in the picture, with that investigation. He might have been the source of police intelligence, providing the names and addresses of witnesses and other vital information. Why? Did Hamlyn have some kind of hold over him too?

Last but definitely not least was Clement Hamlyn himself, plus Claudia Barton-Jones, the latter in trouble with the law in connection with unrelated matters. Or were they? As to the crime writer with a criminal record whose old associates were going down like ninepins, the darkly glowering oaf who now appeared to act out his plots and I guessed lived in a kind of drink-fuelled fantasy world, driven by his need to make more money to pay for it . . . Well, he was as mad as a box of spanners, wasn't he?

Who the hell was orchestrating this poisonous bunch?

Someone else.

I wanted to share this with Patrick but could hardly sit nattering on my phone in a garden in which, strictly speaking, I was trespassing. And, having just arrived for his course, leaving work behind for a few days, he would probably be disinclined to hear my musings on that subject right now. But my guilt at acting alone caught up with me and I rang his number. All I got was the answerphone. So be it.

Another thought . . . In none of her letters had Miss Smythe mentioned going next door and peering in through the kitchen window, or lurking in the garden generally, again presumably when the gates had been left open perhaps because more 'guests' were expected, the reason she had been given the ASBO. Embarrassment? According to her niece she had not been too bothered about it. What else had she done? Her last letter had mentioned that she still hoped to provide evidence, that all-important word.

Evidence. As we had already noted, all the letters had been about things she had seen with her own eyes. Not hearsay, no gossip. If that was the case, on the occasions she had been in the Trent's garden or looked through windows she had seen nothing that furthered her cause. The events she had mentioned had occurred when she was in the tree house. I found myself asking if, after she wrote the last letter SOCA received, Miss Smythe had investigated further but not lived to tell us about it.

It was only a theory but I did wonder what, if anything, this lady could have seen or done that forced them finally to kill her. Something highly incriminating to them. Hard evidence.

I simply had to know who was in the house.

The moon, not full but almost so, made up my mind for me by appearing through a large gap in the clouds and I did not need my torch to walk down the rest of the garden. I took a narrow meandering side path, the tall shrubs on either side of which would conceal me from the house. The realization went through my mind that if a new lock had been fitted to the back door I would not be able to get in. But I did not really want to get in, just find out who was inside.

The light was on in the kitchen, blinds up. Standing to one side of the back door and endeavouring to mask my face with the ivy growing thickly on the wall by it I looked in the window. No one was in the room but through the open doorway I could see that a light was on beyond. Moving carefully – there were plants in pots everywhere here – I turned to the door and, praying that it would not squeak, turned the heavy knob. There was just a tiny click and the door began to open under the slight pressure of my hand. All remained silent within the house.

Then, I heard the clack of high-heeled shoes on the tiled kitchen floor and quickly pulled the door closed, praying that the inner door of the little lobby was shut so whoever she was would not notice. I waited, only realizing that I had been holding my breath when I had to gasp for air. Then, I risked another peep, moving very, very slowly, peering through the ivy.

In the room a slim, fair-haired woman stood with arms akimbo, her pretty face like thunder, nervously biting her bottom lip and looking towards the open doorway into the hall. She was well-dressed as if going out for the evening in a grey sparkly top and black trousers, a small beaded evening bag clutched in one hand resting on the opposite arm. There was a slight tremor about her as though she was either tapping a foot – I could not see – or shivering.

'For God's sake, hurry up!' I distinctly heard her say in a loud stage whisper.

At a snail's pace I moved back, not daring to remain where I was any longer in case she spotted me. Moments later I heard other footsteps, probably a man's, and there was a heated, whispered conversation of which I could only catch the odd word.

'So *now* what do we do?' the woman finally asked, louder.

'We'll have to come back later,' the man replied.

Furiously, the woman said, 'But we can't keep coming in here! Someone'll see us!'

'Keep your voice down!'

I decided that I had every right to join in this conversation, opened the outside door, pushed the inner one wide and went in. For a moment they were so engrossed in their argument they did not notice me. When they did, their expressions were ones of total shock.

'What the hell are *you* doing here?' Hereward Trent shouted.

'Do keep your voice down,' I said, soothingly.

'Who is this?' Sonya Trent demanded to know of him, her mind, I was convinced, racing more along the lines of 'other woman' than anything else just then.

He momentarily lost the ability to speak, so I replied for him. 'I'm with the Serious Organised Crime Agency and please leave out all the stuff about being good neighbours checking on the empty house next door or thinking you saw a burglar in here.'

'But we are checking that all is well with the house,' Trent protested.

'You're lying! You didn't care a toss about this old lady when she was alive!' I raged at him. 'How did you get in?'

Sonya Trent burst into tears.

'It's no good cracking up now!' her husband bawled at her, shaking her by the shoulders and making everything worse as he was hurting her.

I thrust him aside – I loathe bullies – saying, 'It's too late for lies, posturing and denials. Who gave you the key? What are you doing here? What are you looking for?'

Trent sort of deflated. 'I – er – no, it's not – er – what you think. We're—'

'Shall we go back to your house?' I suggested.

Sonya, sobbing, made the decision by marching out through the back door and, after hesitating, he followed. I quickly turned the lights off and locked up, having found a set of keys, including a pair of new-looking ones, on a nearby worktop, and hurried after them. I caught up with them almost immediately as they could not see their way in the dark and went in front, switching on my torch. The thought crossed my mind that if Patrick had not left the gate unbolted they would have had to risk being seen entering the house from the street.

There were security lights in their garden which came on as we approached. I stayed close to pre-empt any notion of slamming their rear door in my face and followed the pair through the conservatory and into the living room where Trent immediately poured himself a large Scotch. He did not ask his wife if she wanted anything and paced stiffly away from us back into the conservatory. Sonya wilted into a chair and carried on crying.

Trent came back into the room, glanced at an ornate wall clock and said woodenly, 'Perhaps . . . we . . . ought to talk.'

'I wonder how many people other than Miss Smythe have died as a result of your little venture?' I said to neither of them in particular, my anger surfacing again. 'Several London mobsters for a start – although you probably don't count them as they're scumbags and beneath your notice. Almost deserve to be finished off really and no problem if they didn't die immediately when someone torched their car with them in it – they could have screamed a bit, but no matter. And the men who were thrown in the Thames might not have *quite* expired after having been shot or their heads bashed in. The same, no doubt, applies to the waste-of-space Spaniard in France who did drown, slowly probably as he could swim, after he'd been beaten up on Cannes waterfront.'

Sonya Trent was gazing at me in absolute horror.

'And then there's your pet psycho,' I continued. 'Hamlyn. He might not have finished off the others but in my view he did murder Miss Smythe – with your certain knowledge – because she'd been watching this place from her tree house. This, as we now know, was mysteriously sabotaged. It collapsed when she was inside it and she broke her leg, also suffering cuts and contusions. That was your first attempt to get rid of her.'

'This isn't *true*!' Sonya shrieked. 'Herry, tell me it isn't true!'

Stony-faced, Trent said, 'Not one word.'

To me, Sonya whispered, 'Hamlyn *isn't* our pet psycho. Just a crime writer we happen to know. He's been here a few times, that's all.'

'Hardly the perfect dinner guest though, is he?' I retorted. 'He has a criminal record, oafish manners and drinks himself into the ground at every opportunity.'

Trent, who had gone a little pale, fidgeted in his seat and, again, looked at the clock. Then he said, 'I know it looks bad but we weren't in the house next door for the wrong reasons. As to everything else you've said, it's nonsense, nothing to do with us.'

'You said you wanted to talk,' I reminded him. 'So, talk.'

'Yes, these are matters that I must clear up with you. I have my reputation to consider.'

'How did you get the keys?'

'From Jane Grant, Miss Smythe's niece.'

'To what end?'

'She asked us to check the place now and again to save her driving over.' He cleared his throat. 'Mrs Grant doesn't share her late aunt's views about us and came to apologize after the police became involved. She said the old lady was in the first stages of dementia.'

'And?'

He shrugged. 'Nothing. That's it.'

'Just now, next door, I distinctly heard you say, "We'll have to come back later" in reply to your wife having asked, "So now what do we do?" Were you looking for something?'

'No. We were – *are* – late for a dinner date and I hadn't had time to look in the loft where the roof leaks sometimes when the rain's in a certain direction and a bucket has to be emptied.' Jerkily, he stood up. 'I don't think we need detain you any longer.'

'Sorry, but it's me detaining you,' I told him, also rising. 'If you like I can arrest you and call out any number of sirens and flashing blue lights and you'll be questioned at the nearest police station. If, on the other hand, you cooperate with SOCA and admit that you're involved with serious crime but are being forced into it by dangerous criminals because they have some kind of hold over you and our investigations prove that to be correct . . .' I smiled at him, leaving the rest unsaid.

'If we—' his wife began.

'Leave this to me, Sonya!' Trent snapped then lapsed into silence for a moment before continuing with: 'Yes, all right. I'll talk to someone in authority – but here, not at a police station, as these are very sensitive matters. Also, it might be very dangerous for us otherwise.'

'Do I really have your word that you'll cooperate with us?' I persevered.

'Yes, you do.'

Watching them carefully, and not trusting Trent for one second, I found my mobile: this was no time to worry about Patrick's preferences and I was praying he would answer this time.

'Farley's Rusks' help desk,' said my husband. He knew it was me as he has programmed his phone to make various animal noises depending on who, in the family that is, is ringing him. Mine's a moo. There was laughter in the background, probably for that reason.

'The Trent's place,' I said. 'Please get here.'

'Now?'

'Now. He's said he's going to cooperate.'

'Are *you* all right?'

'Yes, perfectly.'

'Is it just you and the Trents there?'

'Yes.'

'I'm on my way.'

How long would it take him to get a taxi? How long before he arrived? I guessed it was around ten miles by road and the traffic at this time in the evening would not be light.

Sonya had dried her tears but still appeared to be very shaky.

'This has come as a real shock to you,' I said to her, thinking that keeping up the pressure was no bad idea. 'And you're being blackmailed after the episode at the golf club.'

'You can't know about that!' Trent shouted.

'Someone you've never met does though,' I told him.

Carrying on talking to Sonya as she was the weak link, I said, 'You've been forced to have mobsters in your house, store weapons and stolen property for them, and had to host the kind of gatherings that must be your idea of hell.'

She had her mouth open to reply, probably to tell me that I was right, when Clement Hamlyn strode through from the conservatory entrance.

'Bloody hell!' he exclaimed, coming to a sudden stop. 'It's the little scribbler. What's she doing here?'

'She's with the police and investigating the old woman's murder,' Trent explained tersely. 'Surprised us next door and appears to know what's going on. Thank God you're here.'

It had been a very bad mistake to leave the Smith and Wesson in the car.

'With the *police*?' Hamlyn echoed in disbelief, staring at me. 'Prove it!'

'The Serious Organised Crime Agency,' I said, showing him my ID.

He barely looked at it and began pacing the room. 'Damn! I *knew* that bastard you were with was a cop.'

'Is that who's on his way?' Trent asked me.

'Yes,' I said, adding, and I hoped not as desperately as I felt, 'but not alone.'

I heard approaching footsteps and three men entered though the same way as had Hamlyn: Anthony Thomas by the look of him, his minder, plus a lesser cranially challenged mortal, a dead giveaway due to the fact that his eyes were too close together and about half an inch from his hairline.

There was a lot of shouting, during which Sonya Trent edged away from Hamlyn, obviously completely unable to cope with the situation. Our eyes met and I deliberately then gazed at the group of lights switches on the wall near where she was now standing. She either did not understand or pretended not to.

Silence fell and they were all looking at me.

'Get rid of her,' Hamlyn said to the man from Thugs Central Casting.

This individual walked towards me, sniggering. I forestalled whatever he was going to do by kicking him in a delicate place and then clouted him on the back of the neck with both fists clenched together, the exact spot crucial, and he predictably folded up like a clothes airer on to the carpet. Then I leapt for the light switches, first shoving Sonya into Hamlyn on the way with one hand and slamming shut the door into the hall – there was a light on there too – with the other.

Darkness, a shriek and a loud thump as though Hamlyn had lost his balance and the pair had fallen over together. Someone grabbed me in the gloom – the minder, probably – but I had a hand free and poked him in one eye. He hung on to me, swearing, but I let his other eye have it and was suddenly free. Jinking but staying close to the left hand wall of the room, I made my way towards where I could see dim moonlight through the plants in the conservatory, feeling a tiled floor beneath my feet when I reached it. Then I ran into someone large with stinking breath just short of the doorway to the garden. Hamlyn had thrown Sonya on to the floor, hadn't he?

There was no point in struggling; he would only lose his temper. He lost it a bit anyway, slapping me around the head a couple of times, hard and then, someone having put the lights back on, threw me on to a sofa and hit me again for good measure – a punch in the face this time. I felt my lip split and then life became vague for a while. When awareness slowly returned, my head feeling strangely numb, I had the sense to remain inert, glad – yes, glad – that there were others present so it was unlikely he would rape me.

'He's a damned long time,' said someone, possibly Thomas. 'Are you sure she rang him?'

'Yes,' said Trent's voice. 'She did.'

'What did she say?'

'Not a lot.'

'Not up to much, are they?'

'SOCA won't miss them then,' Hamlyn said with a loud laugh. 'Tie her up and we'll all wait for him outside – I should imagine he'll come in the back. Did you leave the gates open? You lazy bastards usually do.'

They had.

'He looked as if he might be able to take care of himself if in real trouble,' Hamlyn went on. 'But with five of us, OK, four and half with Dessie not too good—'

'My eyes hurt,' guess who whined.

'All right, three and two halves.'

'You can count me out too,' Trent said. 'I've never offered violence to anyone in my life.'

'You're in this!' Hamlyn shouted. 'Right up to your designer-aftershave-reeking neck.'

I opened my eyes to slits in an effort to gauge what was going on. I could not see Sonya in my limited field of vision but did not want to move and reveal that I was conscious. Someone approached and I closed them again. I was heaved face down on to the sofa, my hands wrenched round behind my back and several turns of thick string were tied around my wrists. Too tightly.

In normal circumstances Patrick should be able to survive the odds, even in the dark, I told myself. But Hamlyn, Thomas and his sore-eyed minder were big men and if he himself had been drinking – and why should he not? – it would make a difference. That said, the circumstances, coming into 'enemy territory', would ensure that he was highly alert. And surely he would have his Glock and knife.

Hopeless thoughts, perhaps, as the weapons would probably be locked in the room safe, the course organizers having promised security staff in view of the importance of some of those attending, people like Richard Daws. A tear trickled down my cheek and disappeared into the hugely expensive fabric of the sofa. It was all my fault . . .

I did not witness what happened. A while later I heard yells first outside and then in an adjacent room, Thomas – who had a strong Russian accent – shouting, 'That's the man who was in the pub and caused all the bother when my boys were picked up!'

Just after this Hamlyn came back into the room, gulped down some whisky directly from a bottle on a drinks tray and then hit me again as a postscript.

ELEVEN

I could see nothing and there was an odd humming, rumbling noise in my ears, a vibration with the occasional swinging and swaying to my little world that made no sense. It went first one way and then another when I slid for a short distance, to and fro, on something that smelt sickeningly of fish and rubber.

It took a long time for me to realize that I was lying on the floor of a van being driven at speed. I saw in the dim light what appeared to be – everything was well out of focus – the toes of a pair of shoes a few inches in front of me. Moving very slowly, I wormed myself away from them.

'Lie still!' a man's voice rasped.

I wriggled away a bit more when he spoke again, seemingly behind him to someone in the driving cab, to ask for a cigarette and turned my head slowly to look around me. This seemed to kick all my perceptions awake and my head exploded with pain, the ghastly sensation almost making me vomit. My eyes still would not focus properly but I could just make out a dark shape lying near me. I blinked a few times, inwardly raging with frustration, convinced it was Patrick and not just a pile of sacks, or whatever. It was: after a few minutes my vision had cleared a little and I recognized his gold watch on an outflung arm only a matter of inches from me. By the light of the sudden flare of a match I saw that he was completely still, perhaps unconscious.

The van picked up speed. Where were they taking us? Had we just joined a motorway? The lights of other vehicles, behind and coming from the opposite direction, formed an almost hypnotic rhythmic pattern on the roof of the van. Perhaps I was hypnotized as I drifted off into a kind of fuzzy blackness for a while. Or perhaps it was for days. Or weeks. Or this was hell and it was for ever and ever.

No, no, I inwardly railed, my fuddled brain producing the notion that this couldn't be hell or Patrick would not be right here with me. But hang on, another part of me argued, he *has* killed quite a lot of people. Soldiers do that, stupid, I argued back, they obey orders. The Devil's advocate came back with, you're completely blinkered by your love for this man, he's killed people *without* being ordered to. The fact that he's a clergyman's son doesn't mean anything at all.

'Shut up!' I heard myself yell out loud.

'*You* shut up!' a man bellowed almost in my face.

That they were going to kill us finally dawned on me.

The van roared on and I finally did vomit, the stench of rubber, fish, diesel, cigarette smoke and sweat, never mind anything else,

my undoing. This probably proved to be the deciding factor as far
as our captors were concerned for it was very shortly after this
that they shoved us out of the moving vehicle on to a motorway.

My only recollections of those last few moments before
oblivion were the repeated shouted requests to the driver to slow
down by whoever was struggling to open the rear doors, followed
by the squeal of tyres as the vehicle veered violently to the left,
the driver shouting that a car was right on his tail. Then, brakes
were slammed on and I received a rough manhandling. There
was an appalling impact and then I was rolling over and over in
the road. Headlights, more squealing tyres, wheels missing me
by inches. Then, most peculiar this, the sensation of being slowly
towed, feet first, along the tarmac.

'The M40 can be a bloody dangerous road at night,' a man's
voice said. 'They were damned fools to try to cross it.'

I reasoned from this idiotic remark – surely all motorways are
dangerous to cross whatever the time of day – that there were still
two of us. But he had not said anything about both being alive.
My present environs, judging by the warm fug with tinges of
antiseptic and less pleasant smells, was a hospital.

I opened my eyes and fixed the speaker, who must have
addressed someone who was passing as there was no one else in
my line of vision, with a stare. He had two heads, both with
auburn hair, and four eyes, all blue. His mouth was a long slit
with a ginger fur roof, a bit like a heavily underlined sleeping
cat. This all being a bit wrong, I firmly shut my eyes and then
opened them again and everything resolved itself into a weedy-
looking individual with a moustache and wearing some kind of
green uniform.

'Is my husband alive?' I said, or rather whispered.

'The bloke you were found with?' he queried lightly. 'No
idea.'

'Please find out for me,' I begged.

'Sorry, not my job.'

'Then what the bloody hell are you doing here?' I hissed at
him.

'I'm a porter and have just brought you to this ward with Joe,
over there.'

He strolled away.

Just a little contrite at the way I had spoken to him, I undertook a personal assessment. Other than everything aching as though I had been trampled on by an elephant, a headache that was off the scale and a mouth suddenly feeling several sizes too large, nothing drastic seemed to have happened to me. No bandages, drips or bits of sticking plaster, no splints or Nil by Mouth notices – that I could see anyway. Tomorrow though, I had an idea I would hardly be able to move.

I must have dozed off again at this stage – it did not occur to me that I been given painkillers – and woke up at some indefinable time later, although the ward lights were on this time so my sluggish brain deduced that it was night. It came home to me then that I had been dosed because the medication had spectacularly worn off. The first thing I wanted to do was scream but the five other patients in the little ward appeared to be asleep. Then for some reason I burst into tears, tried to sit up to find some kind of bell push to summon a nurse and knocked over a water jug on the bedside cabinet.

Someone came, a large black woman who made soothing noises and did not mind when I clung to her sobbing, listened to my agonized babbles, prised my fingers from her arm and went away for a few minutes, an eternity, during which time I latched my hands into the sides of the mattress instead. An orderly arrived to mop up the water.

'*Please* tell me that Patrick isn't dead,' I can remember loudly wailing, to my shame, when the nurse returned with salvation in the form of an injection.

'I don't know about him but I'll find out,' she promised, painlessly sliding in the needle.

Darkness enveloped me.

Daylight, bright sunshine on a wall in a different place, drip apparatus in one hand, and the other arm, lying on the coverlet, slightly swollen and with huge hatching bruises. I lay there, trying to think straight and for some reason worrying about looking utterly gormless because that was how I felt. There was a slight movement to my immediate right and I looked round, which hurt.

'Hi,' said Patrick. He was sort of crash-landed in an armchair, staring at me, looking appalled. 'God, you're in a mess.'

My tears took me unawares, again, and we both leaned towards one another and hugged as best we could. We remained like this until I had to disengage to repair the damage from crying with my one usable hand, he handing me a tissue.

'How badly are you hurt?' I asked him, seeing a large graze on the side of his cheek. A shock, too, to see at least four days' growth of stubble on his face. Had we really been here that long?

'Battered and bruised but mobile, after a fashion,' he replied. 'You know me: Sir Bouncealot.'

This set us both giggling, mostly, on reflection, due to the drugs.

'As far as everyone at home's concerned we've been in a car accident,' Patrick continued. 'In an unmarked vehicle. It's not far from the truth.'

'And you've told them?'

He nodded. The anger was there, the need to go and find Clement Hamlyn and do him untold damage.

'I'm really sorry. This was all my fault.'

'Don't think like that. We've got them. Arrest warrants are out for Hamlyn, the Trents, Thomas, and that pair of oafs with him – for attempted murder. Other investigations will automatically follow.'

'Could you identify them then – in the dark?'

'No, I played possum when they jumped me outside and lugged me into the kitchen. It wasn't worth getting seriously beaten up with those kinds of odds – and I wanted to find out what had happened to you. But someone still kicked me in the head when he could see what he was doing.'

'I take it you weren't armed.'

'No, and I should have made the time to go to my room to at least get the Glock, but I didn't. So it's my fault you're hurt.' He paused and looked away. 'I'm thinking of resigning. I can't carry on exposing you to this kind of danger.'

'Please don't resign,' I said. 'You mustn't. It's my choice. Anyway, I don't have to be in on your cases.'

'It sounds very cold to say I can't work efficiently without you but it's true. I think you know what I mean.'

I hoped my swollen face assumed a smile for him, really hoped.

'Greenway made the decision not to call the Trent's place a crime scene after what happened to us hoping that they'll return home thinking they've got away with it. If they see their house is draped in incident tape they may well disappear for ever. He's the sort of bloke to have funds hidden away.'

'What about the children and the nanny?'

Patrick made a visible effort to find the energy to reply. 'By amazing fortune they heard nothing that went on that night as their rooms are in an annex. Arrangements have been made for the two little girls to be taken to their maternal grandmother in Dartmouth, Devon, and there was no reason why the nanny should not go home to Poland, her contract having ended. As far as the girl knows, her replacement had not been arranged. D'you feel like telling me what happened?'

It was a sign of how fuddled I was that I had forgotten he did not know why I had ended up where I had. 'Can I tell you a bit later?'

'Sure. I'll leave you to sleep.' Unsteadily, he got to his feet.

'When can we go home?'

'I'm working on it. I've been told I can be discharged tomorrow but I'm not leaving you here on your own. They don't seem to want the bed. Oh, and Greenway sends you his love.'

Painfully, like a sick man in his eighties, Patrick made his way out, holding on to things to steady himself. I was weak with relief that he was not more seriously hurt, or worse, and at the same time trying to remember what I had wanted to tell him after I had paused to think about the case in Miss Smythe's garden.

Greenway had sent me his *love*?

That same day I had to have a couple of X-rays, which, together with the results of previous blood and other tests, revealed that no serious damage had been done, either internally or to my bones. There remained the question mark of how we were going to get home, from Oxford, as neither of us was in any shape to drive. Having arranged for our car to be collected from Richmond – amazingly, it was still there – Greenway solved the problem for us by organizing a driver and, with superlative generosity, invited us to stay at his own home in north Ascot for a few days. Having checked with the medical staff as to our exact condition he told us, 'You'll frighten the living daylights out of your kids if you go home looking like *that*.'

Also, of course, he wanted the full story straight from the horses' mouths.

The commander carried on being patient and gave us a further twenty-four hours in which to recuperate a little more before asking any questions. By this time the two of us were moving around unaided, albeit hobbling a bit, although Patrick was having to help me shower, which provoked more giggles. As far as the black and blue stakes went, I was the easy winner. The swelling to my face had gone down quite a lot thanks to ice packs, or rather several sessions with a bag of frozen peas.

'I simply don't know how we weren't killed by being run over or when we hit the road,' I remarked at one point.

'Me neither. But the van braked quite hard and the driver was forced over into the slow lane by a vehicle's headlights behind being flashed before we were chucked out so that might have helped. I have a vague recollection of grabbing you by anything I could – it might have even been your hair – and towing you on to the hard shoulder before I passed out.'

'It was my feet. Who called the police?'

'God knows. But someone in another vehicle must have witnessed what happened.' We had been told that the motorway had been closed for seven hours.

We discovered at a later date that the front seat passengers of two cars had reported 'suspicious and large items of rubbish' being dumped by a vehicle that braked hard in the slow lane and a lorry driver had dialled 999 as he was convinced it had been people who had been thrown out. On Greenway's instructions the media had been given the story with the added information that there had been two fatalities but the victims' identities would not be released until their next of kin had been informed.

Greenway gazed at me gravely. 'I have an idea you were very fortunate not to have been raped by Hamlyn.'

I was, but at no stage had Hamlyn been alone with me.

'They've all gone off the planet,' were the commander's next words at this debriefing in his study. He had made a brew of coffee, his wife, Erin, having gone to her French class. Otherwise she might have been sitting in with us as she used to be a detective sergeant with the Met. She is Greenway's second wife. His teenage son by his first marriage, Benedict, was at boarding school.

Greenway resumed with, 'Hamlyn's house is being watched and there's no movement, nor at the Trent's place.'

'No one at Anthony' Thomas's house in Barnes either?' Patrick queried.

'Not a sign of life, according to the Met. Oh, I forgot to mention it, the van was found burnt out but with one readable number plate. It had been stolen from outside Billingsgate Fish Market that same night.' He turned to me. 'Care to fill us in on what happened to you? Take your time, Ingrid – no one's blaming you for anything. At least we've got a nice big charge we can hang on the bastards now.'

'I was supposed to be going home,' I began ruefully. 'Well, actually I fully intended to do that but decided, as I had the keys to Rosemary Smythe's house, that I would go and have a quiet snoop over the wall at the Trents first, just watch for a while. I'd noticed a set of step ladders in the outhouse. But there was a light on at Miss Smythe's. It was the Trents, and I'm still sure they were looking for something.'

I then related the conversation I had had with them as well as I could remember it and what happened afterwards, finishing by admitting miserably, 'It was stupid, stupid, stupid of me.'

Greenway was not interested in my self-flagellation, staring at me intently and saying, 'Obviously the story of checking the house and not having had time to look at a leak in the loft was a load of cobblers and I get the impression from your mentioning that Trent kept looking at the clock that he was expecting Hamlyn and co. to arrive shortly. D'you reckon he strung you along, saying he would cooperate to waste time until they turned up?'

'Yes, on reflection he may well have done that.'

'Yet it would appear that Sonya Trent was dressed to go out for the evening.'

'She and her husband might have been going out for a meal

with Hamlyn,' I suggested. 'And there was to be some kind of meeting first. No, that can't be right as she had her evening bag with her. She might not have been told they were coming.'

'Did she look surprised or alarmed when Hamlyn appeared?'

'Sorry, I didn't notice. But she was already very upset.'

'What d'you reckon they were looking for next door?'

'It's only a tentative theory.'

'I really like your tentative theories.'

'It's possible Miss Smythe wrote another letter to us, which she either hadn't finished, or not posted, or – as how would they know what she was doing? – it's slightly more likely she might have removed something from next door, or their garden, that was hugely incriminating, as proof they were up to no good and they noticed whatever it was had gone missing.'

'A weapon?' Patrick put in. 'A load of money? Drugs? Stolen property?'

Greenway was getting really fired up. 'Which Hamlyn, if he did personally kill her, *was* searching for when he turned the place over.'

Patrick said, 'But according to scenes of crime people he didn't touch the loft, which might be just the place she'd conceal something like that for a short while.'

'He might have been disturbed, say by someone at the door collecting for charity,' I said.

Greenway leapt for a notepad and pen and scribbled rapidly. 'We'll find out – ask the local vicar, he'll know. I really like the sound of all this!'

Patrick then gave his account of events finishing by apologizing for his unprofessionalism in not going armed. Greenway showed no interest in his regrets either; in his mind, I was convinced, he was already rummaging in Miss Smythe's attic.

'It's not quite the end of my daft ideas,' I said into the silence that followed.

'Say away,' Greenway encouraged.

'I almost rang you about this when I was sitting in the garden,' I said to Patrick. 'If I had, mentioning that there was a light on in the house, you'd have come straight over, wouldn't you? Another bad mistake I made.'

'Most probably as the single malt was particularly good I

would have strongly advised you to leave everything very much alone and go home and then called out the cops to deal with it,' Patrick said with a big smile. 'Hindsight's no bloody good, ever.'

'It occurred to me that this group of crooks could each supply something for the whole – for want of a better word – business,' I resumed, knowing he was being kind. 'Trent with his house for meetings, a safe place to store booty and so forth, Anthony Thomas for providing hit men, and Hamlyn as he knows the people they're targeting and also his way around in criminal circles. But he's a heavy drinker and appears to live in his plots, Trent's pathetic and Thomas doesn't seem all that bright. Who's in the driving seat and organizes all this?'

'That is really worth considering,' the commander murmured.

'The senior cop in a spot of bother?' Patrick offered.

'No,' Greenway said quietly. 'He was found hanged in his garage three days ago. There was no point in bothering you with it until now.'

Another death, another victim.

'Did he leave a note?'

'He did,' Greenway said. 'Admitted receiving payments in cash from criminals in exchange for information – no details unfortunately – and that he couldn't live with the shame of letting down his colleagues any longer. His wife said she knew nothing about it but wasn't all that surprised, in her words: "Recently he'd become unrecognizable as the man I married". He'd refused to talk about what was worrying him but they already had money problems as he'd been a compulsive gambler for years and apparently she'd been planning to divorce him over it.'

'Someone must have found out about that,' Patrick said. 'But surely it can't have been Hamlyn in this case. Trent? They were friends. It was he Trent complained to about Miss Smythe and she ended up with the ASBO. But somehow I can't see Trent being up to putting the screws on him. As Ingrid said, he's pathetic, as well as presumably already having had his own reputation on the line. And all our late cop needed to have done was report him for trying to bribe a police officer, money worries or no. It doesn't quite add up.'

'OK, we'll work on it from the point of view that Trent was aware of the money worries and merely gave the information to

someone else,' the commander said. 'Who? Who's in a position
to put pressure on a fairly top cop?'

'A fairly top mobster he once put inside on phoney evidence
and who might have even been his snout when he was in a more
junior, hands-on role?' I hazarded.

'The imagination of writers,' Greenway whispered, getting up
to shake my hand gently. 'That is so neat, so splendidly possible,
Ingrid, I feel like crying. I'll work on it from here. You both look
exhausted so please go and rest while I get on the computer and
I'll keep you right up to date.'

I followed this advice but Patrick stayed put, although I gather
he dozed off in that warm, quiet room, the only intrusion the soft
sound of the commander tapping keys. The information Greenway
was to gather would, predictably, be highly complex and extensive
and, later that day, he wasted no time in sending everything he had
found so far to his team at HQ to ensure that it would be waiting
for them in their in-boxes on Monday morning. That would be just
the start. Before he began, I also found out later, he arranged to
have Miss Smythe's house resealed and ordered that someone be
on duty there at all times until it was searched.

The next day Hereward Trent's battered body was found dumped
in reeds at a nature reserve at the northern end of Hackney
Marshes recreation ground. After a vicious beating he had been
killed with a single shot to the head. Forensic examination would
soon reveal that he had been dead for several days.

TWELVE

'In Greenway's opinion he paid the price for having cold feet,'
Patrick said, placing his mobile back on the table.

We were at home having been given strict orders to return
to Hinton Littlemoor for forty-eight hours, the commander having
said, 'No, don't argue, see your family and recover a little more.
Travel first class on the train and taxis everywhere else, on
expenses. Your car'll be fine right here at my place.'

The news had come through during the rail journey and I had wondered if, had we been in the Range Rover, Patrick would have turned around and gone straight back. I admired the commander's tactics in reducing our mobility at a time when neither of us was really fit enough to drive for long distances. With this latest news I now found myself utterly sickened by the case and the thought of returning to London to tackle it again was awful.

Family members, of course, were horrified by the visible signs of our 'accident', Vicky, the second youngest, hiding from 'Mummy's and Daddy's hurts', and Patrick's father, John, insisting on a laying on of hands in the church and offering up a healing prayer for us which, for reasons that I simply cannot explain, helped me enormously. Vicky soon recovered from the shock of our appearance having been given a ride around the garden on Patrick's shoulders, her absolute favourite occupation in life right now.

'I shall really have to go and buy that delightful child a horse,' Patrick said ruefully as he dropped into a chair.

'She can have little rides on Fudge soon,' I said. 'And you ought to have been given proper sick leave.'

'We can have proper sick leave. It's just that . . .' He broke off, shrugged, then muttered, 'Ouch.'

'It's perfectly understandable that you want to get on with the job so these wretched people are arrested as soon as possible.'

'Yes, only they're scum, not people. But what I really want, right now, is *Hamlyn*, preferably my hands around his throat,' Patrick said thickly and quickly left the room, limping a little.

It is never far from my mind that most men who have laid hands on me in the course of our working together have ended up extremely dead.

'There are some forensic details that are interesting although, as we're both aware, it's too early for DNA and other test results to come through,' Patrick said the next morning after another call from Greenway. 'As we already know, Trent had been dead for around three days. His body shows signs of dehydration and there's nothing in the stomach, which suggests that he was confined somewhere without food or water before he was killed.'

'I'm worried about Sonya,' I murmured. 'I didn't get the impression that she was willingly involved.'

'You don't have to come back with me tomorrow.'

'Does it show that much?'

'I have known you for rather a long time.'

'If you mean "known" in the legal sense, meaning sexually I was fifteen.'

'Please don't remind me.'

When I had told him my age – we were both quite strictly brought up – Patrick had attained a shade of paleness that up until then I had assumed to be humanly impossible. This was after most of a whole summer of passionate love-making on an unusually sunlit Dartmoor. Until then he had merely been the Head Boy at school in Plymouth, a figure as remote to me, being three years older, as though we lived in different countries. Then, our fathers being good friends, Patrick had been cajoled into coming round one evening to help me with my physics homework, with which I struggled, whereupon he had sat opposite me at the kitchen table, stared across with those fine grey eyes, and simmered. What had happened next was not physics but chemistry and, holding his gaze, I had known that here was the man I wanted for ever and ever.

He had thawed rapidly and over the next few weeks we walked the dogs, rode our bikes and I discovered that his greatest attraction was his ability to make me laugh. He is a born mimic. And then one day we laughed ourselves helpless, hugging one another under the hot Devon sun and I felt the way his wiry body moved under the thin material of his shirt. As children one minute then and as close as two people can be the next, a little later gazing breathlessly at one another, speechless with amazement at the sheer gorgeousness of what we had just experienced. In short, we were made for one another. Thinking back it still amazes me that I did not become pregnant.

I would go back to London with him.

There was no reason to enter Miss Smythe's house through the back this time, and Greenway, who had not visited the murder victim's home previously and germ warfare would not have kept away, wielded the front door keys with aplomb. I was already having horrible sinking feelings about it, the writer's imagination presenting me with the hostile stares and mutterings of these SOCA personnel who had been summoned for duty on a Sunday should we find absolutely nothing.

Jane Grant had been extremely surprised when asked to attend the search but had arrived on time and now stood with us in the spacious hallway. I had half expected her to have gone the way of all the others, that is, disappeared, but here she was, outwardly composed but with a nervous smile. Initially it was thought risky to ask her along in an effort to find out if she was complicit in what had gone on as she would then be able to report to her 'friend' Hamlyn that Patrick and I were still in the land of the living. Then the decision had been made that it was imperative to establish, now, how involved she was with his activities for her own sake if nothing else.

Greenway led the way into the sitting room and suggested we seated ourselves for a few minutes while his team got themselves organized. He had already jokingly assured Mrs Grant that there was nothing alarming in the battered state of two of his staff – who were still on fairly powerful painkillers – which was down to a traffic accident. She had promptly flashed us a very alarmed glance, gone on to offer her sympathy, and then concentrated on what the commander was saying to her.

Patrick had stretched back in his armchair, winced, forgetting for a moment, and then assumed his usual, almost catlike passiveness of the one not doing the interviewing – yet. This tends to make people forget all about him until the moment he chooses but I did notice Jane Grant's gaze drifting towards him now and again as she began to relate her findings when she went through her aunt's papers. Nothing unexpected or out of the ordinary, that is.

'This isn't mere nosiness on my part, you must understand,' Greenway emphasized, pushing the door closed to muffle the clumping of feet up the stairs. 'We're just wondering if there were any letters that might have been started and not finished, or sealed ready for posting and still among her documents.'

The woman shook her head. 'No.'

'Are you quite sure? This is very important.'

'No, there was nothing like that. Just her birth certificate, a copy of her will and other family papers, a few old postcards, family photographs and nostalgic bits and pieces from her teaching years, the things one would expect to find.'

'Have you finally established whether you're a beneficiary in your aunt's will?'

'Yes, I have. Other than a couple of modest bequests to the local church and a children's hospice round the corner she's left everything to me. I've contacted her solicitor to make sure that everything's correct and he assured me that it is.'

'Are you aware that your aunt had written around a dozen letters to the Serious Organised Crime Agency with her suspicions about the people living next door?'

Mrs Grant sat up poker-straight. 'As many as that! Oh, my goodness! I knew she'd sent off at least one because she was writing it when I came to see her one day. I'm afraid I told her she was wasting police time and she got a bit short with me so I didn't mention it again.'

'For reasons that we'll explain in a minute or so we want to search the attic rooms here. Scenes of crime personnel did not do so for reasons best known to themselves but mostly, I understand, because it was fairly obvious from the completely undisturbed layer of dust up there that the murderer had not penetrated that far. We think he may have been put off, panicked perhaps because someone rang the doorbell and he'd left the back door open. I'm curious: your aunt appears to have been a very house-proud lady but she didn't seem to have bothered with the loft. Was there any reason for that, do you know?'

'She kept saying that she was going to have a big turnout,' said Jane Grant. 'But never did. I think the knowledge of what was involved made the job just too much for her to contemplate. A lot of her parent's things are up there and if the truth were known she couldn't bear to get rid of, or even disturb them.'

'A little under a week ago the Trents were in this house, looking for something. Have you any idea what that might be?'

'The Trents! No, of course not. But what—'

Greenway interrupted with: 'They said you'd given them a set of keys, which included the new ones for the back door, so they could check that all was well here. Something about a possible leak in the loft?'

'But I didn't . . . haven't.'

'They said you had – while talking to my assistant here.' He indicated me.

'That's not true. I wouldn't expect the Trents to keep an eye on the place, I hardly know them. Besides, there aren't any leaks in the loft that I know of.'

'So you gave the keys to someone else?'

'Just . . . a friend.'

'Was that the same friend who visited you a little later the same morning Mr Gillard interviewed you the first time?'

'Why am I being *grilled* like this?' she suddenly demanded to know. 'And why the *hell* were you watching me?'

'Please answer the question.'

He chin came up. 'Yes, it was.'

'Why did you give them to him?'

She shot to her feet. 'This is intolerable. I refuse to answer any more of these stupid questions.'

'Are you frightened of him?' Patrick asked.

He had spoken very softly but nevertheless she jumped out of her skin on hearing the different voice. 'No!'

'I think you are. Please sit down.'

Slowly, she reseated herself.

'Answer the question,' Patrick said. 'Why did you give him the keys?'

'There's nothing wrong about it. He's a writer and in the middle of a novel set here in Richmond. He wondered if he could have a look round in here to get the atmosphere of a local Victorian house. There was no reason for me to refuse. It's not often one gets the chance to talk to a famous author.'

'He just knocked on your door out of the blue and asked?'

'No, of course not. He'd previously called round to give me the Trents' and his condolences. His name's Clement Hamlyn and he's a friend of theirs.'

'We know his name. Did you ask yourself how he knew where you lived?'

'I did wonder at the time but thought that Auntie could have told the Trents before everything became so difficult.'

'He had probably followed you home one day. Mrs Grant, it's important to tell you at this stage that your aunt was right about these people. They're dangerous criminals – Clement Hamlyn has a criminal record.'

She just stared at him. Then, probably the last thing anyone was expecting, her eyes filled with tears and overflowed down her cheeks.

'I'm really sorry,' Patrick whispered.

She fumbled in her bag for a tissue and wept silently for a few moments. Then, with a supreme effort, she pulled herself together and said in a choked voice, 'I feel such a fool. I suppose he turned my head a bit. Perhaps he wouldn't have taken me out to dinner at a West End restaurant after all.'

'No, I don't think he would.'

'Sorry, I'm finding this very hard to believe.'

'An arrest warrant is out for him in connection with attempted murder.'

'Who, *Auntie*?'

'He is a suspect but in this case no, me. And my associate over there.'

Gazing at one and then the other of us, she shuddered.

'Did he say anything that, now, in hindsight, would lead you to wonder if he was trying to find out how much your aunt had told you about her suspicions?'

'He knew the tree house had fallen down. Hereward had told him, he said. Did I know what had caused it? I told him what I thought, that it must have been rotten.'

'It had been sabotaged by someone sawing almost right through the timbers.'

'Oh, no,' Jane Grant gasped. 'Oh, poor Auntie.'

'Did he question you further? Surely he must have commented on the fact that your aunt had got into trouble with the police for snooping around in the garden next door on occasions when the gates had been left open.'

'He said it had all been very unfortunate and how sad it was that she'd been getting confused in her old age. I didn't disagree with him. Yes, I've just remembered, he then jokingly said he hoped I hadn't believed any of "the nonsense", as he put it, and I told him I hadn't.'

'Has he contacted you recently?'

'Yes, yesterday.'

I think the hairs on the back of my neck stood on end.

'D'you mind telling me what he wanted?' Patrick went on to say in casual fashion.

'He said there had been a small fire at his house and he had nowhere to live until some work had been done. He asked if he could stay with me for a few days.' Bravely, just a tremor to her voice she added: 'He said we . . . we could go out for dinner and to a show.'

'What was your reply?'

'I said I was sorry but my cousin was coming for a week and there were only two bedrooms. I suggested he could book into a hotel and we could still go out. He said he'd think about it but I haven't heard back yet.'

Patrick looked at Greenway and some kind of telepathy must have passed between them because the commander imperceptibly nodded.

'I'd like you to phone him, now, and tell him you've changed your mind as your cousin can't come after all.'

She began to protest.

'Listen,' Patrick interposed with a smile. From his manner I knew he was certain she was innocent – or as certain as anyone could be at this stage. 'You won't be at home. When you leave here someone'll accompany you and you can pack a bag and be taken to a safe house until Hamlyn's been arrested. Your cousin can go with you.'

'Oh, it wasn't true. I didn't want him staying in my house. Dinner's one thing but . . .'

'You *are* frightened of him.'

'He's always all smiles but for some reason I felt uneasy the last time we met. And – I know this sounds horrible of me – his breath smells terrible.'

'Will you do it?'

'Now you've told me this I shall be all jittery and not know what to say,' Jane Grant said desperately.

'I'll tell you what to say.'

'Very well,' she agreed after a long pause, during which she had stared unseeing into space.

They went into a smaller room which would provide the same kind of snug-sounding resonance as her own home and where there was no danger of anyone else present sneezing or knocking anything over. Greenway called for silence upstairs. Patrick told me later that she had carried off the call very well but she had obviously had another little weep afterwards as she was drying her eyes when she back into the sitting room and he had his arm around her. Why should I mind? A little comfort was due to her from somewhere in this whole black world in which she now felt she was living.

Hamlyn had said he would arrive at her cottage at around nine that evening and she had told him that she would leave the front door unlocked.

'Well?' Greenway said a little later after restarting the muted thumps and sounds of furniture being shifted upstairs. Jane Grant had departed in an area car with a woman PC and her reassuringly beefy male colleague. 'Is she OK or just a good actress?'

'Real tears,' I commented.

'Because all the plans are coming apart, or am I being a nasty old cynic?'

'One of the oracles of murder,' I continued, 'is, who stands to gain? She already gains by being the main beneficiary in her aunt's will. Why involve others?'

'She might have been forced to.'

'In which case, surely she would have bared her soul to us when she knew the truth. My only reservation is that I can't understand why she was remotely charmed by Hamlyn in the first place. Unless she's so desperately lonely that anyone will do.'

'Patrick?' Greenway invited.

Patrick rose stiffly and went for a little walk around the room to loosen up. 'Does it matter? She's only a small player even if she is involved. I'm actually more interested in why Hamlyn seems to want to lie low at her place. My gut feeling is that he doesn't.'

'What does he want then?'

'To kill her.'

'Living in his plot again perhaps,' I murmured. 'Our hero is on the run from the cops and outwitting them all, planning to finish off the last person who stands between him and some kind of insane, ghastly, self-righteous, blood-boltered glory.'

'God, how I wish you could write the end of his damned book and make sure he's banged up for just about ever!' Greenway burst out with.

'It wouldn't stick to the rules,' I said, having to smile at his fervour. 'Fiction hardly ever does.'

'What rules?'

'Real-life police rules.'

The man in charge thought deeply for a full half minute. Then he said, 'How far would you want to bend them?'

He was not talking about fiction this time.

'Up to national security standard – perhaps a fraction more.'

'You mean you'd like to work as you did for MI5?'

'Yes.'

I feel bound to make it clear at this point that my husband was drinking in my every word.

The commander thought about it again, probably desperately missing his paper clips. 'In my opinion these people require different measures,' he concluded finally. 'But I doubt whether—'

'Sir!' came an urgent call from upstairs.

'Yes?' Greenway yelled.

'We've found a sub-machine gun, sir – a Heckler and Koch MP5. It was under a loose floorboard behind an empty chest of drawers.'

The commander swore and then, already halfway to the door, said jubilantly, 'We've got them!' He came to a sudden halt, turned, and added: 'Finish his book, Ingrid. You can begin, if you feel well enough, by being present when we arrest him tonight.'

The old long case clock in Jane Grant's hall had quite a loud tick, audible over the radio in the living room which was tuned, quietly, exactly as it had been left by its owner, to Radio Four. The clock struck the half hour, eight thirty, and automatically I checked my watch, having to turn it slightly to the light provided by one of the two small table lamps, this one on a bookcase in an alcove by the fireplace. The other was on a small table at one side of what I assumed was Jane Grant's favourite armchair.

I was seated on the sofa. It was on the same side of the room as the window, the archway into the hall being over to my left.

The heavy curtain that could be drawn to keep out draughts had been pulled across. It was a very dull evening, a mist seemingly having drifted up from the river, swirling in almost Dickensian fashion around the trees on the tiny church green nearby when we arrived. I got up to close the curtains, careful not to place myself right in front of the window as I did so.

My worry was not that Hamlyn would arrive early, as he might, hoping to catch the occupant unawares, but that my working partner was simply not yet fit enough to carry out what we had decided to do. I was not sure of my own ability either as the room was warm, the slow tick of the clock hypnotic, the music on the radio soothing and I had just caught myself beginning to doze off.

Half an hour later I was still sitting there, the church clock having just accompanied the grandfather in the hall in striking the hour. I was wide awake now with the jitters because the radio, which we had switched on to make everything sound normal, was making it hard for me to listen for anyone coming in. The only real change we had made in the room was to shift an antique card table out of range of possible damage should there be any violence.

How can thirty minutes seem like an eternity?

Another ten went by: he was not coming.

Patrick appeared through the curtain. 'Shall we give it a bit longer?'

'Please switch off the radio. My heart almost stopped when you came in.'

In the end we waited for almost another hour: nothing.

THIRTEEN

'It was a bit of a long shot and he must have suspected something,' Greenway commented as we walked back to the cars, the crew of an area car that had been brought along as back-up in our wake. Patrick and I had not known that he would decide to be in the vicinity. 'But I can't see it being too long before

Anthony Thomas is picked up and he might know where he is. Thomas is going to be charged with the attempted murder of you two for a start so can be neatly filed on remand awaiting the rest. The Met have two of his yobs already who might be persuaded to drop him in it in exchange for a lesser charge – the ones who were arrested after the pub brawl.'

'The real brawl took place in an alleyway at the back,' Patrick reminded him.

'You love starting fights, don't you?' his boss observed with only a hint of disapproval.

'It mostly happened because the bloke I had won a lot of money off pulled a knife, wanting his cash back, but it was one of the first things I was taught in training for Special Services and can get you out of real trouble.'

'But you still got yourself arrested.'

'And your point?'

'Oh, I see.' Greenway chuckled.

'Sonya Trent,' I brought them back to earth with. 'Where is she?'

'Was she in the van?' the commander wanted to know.

'No,' Patrick answered. 'Although I can't say for sure. I heard Thomas's voice and am certain he was shouting from the cab. So if he was driving with Trent in the passenger seat and both yobs were in the back with us there wouldn't have been room for her, unless she was somehow jammed in the driving cab. I find that unlikely. Hamlyn had stayed behind, at the Trents' place.'

'Yes, with Sonya,' I said. 'I have a horrible feeling he raped her – turned on by the violence.'

Greenway said, 'Although the house wasn't treated as a crime scene for reasons I think you already know about someone did have a careful look round and reported that there was no sign of anything like that having occurred. He could have taken her off in his car though. He must have known that the nanny and children were in the house.'

'If he went on to kill her . . .' I muttered.

'He's had plenty of time to dispose of the body. But I suggest we remain optimistic and work on the assumption that the woman's still alive and try to find her.'

'Will you give it priority?' I persevered. 'Even if it means using members of your team for that rather than first looking for Anthony Thomas?'

We had reached the vehicles. Greenway found his cars keys in his pocket and paused with them in his hand. 'I think I'm prepared to give it two days – but no longer. And you? Are you fit to do a little, less stressful, routine work? It was a pity your MI5 approach with Hamlyn came to nothing before it even got off the ground.'

'We haven't started yet,' Patrick said. 'We'll find Thomas.'

'He's not at his place in Barnes,' Greenway said. 'Sorry, I should have mentioned earlier that it was searched this morning.'

'According to his website Thomas's interests are classical music and going for long country walks,' I said, back at our hotel. 'I thought that was hogwash when I first read it and I do now.'

'But he *is* Russian,' Patrick demurred. 'They wrote some of the best classical music in the world. And just because he looks a bit stupid and his grasp of English might not be too good – I heard him talking in the pub – it doesn't mean he fails to appreciate the finer things in life.'

'So we comb London listening out for Borodin and Rachmaninov?'

Patrick impatiently shook his head, thinking my joke sarcasm. 'You probably don't read the sports' pages of the newspapers, but I do. He's livid right now. Another Russian's bought the football club he was one of the directors of and he's been slung off the board, the new owner saying he didn't want any connections with mobsters. Obviously word gets around.'

'He's presumably still involved with boxing.'

'And the last thing I want to do at the moment is present myself at a place where there are any number of super-fit younger blokes, thank you. No, we get him right where he lives – in every sense of the expression.'

'Dinner?' I queried, interrupting what had every appearance of developing into a dark brood and praying that the final showdown in Sussex was not still preying on his mind.

'Good idea. Fuel for a nocturnal venture.' I must have looked a bit pained at this for Patrick added: 'Your idea, working as we did for D12.'

Ye gods, I did *not* want to go out again tonight.

No, I would *not* go out again tonight.

I was surprised then when, after we had eaten and gone back to our room, I thought for him to change into something more suitable – I had not told him yet but was *damned* if I was going out again tonight – he appeared to be getting ready for bed. That is, removing all his clothes and staying that way.

'Change of plan?' I wondered aloud, aghast at the still black and blue state of him.

'No.'

'When's the nocturnal venture then?'

'Now.' This with a big grin.

'You appear to be fully prepared,' I commented, getting undressed – nay, stripping off – with scant regard to a rather good dress.

He was, magnificently so.

I suppose at this stage that if I had been writing one of my novels I would have composed a few slightly raunchy lines about my heroine's sensations before leaving everything to the reader's imagination. In real life, however, my only reaction to events right now was to be totally gobsmacked at the miracle wrought in my man by fillet steak and chips.

It has to be said that we made love very, very gently.

The Met removed their surveillance of Anthony Thomas's house in Barnes, partly because he had never shown up there but really due to overtime costs and a lack of personnel. With regard to the protracted no-show, it had occurred to us that the owner of the property opposite, from the loft room of which the watch had been carried out, might not be a disinterested party. We proposed to find out.

First reactions would be important.

'Serious Organised Crime Agency,' Patrick said crisply to the middle-aged, pyjama-clad man who answered the door holding a brimming mug of sludge-coloured liquid that might have been tea.

'They've gone.'

'Who's gone?'

'The cops who were watching the place opposite.'

'I know. May we come in?'

'Is it important?'

'It might be.'

Grudgingly the door was opened a little wider and the man slouched off, his slippers scuffing along the carpet. We followed him into an untidy, stale-smelling living room where he flung open the curtains, shifted a couple of empty ash trays from the arms of chairs on to a side table and dropped with a heavy sigh into a sofa.

'What's it all about then?' he wanted to know.

Patrick introduced us, as usual giving the impression that I was merely his minion note-taker, established that the householder's name was Norman White and then said, 'Do you know the man who lives over the road, Anthony Thomas?'

'I was asked that. I only know him by sight.'

'D'you know anything about him at all?'

'Not a thing. They asked me that too.'

'He doesn't appear to have turned up the entire time the place was watched.'

'A waste of public money then, wasn't it?'

'Before the police were here how many times had you seen him?'

'Only now and again.'

'Was he alone or with other people?'

'Sometimes on his own, once or twice with a few blokes. They were quiet, not the kind of folk to make a nuisance of themselves.'

'Has there been any kind of activity since the police went?'

White began to show signs of impatience. 'Not that I've noticed.'

'Did you know that he's Russian?'

'Well, he has quite a heavy accent so—'

'You have spoken to him then,' Patrick interrupted, having hooked his fish.

'Er – once now I come to think of it. He asked me about the refuse collection day when he first came here.'

'When was that?'

'Around a year ago.'

'I suggest that he might have told you quite a bit about himself. I have an idea he could be a charming character when he so chose.'

'He didn't tell me anything – but was pleasant enough when he asked about the bin day.'

'He's involved with boxing promotion and until very recently was the director on the board of a football club. Before that he was some kind of film star. I've no doubt he's a good actor.'

White shook his head. 'That's all news to me.'

'You seem to have a photograph of the football team signed by the players on the DVD storage unit over there. They can't be all that easy to come by.'

'So I – I – support that team,' White blustered. 'It's not against the law, is it?'

'I suggest you tell me the truth before I arrest you for being an accessory to serious crime.' Patrick followed this up with one of his stock-in-trade star-of-*Jaws* lookalikes.

'I've heard about cops like you!' White said hotly. 'And on the telly. Bash the door down and frame some poor sod for any number of crimes.'

My husband tends not to get really nasty with those he has wrong-footed who are middling stupid. 'Mr White, Anthony Thomas, once known as Anatoli Tomskaya, is wanted for attempted murder. If it's found that you're protecting him—'

'He said the cops'd say he was wanted for something,' White triumphantly butted in with. 'So he was right.'

'Why did you believe him?'

'Why shouldn't I?'

'Especially if you accepted a handful of tenners as payment for the nod if the police came nosing around looking for him.'

'No!' White shouted.

'I'm utterly fascinated by this. What was the *reason* he gave you that the police would lie to get their hands on him?'

'I can't tell you,' White muttered.

'Why not?'

A woman wearing a pick fluffy dressing gown came into the room. 'Norm, I heard you shouting. What's going on? What do they want?'

'It's a different lot of cops. They're on about Thomas – the bloke over the road,' White told her. And on an afterthought, 'My wife, Debbie.'

'*Tony?*' She rounded on us. 'You can't leave him alone, can you?'

'You seem to be on first name terms with him,' Patrick said.

'No, not – not really. We just wave if we see one another . . . outside, you know, parking our cars.'

Patrick looked from her to the pot-bellied, unshaven ruin on the sofa and back again and smiled a little smile, a good paragraph's worth of insinuation. Then he said to White, 'Answer the question – how did he explain his statement that the police would lie in order to arrest him?'

'As I said, I can't tell you.'

'I insist that you do.'

'I can't! It's sort of – secret.'

'Like the Secret Services, you mean?'

'Yes. I can't tell you. He made me promise. I'm the only person who knows other than his . . .' White shook his head. 'I'm not saying another word.'

'Handler?' Patrick asked sharply.

'You know about such things then,' White said in surprise.

'Yes, we used to work for MI5.' Patrick leaned forward and spoke in a whisper. 'Look, we've both signed the Official Secrets Act. You can tell *us*.'

'You're not the only person,' the woman said indignantly to her husband. 'He told me too – said *I* was the only one who knew.'

'While he was screwing you?' White bawled. He had not missed Patrick's little bit of theatre – not that it had been intended he should.

'I have *not* been carrying on with him! How the hell could I? He's hardly ever at home. We've just had a couple of little chats, that's all.'

'Has this man told you both that he's some kind of spy?' Patrick asked, an edge to his voice. When nothing was immediately forthcoming he bellowed, in his parade ground voice, 'Tell the *truth*!'

They both started violently and then White blurted, 'I knew you were a bloody bully! All right, he said someone's reported him to the security services as one, industrial secrets and all that. But he's a double spy and MI6 know all about him. He said I was serving my country by helping him.'

'Did he offer you money?'

'Yes, but I refused it. I used to be in the Territorials so wouldn't take money for something like that. But I accepted the photo of the lads at the club. They're real signatures, not photocopies.'

'You're not going to believe me if I tell you that he left Russia with the Moscow police after him and is now on the Metropolitan Police's Most Wanted List as he's a mainstream mobster, are you?'

White, looking completely baffled, remained silent.

'No spy of any kind would have given you all that information about himself,' Patrick pointed out.

The woman sighed. 'He seemed such a nice bloke and we have a little chat and laugh about our secret and he asks me how I am and . . .' She tailed off and then snapped, 'But he lied, didn't he? About me being the only one who knew. And when men lie about one thing they've probably lied about loads of other stuff as well.' This with a glance at her husband and the certainty of bitter experience.

'You have his mobile number then?' I said to her.

There was a slow nod.

Her husband fixed her with a furious stare. 'You've been phoning him too?'

'Why not?' Debbie practically spat at him. 'At least he knows how to speak nicely to a lady. I talk to him quite a lot actually.'

Patrick interrupted more pending warfare with, 'Have either of you let him know that the police have left here?'

'No, they only went last night and I couldn't get hold of him this morning,' White replied.

'Mrs White?'

'Not me. I leave all the boring stuff to Norm.'

'Please try contacting him again now,' Patrick said to White. 'Tell him.'

'I'll phone,' the man said, getting up to use the landline phone on a small table.

'Are you going to arrest us?' Debbie White said in a small voice. I am afraid this author had earmarked her for a sparkly, hard and shallow character in her next novel.

Patrick put his finger to his lips while the call was made. Then he said, 'No, of course not. Being manipulated by a good actor isn't a crime.' More accurately, it simply was not worth the hours of paperwork.

'He told me, boasted really, that he knew all kinds of people in showbiz: pop stars, actors, even a top author who writes crime stories, Clement somebody or the other. That was all lies as well, I suppose.'

'Clement Hamlyn,' I said. 'Yes, he does know him.'

'He once said that the bloke's right off the wall, whispered that he might have even killed people. I think Tony had been hitting the vodka, mind.'

'Time will tell,' Patrick said with a smile.

White reseated himself, looking grim. 'As you heard, I told him,' he said, resuming his seat. He picked up his cold tea and then replaced it on the table with a grimace.

'Did he make any comments?' Patrick enquired.

'Not really. Thanked me and said I might see a bit more of him from now on.'

'Then we'll thank you too and leave.' Patrick got to his feet.

'He said he was having a few days off and enjoying a walk in the country – Virginia Water. But that's here in London, isn't it? Got his wires crossed. Hope he goes down for a good stretch.'

I wondered if being manipulated by another good actor would cost White his marriage and then realized that I did not care: one bit. But at least he had handed us the man on a plate.

This not being a James Bond movie we had no intention of going after the Russian ourselves, present weakness apart we were also aware that it was unlikely he would be alone but have a couple of minders, possibly armed, in attendance. Not only that, Virginia Water, a large lake situated in parkland and gardens in a corner of Windsor Great Park that was a playground for the Royal Court during the early nineteenth century, is now a very public place. Patrick passed on the information we had been given to the relevant parties together with a reminder of the registration number of Thomas's silver Mercedes which he had made a note of from the man's file.

I did not envy whoever would be in charge of endeavouring to apprehend him. Patrick thought the right tactic would be to carefully shadow him on foot while he was in such a public place and then follow him in unmarked cars when he departed before setting up roads blocks some distance away. This would also be difficult due to the constant heavy traffic.

'Good, no obvious cops,' Patrick said, having paid off the taxi that had taken a frustratingly long time to get hold of. We had asked to be put down near the entrance to the main car park and from where I was standing it looked quite full. Without needing to confer we entered and strolled along the rows of cars – content to walk slowly and also not wishing to draw attention to ourselves – looking out for Thomas's Mercedes. This being a wealthy district every other car seemed to be either that or a Range Rover, Porsche or BMW, so I stopped looking at badges and concentrated on registration plates.

Ten minutes later when we had not found it I said, 'Perhaps Thomas didn't tell White the truth.'

'That has to be factored in,' Patrick agreed.

'From childhood memories I have an idea there's a road that people park in partly to avoid paying here.'

'Where the really rich leave their cars?' Patrick wondered.

'Especially the really rich. It's near one of the lodges on another entrance.'

'How far around the lake?'

'I can't remember exactly – I was only eight years old. At least a couple of miles away.'

'Bloody hell,' he muttered. 'Can you walk two miles?'

'No. How about getting an update before we decide what to do, if anything?'

Patrick paused in finding his mobile, gazing into the distance. 'Those two vehicles parked over there not in proper spaces . . . unmarked police cars unless I'm losing it.'

No one was in the cars. Patrick rang for the latest information and all the Met could tell him was that a low-key search was being carried out by plain-clothes personnel but neither Thomas nor his car had yet been located. Patrick mentioned the road, Blacknest Road as it turned out, where the vehicle might be but that was one of the first places that had been reconnoitred. At present there were five teams of three commencing to walk the lakeside paths in different directions and if that drew a blank then the search would be extended into Windsor Great Park itself.

'There's an armed response group on standby and mounted cops arriving very shortly in the park,' Patrick finished by saying. 'Perhaps they ought to give the horses to the blokes with guns.'

'We're a bit superfluous,' I observed. 'The park's absolutely vast, around a thousand acres.'

We carried on with our trawl through the car park, just in case, but did not find the vehicle.

'OK,' Patrick said, coming to a halt. 'We out-think this mobster. As you pointed out he could have been lying to White but had no reason to unless he suspected him of selling him down the river. White could have been lying to us but I don't think so. So, Thomas goes for a walk, jog, whatever but always being wary of the law, especially now after what they did to us, he does not leave his car in an obvious place. Perhaps, when possible, he never leaves it in obvious places. What time is it?'

'Eleven fifty.'

'I'm wondering if he's parked where he's planned to have lunch. Where's the nearest pub?'

'Practically next door. But that's still quite an obvious place.'

The silver car was not obvious at all as it had been left in a far corner of the pub car park partly screened by overgrown shrubs and beneath a huge weeping willow tree, some of the trailing branches of which had been draped over the vehicle. We observed it from the middle distance, Patrick reported the find and then we left, hoping that if Thomas and any henchmen were inside the building they had not seen us.

'No, you're right,' Patrick said. 'We're superfluous and if they're in the pub simply can't risk being spotted and flushing them out before the cavalry arrive. D'you want lunch – somewhere else?'

'I wouldn't mind ten minutes fresh air by the lake,' I replied. To sit on a seat with the sun on my face and think of happy things: the garden at home, the children, the kittens, a few day's leave with the man I love . . .

As the full car park had indicated there were plenty of people around: women pushing buggies, cyclists, joggers, very smart dogs being exercised by exceedingly smart people. We turned right and headed along the shore where it did not seem to be so crowded and then sat on a bench for a while. I found it impossible to relax so suggested carrying on for a short distance. It is an idyllic place, the sun sparkling on the lake, waterfowl dipping and diving, fresh new leaves on the trees.

'As a child I was taken to some ruins here,' I recollected. 'My father was really keen on seeing them – I think he said they came from North Africa.'

'All by themselves?' Patrick queried. I was sure he had not closed his eyes for a second either.

'No, silly. Someone gave them to the then King as a present.'

'That sounds like George the Fourth. He was really in to follies and grand pavilions. Where are they?'

'Sorry, I really can't remember after all this time.'

'Never mind, let's just walk a little farther along here and then go and find something to eat.'

'Will we do things like this when we're old and retired?' I mused aloud after a few minutes of mutual reflective silence. 'Feeling as we do now: battered, worn out, with aches and pains, having to have little rests now and again?'

'God, if I don't feel a damn sight better than this when I'm old and retired I'll go out and bloody shoot myself – that's if I live that long,' was the heated riposte.

I took his hand.

For some reason – the serenity of our surroundings must have worked its magic on us – we carried on walking and I felt the tension beginning to seep out of me. Some time later, not very long afterwards, we arrived at England's small share of the ruins of Leptis Magna.

FOURTEEN

I noticed the pedimented columns in the distance before my partner did. His attention was firmly on a group of three men rapidly approaching us along the sandy path. They were casually dressed: jeans, leather jackets, trainers, one wearing a baseball cap, the uniform of non-uniform police and at a fast walk, two staring about gimlet-eyed, the third, binoculars around his neck, talking grimly into his mobile phone. The little army crunched by.

'Any sign of him?' Patrick called to their retreating backs.

They came to an abrupt halt and turned to face us and for a moment there was silence but for the hoots of waterbirds and the faint drone of a Heathrow-bound airliner.

'SOCA,' Patrick went on to say, walking closer, speaking more quietly.

'No,' one of them answered.

'You're looking for a bloke out for a walk or jog but at that rate you'll be after someone hiding under bushes. For God's sake, don't look like cops.'

They stared at him for a moment longer and then one jerked his head and they marched off again.

We both sighed.

'OK, keep out of it,' Patrick muttered. 'Mind my own effin' business. Yes, ruins – fascinating.'

He came off the boil as we got closer and began to read the explanatory notices.

'It's fairly recently been restored as much as possible to the ruinous state that was first created when it was re-erected here at the beginning of the nineteenth century as a temple in the King's pleasure gardens,' I said, being annoying by reading a different one to Patrick. 'Vegetation had grown over it and vandals severely damaged everything by pulling over some of the walls and pillars.'

'I'm thinking of the work involved in bringing something like this from Libya to Surrey in those days.'

We wandered along the central path between low railings with spikes, blunt, on top, on either side that now prevented public access – no doubt intended as a deterrent to modern vandals – and again I paused, half shutting my eyes and trying to picture these shattered remnants as they had been in their days of glory. But for once my writer's imagination failed me and all I could see was the reality: elegant stonework in a woodland glade with neatly mown grass round and about it. The harsh cry of a jay as it flew from an oak banished for ever any imaginary pictures of hot African sunshine and I walked on.

Gates in the railings permitted access for gardeners and other

maintenance personnel and I noticed in passing that the two in
view were open – that is, the padlocks that presumably fastened
the securing chains were not there. In the fenced-off area over
to my left a wheelbarrow containing a few tools was rather
incongruously parked where one might have expected an altar
to have once stood. Had the police suggested to the park author-
ities that they withdraw staff as a safety measure and those
working here had forgotten to lock up?

'George the Fourth wasn't able to close the main road then,'
I said to myself, following Patrick beneath an old bridge under
the A30. Ahead lay more of the ancient Roman city, darker,
with taller trees and, despite the traffic thundering above my
head, brooding, somehow dangerous. The jay was still nearby,
its raucous *kaaa* amplified by the narrow space in which we
were standing, and the bird could be glimpsed among the
greenery ahead of me. It was watching something, not us. I
felt a sudden jolt of alarm.

'As wary as magpies,' I heard Patrick whisper tautly just as I
was about to share my concern. 'Is anyone around?'

'I can only see an elderly couple about forty yards away back
the way we've just come,' I told him.

'Please go and stop them coming any closer. Hurry. Stay away
until I say otherwise.'

I hurried as well as I was able, told the pair that the gardeners
were spraying chemicals and had come without warning notices
and managed to usher them away. Then I looked back towards
the bridge and could see no sign of Patrick. Despite what he
said I had no intention of staying away, actually feeling very
exposed on this open pathway with any number of hiding places
among the ruins on almost every side of me.

Hearing footsteps a short distance behind me towards the lake
I turned and saw another threesome of police coming from the
opposite direction to the others, having to look again to establish
that it was indeed different people. It was, the man nearest to
the water being rather overweight. Did I hurry over to them and
suggest they search the ruins? Was the resulting three-ring circus
necessary – if indeed there was a real chance that the man
everyone was looking for was there and not a bad case of SOCA
heebie-jeebies – with sniffer dogs, police marksmen, and given

half a chance, the King's Troupe, when a little stealth might suffice? I thought not.

The miniature cohort of cops slogged off.

There was no point in my going through one of the gates into the relics of the ancient world on this side of the bridge as the embankment carrying the road would block my path and I was convinced Patrick was on the other side of it. Moving as quickly and quietly as possible I went back, keeping well to one side of the arch when I reached it and not yet moving forward so as to be plainly visible from the other side. Inwardly cursing the slight sounds I made I took the Smith and Wesson from my bag, then risked going back a few paces to where I could put the bag over the railings and conceal it behind the base of a broken column.

I could hear the alarm call of a blackbird somewhere ahead of me. During the training that he had added on to that which I received before working for MI5 Patrick always impressed on me the importance of watching and listening to wildlife when hunting in the countryside, whether it be for foe or the cooking pot. And, he had said, time used being still, using all your senses, absorbing what is going on around you is never wasted. The word came back to me again: stealth.

Ahead and over to my right a twig snapped, a biggish twig, smallish branch sort of noise made by a human being or heavy animal treading on it. I recollected the gap in the columns I had seen the first time with a view into a wooded glade beyond and risked a quick peep around the end of the arch.

A man carrying a hand gun of some kind was furtively walking to the rear of a broken-down wall – I could only see the top two-thirds of him – that was at right angles to the embankment, the top of which was screened by the branches of trees. Slowly making his way in the direction of the centre of the glade he looked around nervously as though trying to find out if anyone else was there. I froze as he glanced in my direction but he did not see me and left the wall behind, walking away from me. Then, slightly over to my left, another man emerged from between the end of a row of columns set on a raised dais and a tall group of shrubs, paused for a moment, a matter of five yards between him and the other man, and then swiftly closed the gap and struck him down from behind with a blow to the neck.

Just a rustling sound, as of dry leaves blown in the wind, no more.

Patrick removed the handgun from the inert hand, looked over his shoulder, saw me and gave me a cautionary sign, again, to stay back. I raised my hand to tell him that I had understood and he disappeared back the way he had come.

To understand is not necessarily to obey though.

My quandary lay in knowing that I cannot move as silently as Patrick does, especially right now. The worse thing to do then was to follow him. Therefore I would head for where I had seen the man emerge, the broken down wall over to my right. Praying that the hinges of the little gate in the railings would not squeak I opened it, they did not, went through on to the grass and over to the prone figure. My delight upon discovering that it was the mobster from Thugs Central Casting to whom I had given a significant bruise in the groin was boundless. Patrick must have recognized him. He would only be unconscious for about ten minutes, depending on his constitution. As I reckoned this to be rock-bottom it would possibly be longer.

I was still praying hard; that I would not also snap twigs, trip on an overlooked chunk of antiquity buried in the leaf litter or be taken unawares by Anthony Thomas's minder. It seemed logical to assume that he was present, a scary individual with eyes like a hungry hippo – no doubt still bloodshot after what I had done to them – who had the presence of someone who thought nothing of killing with whichever weapon first came to hand.

There was no intention on my part to go in for any heroics. I was merely back-up, my role to watch and wait. Perhaps the hapless mobster had been sent out to see if the coast was clear. Had Thomas spotted the police presence and retreated here or merely paused in his exercise due to curiosity about the ruins? His henchman had appeared to be highly nervous so my money was on the former.

I went around the end of the wall and turned sharp right to walk at the base of the embankment. The ground rose and would eventually be only just below road level. Pausing behind the trunk of a nearby beech I gazed around, trying to listen but with the road just over to my right this was now very difficult. A light breeze blew on to the left-hand side of my face and brought with it a strange scent: pleasant, lemony, smoky. I had smelt it before, a long time ago and stood there, ransacking my memory.

Russian cigarettes, Sobranie Yellow citrus menthol Russian cigarettes to be precise.

He, or they, were quite close by. Carefully watching where I put my feet I moved away from the tree and made my way towards a clump of thick greenery a short distance away, glad that the breeze would blow any trace of the perfume I was wearing away from them. There was very little alternative cover other than a small group of silver birches, too skimpy to be useful.

In very, very slow motion I reached the clump, actually a towering Rhododendron *ponticum*, and managed to get myself inside it – old specimens are often like umbrellas with no foliage in the middle. Looking between its large leaves I saw Thomas and his henchman around fifteen yards away across another little glade, the pair seated at an angle to me with their backs against a large, fern-bedecked fallen tree. Thomas had what looked like a small vodka bottle in one hand which he now passed to his minder, who took a hefty swig, finished the last drops as an afterthought and threw the bottle hard so that it bounced off a tree and fell down with a thump. They were chuckling softly.

Thomas drew on his cigarette and, on the light wind, I heard him say, 'The fool's lost himself.'

'Probably can't even find his own arsehole when he's had a shit,' growled the other man.

They both dissolved into more chortles and then the Russian shushed frantically, a finger to his lips. 'No noise. We go now. To hell with Dessie, he finds his own way back.'

'Those blokes we spotted in the distance can't have been the filth but just fitness nutters doing their thing.'

'You're right. You were too nervous.'

'I thought it was my job to protect you,' was the truculent reply.

Thomas clapped him on the shoulder and stood up a little unsteadily, brushing leaves off himself. 'You are right, Ricky.'

'I wouldn't mind the pay you seem to keep forgetting about.'

'You shall have it.'

Ricky struggled to his feet. 'When?'

'When I give it to you!' Thomas retorted sharply. 'Now, go on ahead. Have a good look round while I stay here and tell me when it's safe.'

'If it wasn't for that madman Hamlyn we wouldn't have to—'

'Just do as I tell you! Go!'

Alone, Thomas relieved himself by a tree and then lit another cigarette. I held my breath when he flicked the match aside, thinking he might start a fire but there were no thin trails of smoke.

The breeze sighed in the branches, making them dip and sway, and Ricky did not come back. Thomas began to pace nervously up and down, making enough noise scuffing through last year's leaves to cover the sounds I made as I shifted position slightly to try to ease the cramp in my right leg.

It seemed to me that at least another five leaden minutes went by, but, more realistically, it was probably two. Then, silently, Patrick appeared without warning on the far side of the glade. Other than having the Glock in his hand he was relaxed and gave every appearance of having known the Russian was there all along.

'But you're dead!' Thomas gasped.

'Not *yet*,' Patrick said.

Thomas then grabbed a gun from his coat pocket but I had already taken aim and now put a shot into the ground near his feet. Ye gods, we have rehearsed scenarios like this enough times and I had pushed a hand through the greenery and waved to show Patrick where I was. The man threw down the weapon as though it had suddenly become red hot.

'You're under arrest,' Patrick said quietly. 'If you resist and try to run my partner will put a bullet in you – itching to actually, aren't you, petal?'

Petal resolved to tackle him about this designation later and left her hiding place.

'I want Hamlyn,' Patrick murmured, getting a big handful of the front of the Russian's designer shirt together with his tie. 'Where is he?'

'I know nothing of that lunatic,' Thomas scoffed.

'Otherwise, in the short time before there's a police reaction to that shot having been fired I shall take you apart. To explain your resulting injuries I shall say that you tried to escape by climbing that tree down there by the archway to get up on to the road above and sadly fell out of it. What shall we say? Broken ribs, punctured lung, broken arm?'

A little shake was administered but sufficient to make the mobster's teeth rattle together.

'You – you can't do things like that,' Thomas stammered.

'I know you've heard of the NKVD,' Patrick continued silkily.

'Almightly God, yes.'

'I work like that – do things that the ordinary police are too . . . squeamish to handle.'

Another shake, more meaningful this time.

'All I want from you is Clement Hamlyn.' And when the other remained silent, Patrick yelled, 'The man assaulted and then tried to kill my working partner, damn you!'

Thomas's eyes swivelled to me. 'This woman?'

'Yes, this woman.'

I could almost hear Thomas's thoughts. He too, plus his henchmen, had been involved in trying to kill this woman . . .

'She is . . . formidable . . . and beautiful,' he whispered. 'Hamlyn is mad and someone has to stop him. He is at a *dacha* he has in the country.'

'A holiday cottage in the countryside?'

'Yes.'

'Where exactly?'

'By the sea, in the south somewhere.'

'*Where* though?'

The man performed a shrug as well as he was able due to the restriction in his shirt front.

'Think!'

The Russian shook his head helplessly. 'That's all I know. Except that there was a murder there, more than one perhaps. He bought it because it . . . amused him.'

Then, and I am not mistaken about this, Thomas shuddered. He looked quite relieved when Patrick formally arrested him.

There were a few raised eyebrows when the rest of the trio were retrieved from a deep, steep-sided ditch at the base of the road embankment, a few fallen branches, other pieces of wood-land detritus plus a couple of small chunks of the Roman Empire having been loaded on top of them to discourage attempts to climb out. The men were conscious when found but because of the circumstances, helpless, their language appalling. That of their captor when remonstrated with about possible infringements of the suspects' human rights, I have to confess, was more inventive but worse. The one who had been referred to as Dessie was then promptly threatened with an additional charge of assaulting a police officer having aimed a kick at the constable concerned for his welfare who had been assisting him from his hole in the ground.

Patrick owned up to firing the shot – it is still iffy as to whether I am supposed to have the ex-MI5 Smith and Wesson – and no one checked his Glock. He made a short statement to the officer in charge of those at the lake, promised to put it in writing to his immediate superior, the temporary cordons keeping the general public away were removed and everyone but Patrick and me departed.

'Sorry, you're too heavy for me to give you a piggyback,' I said sympathetically to a beyond exhaustion husband. 'But I did see a wheelbarrow somewhere over there.'

Patrick had got as far as the raised dais and seated himself on it. He smiled wryly up at me.

'That was really clever,' I told him. 'Appealing to the romantic side of that hoodlum. No one's called me formidable and beautiful before.'

'I've told you you're beautiful,' he protested.

'No, you haven't.'

Then the gardeners returned and, obviously completely oblivious of what had taken place, irately told us that the public were not permitted to enter the enclosed areas and ordered us to leave immediately.

Patrick made it back to the pub.

We were not directly involved in the continuing hunt for Clement Hamlyn. It was left to the various police forces whose jurisdictions stretched from Margate to Land's End. Over the next few days it was established that no less than sixty-nine properties near the south coast – Brighton had a tally of twenty-four – had been connected with murder cases, and that only during the past fifty years. These were duly investigated, which took over a week, during which time Patrick and I went home.

Patrick's mother, Elspeth, had taken one look at her son's continuing haggard and weak appearance and declared that I was not feeding him properly. His protests that it was not my fault as we had been living in hotels and eating out fell on deaf ears. While this was perfectly true he still seemed to be having very dark moments, sometimes for a couple of days at a time, torturing himself, perhaps subconsciously punishing himself, for what had happened at the culmination of the Sussex assignment. In my view he was not consuming enough to keep a gnat alive. Vast steak and kidney pies, shepherd's or cottage pies, were placed before us at dinner by Elspeth, a roast at the weekend, followed by perhaps an apple, treacle or chocolate sponge pudding. I was not at all offended and prepared all the trimmings and vegetables as I had fielded the wink this very wise woman had sent in my direction, becoming part of her conspiracy. And of course I paid her for the extra food. So with the children demolishing all this at speed and under the gaze of his wife Patrick started to eat.

Hamlyn was finally discovered, dead drunk, in a remote, and filthy, barn conversion in Dorset. He was sobered up, ordered to have a bath and pack a bag and brought to London. Once there, and having recovered some of his usual arrogance, he insisted on making an off-the-record statement, refusing to answer questions until his wish was granted. Commander Greenway, when sounded out about this, confessed himself curious.

FIFTEEN

'You're both *dead*!' Hamlyn raged when he could speak for shock.

'Anthony Thomas said that to me when I arrested him too,' Patrick replied.

'So you *are* a cop.'

'Sort of.'

'Why is *she* here?' This with a crude gesture in my direction.

'We work together. You should have realized that by now.'

'I demand to see someone else.'

'You've got me, and as you requested, it's right off the record. But the fact that this interview is taking place has been noted in the case file and if I have to give evidence in court I shall have no choice but to tell the full story. That's as far as we can go or we'll be in breach of regulations. Also, I shall use what you say to me as groundwork for when you're officially questioned, perhaps in a couple of days, by me and also others.'

'That's not good enough.'

'You've already been treated far better then you deserve.'

'Is this being recorded?'

'No. Which means that I can say this to you: forget the police, forget SOCA, this is me with a personal mandate to put you and your assorted scumbags out of business. Personally I don't care if the whole lot of you end up in the Thames like some of your recent victims.'

This conversation was taking place at the remand centre where Hamlyn was being held. He looked pale and nervous, his hands a little shaky, but that might have been because he could have no alcohol here.

No one here had said that I should not be present having seemingly not realized that, along with the prospective interviewer, I was actually one of the suspect's victims. But I had been told, by my husband, whose run in with Hamlyn seemed to be regarded as being all part of the job, that I should not take notes, not a tragedy as I have a very good memory. In early days I was PA to an elderly, and forgetful, director of a family-run company and this had given me excellent training.

'If you're hoping to frame me for the attack on da Rosta I was *not* responsible for that,' Hamlyn said.

'No, I know who that was,' Patrick informed him. 'And now you've mentioned it I'll tell you that it was very useful, just a flesh wound that'll keep him nice and safe under police protection until he's jailed after helping with enquiries in connection with an unrelated murder case. We know from him that you'd been demanding money with menaces and the proprietor of the club he frequents saw a man closely fitting your description talking to him. Then there's the matter of the jewellery.'

'What damned jewellery?'

'Miss Smythe's jewellery that you stole the night you killed her: a gold watch chain, another chain with a locket and a diamond ring. Da Rosta said you offered him the two chains in exchange for a discount on the money you were trying to force him to pay you.'

'Well, he's lying, isn't he? Setting me up.'

'Odd then, that his description exactly matches that of missing items that he cannot have known anything about. He said he thought they were hot. They were. How did you manage to get rid of them in the end?'

Hamlyn just shook his head.

'And the diamond ring,' I interposed. 'Did you give that to your somewhat bandy-legged girlfriend?'

He still said nothing but his restlessness increased, his limbs making jerky movements.

'Do you want to make your off-the-record statement now?' Patrick enquired.

'You have no case against me. That's the gist of my statement.'

'That sounds like time-wasting and self-aggrandizement to me. OK, none of it's anything to do with you. Right, we'll discount for the moment the deaths of Tom Berry, or Jerry, Fred Jones and a guy calling himself Rapla on the grounds that the world is a better place without them, postpone until later the murder of Alonso Morella in Cannes and consider the brutal killing of Miss Rosemary Smythe. You killed her and that's quite enough to send you down for life. But first tell me why you changed your mind about staying with Jane Grant, her niece.'

'I just did.'

'You told her you'd had a fire at home. I was there when she rang you and suggested what she said. There's no damage to your house. The police have been watching it for getting on a fortnight.'

'Damn you.'

'I suggest that you were going to kill her. You're hooked on killing.'

'Don't be a fool.'

'What were you ultimately hoping to get from her? Money? Some of her inheritance? To find out for sure that her aunt hadn't told her exactly what she'd seen going on at the Trents' place?'

'I'm not answering any more questions.'

'Their house is being searched this morning, right now, in fact, and it's expected that weapons and possibly drugs and stolen property will be found.'

'Nothing to do with me.'

'So what's the reason for all this, if indeed there is one? Is it just revenge for past perceived slights and injuries or a good way to earn some readies on the side to pay for all that booze?'

'Go to hell.'

'We don't think you're the brains behind this now, even though you might have been in the beginning, mostly on the grounds that some of your thinking processes are now severely compromised.'

'They are?' Hamlyn hooted in surprise 'How d'you reckon I write the books then?'

'Oh, there doesn't appear to be anything wrong with your imagination. Let's talk about the book. How does it end?'

'With your deaths,' Hamlyn said through his teeth.

'I'm writing the end of your novel for you,' I interrupted sharply.

'You're not listening. I've already done that,' Hamlyn retorted, staring through me in the most unsettling fashion. He tapped his forehead. 'It's all up there.'

'I think you've written in Jane Grant's death. She's staying alive.'

'She can't. She's Clive Grant's wife. She told me his name.'

'They're separated and he's living in Luton.'

'No.'

'No?' Patrick said quietly.

'He's as good as dead. He has to be – he used to be with Fred Jones's mob.'

'The man's a civil engineer!'

'Not a chance. The pair of them, him and her, were right there when I was grassed up for a murder I didn't commit.'

'Who was murdered?'

The crime writer shook his head. 'I've forgotten – it was back in the bad old days.'

'But you've never done time for murder.'

Hamlyn seemed to emerge from a daydream. 'Er, no, you're right.'

That happened in the fourth of his novels, I seemed to remember.

'And Clive Grant?'

A shrug.

'You were going to kill Jane Grant and then go and look for him.'

'I might have done.'

'Who told you he was a member of Fred Jones's gang?'

'I just knew.'

'Was it Anthony Thomas?'

'Bloody hell, the man's little more than a posing imbecile! Look, I said I didn't want any more of your damned questions!'

'So you're going to take the blame for all these killings?'

'Blame! What d'you mean, blame? I merely *created* them.'

'Which is why they're in the book,' I said.

'Of course. It will come right then. Completely on the line, a brilliant crime story written with hands-on experience.'

'How long have you been drinking heavily?'

The man again appeared surprised. 'Another stupid question from a stupid woman. Always. All writers drink. If you drank more you'd write much better novels.'

'As has just been mentioned, it appears to be affecting your mental stability. Had that occurred to you?'

Slowly, he shook his head. 'No. Why should it?'

'Tell me exactly how the book ended before I rewrote it,' I requested.

'How can I now?' he suddenly roared, making me jump. 'OK, I lied, it *was* all in my head, very neatly too. But you've shitted it up. Da Rosta's alive without paying a penny and apparently that idiot Morella drowned when he was supposed to swim to safety and tell the police that Danny Coates had tried to kill him. And now *you're* still alive!'

'We didn't have anything to do with Morella,' Patrick said.

'You did. You gave him the kind of look that stopped him from throwing the pair of you in the harbour.'

'Daniel Coates wasn't responsible for his death?'

'No, why would he be? Morella was his eyes and ears. I didn't find that out until after I'd hired him to do a little work for me.'

'But you wanted Coates framed for his attempted murder? No, don't tell me, it was in the book.'

'Of course it wasn't in the bloody book, you idiot!' Hamlyn shouted.

'Is Sonya Trent in the book?' I asked.

'No.'

'Where is she?'

'God knows.'

'You haven't killed her too?'

'No, why on earth should I?'

'But you did attack Morella,' Patrick persisted.

Hamlyn shot to his feet. 'I'm going.'

'You can't until I say so,' Patrick told him.

Whereupon the man, his face twisted with rage, hurled himself at us and it took four of the remand staff who had been standing by outside the door to subdue him even after Patrick had been forced to defend the pair of us by hitting him hard with the flat of his hand around the side of the head.

'Patrick, that man's so dangerous he's going to end up in Broadmoor!' I said to him shakily afterwards, finding myself clinging on to his arm.

Even so I was wondering what Hamlyn had meant when he said that wanting Coates framed for Morella's attempted murder was not in his book. There seemed to be only one logical – if indeed anything approaching logic existed as far as Hamlyn was concerned – answer to that.

The hoard of weapons, drugs, stolen property and money discovered in different parts of the Trents' house was impressive, the currency in several different denominations so contaminated with drugs that it would never go back into circulation. Various hiding places, including the children's bedroom, had been utilized but most finds were in Hereward Trent's study: the money in a wall safe, and a medium-sized crate of assorted firearms and ammunition in a cupboard concealed behind a bookcase. Boxes containing stolen silver and silver-gilt items packed together with Chinese porcelain, the latter becoming increasingly valuable as the Chinese are buying back their heritage, were discovered in a garage.

The search had taken all day, someone apparently having been overheard saying that the only police departments not involved in these cases now the Art and Antiques Squad had been called in were Human Resources and the stationery office.

It was another three days before we formally interviewed Hamlyn in the extremely secure basement custody suite at SOCA HQ where suspects can be brought from either police stations or remand centres. Meanwhile, he had been assessed by a psychiatrist and found to be, in Greenway's requested translation of the technical terms, 'in cloud cuckooland, probably partly brought on by a serious alcohol addiction, in and out of a dream-world of his own but with a sufficient grasp of reality to remember what had recently occurred including his own actions. Caution is urged when questioning this man as he has the potential to be extremely dangerous'. This, I think, we were aware of already.

In view of this the commander had asked me if I wanted to be present on this occasion.

I told him I did, adding: 'Unless you think my presence would be likely to wind him up so that he becomes violent again. And I would like to point out that Patrick can't be expected to restrain him on his own if he does.'

Although eight days of good home cooking had made a visible difference to Patrick, right now I was not sure if he was strong enough yet for his stamina to be sufficient for any further prolonged resistance to questioning. Signs of this were the fact that the blow around the head he had meted out to Hamlyn at the last meeting should have floored him and also his having asked Greenway if he would prefer to carry out the interview himself. Smiling, the commander had shaken his head and said, 'No, you're the interrogation expert.' A touch of Daws' ruthlessness or something quite the opposite?

'Don't worry, I'll only be in the next room with several other strong bods and the remand people who brought him will be on call as well. It goes without saying that he's seriously mentally ill – what I really want to know is whether he's behind all this and, if not, who is.'

The interview room has the facility for other investigators to watch and listen to what is going on next door, courtesy of microphones and a window that appears to be a mirror on the other side. I had already known that Greenway would not be alone, present also would be CID investigators from the Met who were involved with trying to solve the various gangland murders, most of which, having occurred some time previously to Miss Smythe's, had not come within SOCA's remit. They would question Hamlyn later, but not necessarily all today. Such were the number of cases that a liaison officer had been appointed.

When Patrick saw me making my way towards the interview room – he had been requested, by Greenway, to write a report on possible Met failings at Virginia Water – he asked me the same question as had the commander.

'I want to see this man locked up forever,' I told him.

'And you are, after all, a formidable and beautiful woman,' he said with a grin.

Clement Hamlyn was already present when we arrived and subjected us to a black-browed stare, as though we had never met before. Patrick completed all the formalities, noted that the suspect had declined the presence of a legal representative, and switched on the tape machine. The interview would also be recorded using a concealed video camera.

'It helps a lot that you're still sober,' was Patrick's opening remark. 'Most of our previous encounters have been marred by the fact that you were rat-arsed.'

The author muttered a few obscenities and stared somewhere over my right shoulder.

'And despite the fact that when we last met you virtually admitted killing any number of people what I said still stands and that conversation can't be used in court as evidence against you. So now it remains to establish exactly how many you've murdered so you can be charged accordingly.'

'I was unwell when I said all that,' Hamlyn said. 'That remand centre's a real dump and I'd caught a bug of some kind.'

Stolidly, Patrick continued: 'Other people will question you about the deaths of those I'll refer to as career criminals but I want to concentrate on the murder of Miss Rosemary Smythe at Richmond and the associated organized crime that it is connected with. I take it you have a fairly clear recollection of that.'

'You're wasting my time and I didn't kill her.'

'This all starts after she wrote around a dozen letters to us, SOCA, as she thought her neighbour, Hereward Trent, was involving himself with criminals.'

'She wrote to you? God, she was an interfering old bat. Hereward said she was a neighbour from hell.'

'Do I add him to the list, by the way?'

The man's gaze fixed on the speaker. 'Trent? No, of course not.' Then, 'Why, is he *dead*?'

'His body was found dumped at a nature reserve around ten days ago. Before you were arrested too. He'd been beaten up and then shot in the head. Threatened to turn you all in, did he?'

'Look, I hadn't even seen Trent since that night we—' He abruptly stopped speaking.

'Chucked the pair of us out of a van on the M40?'

'I wasn't there!'

'Time will tell where you were, or weren't, but you ordered it.'

'I did *not*!'

'So who's the boss man? Thomas?'

Hamlyn gazed despairingly at the ceiling for a moment and then said, 'I can distinctly remember telling you that the man's an idiot, *thick*. He just makes a living hiring out hit men even more stupid than he is. The boxing thing is just a front.'

'And yet I saw him and his minder getting out of a car driven by you outside a pub in Shepherd's Bush.'

'I was only giving him a lift.'

'I'm glad you can recollect that. So who is in charge?'

'Thank you, but I prefer to stay alive, even if I have to do time.'

'You want to go down for life to protect this individual?'

'No, but it's necessary to protect . . . others.'

'Claudia Barton-Jones, for example?'

Hamlyn mutely shook his head.

'We're back in your novels again,' I said. 'You're the kind of man to boil down his own mother for glue. Why did you kill Rosemary Smythe?'

'Who's saying I did?'

'The Trents were looking for something in her house – you'd given them the keys that you'd tricked Jane Grant into letting you have. I have a theory that on the night you killed that old lady you were beside yourself because it was thought she'd gone off with something highly incriminating from the Trents' garden that had been left lying around. You burst in through the back door, obviously well-fuelled on whisky, and demanded to know what she'd done with it. She refused to tell you and you then drunkenly rampaged around the house trying to find it but were actually too drunk to look properly. Failing to locate it, you lost your temper and threw Miss Smythe down the stairs. Then, discovering that she was still alive, you strangled her.'

'Your books are lousy and so's that fairy tale,' Hamlyn sneered. 'Two out of ten for trying though.'

'But we found it,' Patrick informed him. 'In one of the attic rooms under a loose floorboard. A Heckler and Koch MP5 sub-machine gun. I understand from one of Miss Smythe's letters that a Thomas thicko-for-hire had played soldiers in the garden with weapons. Was that the chap who sabotaged the tree house or did you do it?' When Hamlyn remained silent he continued: 'You've told us that Thomas is of no account and isn't the one issuing orders so why protect him and those working for him? Are you intent on taking the blame for everything that's happened?'

Still Hamlyn remained silent.

I said, 'Someone's well aware that you have an alcohol problem and most of the time have real trouble telling the difference between fact and fiction. He's known that, and you, for a very long time and has been using you for his own ends, for money and to settle old scores. Some of the old scores could well have been yours as well so you were quite happy to go along with it to begin with. But then it all started to get out of hand and—'

'Shut your idiot mouth!' Hamlyn shouted at me.

'We're obviously getting somewhere,' Patrick murmured. 'It seems to bother you more that someone's using you than I would have thought sensible. Who sabotaged the tree house? Was it you? D'you have a thick blue sweater with a hole in it after catching it on a rose thorn climbing over the wall or have you chucked it away?'

'I—' Hamlyn bit off the rest of what he had been about to say.

'Chucked it away? I thought so. It's just your style, that tree house. No trouble at all getting into that with your height and long arms. You're probably a practical sort of bloke too and unlike Trent, Thomas and his assorted gutter rats you'd know where to saw and by how much. It's possible it didn't fall down with the old lady in it for a while so you had another go. She apparently heard someone in her garden one night.'

'You can't prove any of this.'

'And then there's the oil that a leaking mower had deposited on the Trent's lawn that you walked through on the night you killed Miss Smythe that was deposited, together with grass cuttings, on her hall carpet. The shoes you were wearing will probably still have minute traces of oil on them and you probably won't have thought of throwing those away.'

The author pointed an accusing forefinger. 'You're just making all this up.'

'Give me *your* story then.' Patrick leaned back in his chair with a chilly smile.

Hamlyn took a deep breath and then spoke angrily and jerkily. 'All right. I admit I'm involved with these people. But only as a sort of observer. It's research. But no one's using me and I was not involved with any of the crimes that were perpetrated – by them.'

'We've already established that you threatened Angelo da Rosta. He was alive without paying you a penny, you complained.'

'You've established nothing. What I said the other day is anyone's guess. You said yourself that what passed between us then can't be used in court as evidence against me.'

'He's prepared to swear in court that you did.'

'Any brief worth his salt'll throw that out. It's the word of a third-rate mobster against mine.'

Here Hamlyn bared his horrible teeth at Patrick in a triumphant grin.

I said, 'It's good to undertake research, isn't it? Go to places, get the feel of the streets you're writing about and beat up women so you know what it feels like. That's why you asked Jane Grant if you could have a look around Miss Smythe's house, because although you wanted to carry on with your search for the sub-machine gun a place like that is in your novel.'

'You deserved a smack but basically, you're right. And congratulations, you're learning fast,' Hamlyn said.

'But then you gave the keys to the Trents as you'd had second thoughts about entering the house yourself in case you were seen.'

He just stared through me.

'Hereward Trent wasn't behind all this, was he? His home was being used as a safe house.'

'He was a pathetic fool and pathetic them. deserve to be used. I felt sorry for him – sometimes.'

'The man was so nervous it was obvious he was under huge duress. Threats to his family?'

'It's always a weak point with fools, something I've discovered during my research. I can always influence them. I admit I leaned on him. I – er – was asked to as he seemed frightened of me for some reason.' This with a smirk, craning his neck a little in the direction of the mirror as though he was trying to admire his reflection in it.

'How did you find out about his spot of bother at the Essex golf club that was one of the reasons they moved to Richmond?'

'Oh, that. Someone I know had heard about it.'

'You used it to blackmail him.'

'I'm admitting to nothing. Some bastard'll only frame me for his murder.' This with a contemptuous glance at Patrick.

'It makes you feel big having a hold over others, doesn't it?'

'It's professional. I like to get right under the skin of my characters.'

'I understand you sometimes threaten people with rape.'

'Why ask, d'you fancy it?' the man retorted with a leer.

'Your leading character does that too.'

'So?'

'He's a complete shit. Like you.'

He actually gaped at me.

'Did you rape Sonya Trent?'

'I – er—'

'Offer to get her out of the house in case a neighbour saw something suspicious and called the police? Drive her off in your car, did you? Take her to a quiet place where you raped her?'

'Er—'

'I think you did. I asked you this the other day. Where is she?'

Hamlyn responded with an extravagant shrug.

'You really don't know?'

'No.'

'I don't believe you.'

'I don't know where she is!' Hamlyn shouted. 'She – she ran off.'

'After you'd raped her.'

'OK, yes, but I really don't know where she is.'

'And you're not really interested because, as you said last time, she wasn't in the book either.'

The man shook his head, eyes closed. 'Now you're deliberately trying to confuse me.'

'No, I'm trying to get inside your crazy world. The other day you said – and you do seem to be choosing to remember some of what was said – that getting Daniel Coates framed for Alonso Morella's murder wasn't in the book. If you don't know where Mrs Trent is and that's not in the book either it suggests that those are the things you have no control over.'

'I could have said anything the other day. As I said before, I wasn't well.'

'You were examined by a doctor at the remand centre to see if you were fit to be interviewed and he reported that there was nothing physically wrong with you except symptoms of alcohol withdrawal. According to the psychiatrist who also saw you, you go in and out of a psychotic state so I suppose it's a bit like using a revolving door. And when you're like that you're a serial killer – bragging about it too.'

'Get this bloody woman out of here!' Hamlyn bawled to Patrick.

'She stays,' Patrick whispered.

I continued: 'To you, sane or otherwise, everyone's a fool, stupid, an idiot or an imbecile. That sounds like the reaction of a man who knows that, deep down, he's the biggest moron of the lot for being outmanoeuvred by someone who's got right inside his raddled brain. He's controlling everything, and especially, *you.*'

'This is all utter make-believe!'

'Yes, despite what you said I'm quite creative too. But I think I've got this right. You need this person because he's your mental prop to remaining the famous author who writes amazingly authentic novels. You have to keep him sweet or he'll blow you and your illusions to bits by grassing on you to the police. And he's playing with you: he made you go and find him in Cannes to get the money he owed you. I did a little bit of research and discovered that you haven't bothered to attend a literary festival before. Too boring? Too many idiots there?'

The crime writer leaned across the table towards me. 'One day, I'll find you, and then . . .' With a triumphant smile he left the rest to my imagination.

I smiled back. 'There you are, Big Jake – that's his name isn't it? Big Jake, the all-powerful, right under the thumb of a shitty little mobster. I'm pretty sure it's Daniel Coates – directing everything from his boat somewhere in the Med and on rare visits to this country using a stolen identity. Coates, showing you up as the truly pathetic man you really are.'

It came as a shock to me when I saw this remark strike home.

I continued: 'Did he laugh at you on that boat while holding a gun on you before throwing you just some of the money you'd told him he owed you? Laughed at you while you scrabbled on the floor for it? You missed one of the fifty euro notes. Then he probably carried on laughing while forcing you to leave the boat by clambering on to the one moored next to it and from there up on to the outer harbour wall. It was quite a long walk back from there, wasn't it?'

'I shall kill him for what he's done,' Hamlyn said slowly. 'And you and your screwing mate.'

'You can't, it's not in the book now. I've rewritten it. And the end now is that Big Jake's going to end up in a secure mental hospital.'

'You can't do that!'

'I've done it. I *know* it's true. You're finished.'

The man sat there motionless, his face set.

'Tell me it's Coates.'

'I'll tell her if you promise to kill him,' Hamlyn said to Patrick.

Patrick shook his head. 'No. Tell her and we'll arrest him instead.'

'But . . .' He gazed helplessly from one to the other of us. 'If you've rewritten the end . . .'

'I'll delete it if you confirm that it's Daniel Coates,' I promised.

'But . . .'

'You're finished!' I yelled in the man's face. 'Tell me it's Coates who's responsible.'

'It's Coates,' Hamlyn said in so low a voice as to be hardly audible. And then, shockingly, his heavy features crumpled and he sobbed, the tears running down his face.

Outside the room I found I was shaking so much my teeth chattered. Patrick put an arm around me and steered me to the canteen where I was treated to a steaming mug of hot chocolate.

SIXTEEN

'Well, as you know,' the commander said, 'Hamlyn was questioned again this afternoon by a Met DCI and his sidekick working on the Berry, Duggan and Rapla murders and they did, at my request, slip in asking him about the whereabouts of Sonya Trent. He was a bit more composed by then, perhaps had slipped back into his comfort zone of telling himself he was undertaking research – what it's like to be grilled by the nasty mob – and although the question took him unawares he still said he didn't know. I said I'd give looking for her priority for two days and I have. There's no sign of the woman. We have no idea who her friends are. Her parents in Dartmouth have been questioned and they can't suggest where she might be. They're frantically worried, of course.'

'The poor woman might not even know that her husband's dead,' I said. 'What was reported in the media?'

'That the body of a so far unidentified white male has been

found near Hackney,' Greenway answered. 'I can't believe she would think it was him if she read or heard about it. D'you reckon Hamlyn killed him?'

'He was pretty convincing at being surprised by the news.'

The commander rose from his chair, stretched, his hands brushing the low ceiling and then said, 'Coates. I haven't congratulated you yet, Ingrid, but that was a fine piece of work.'

'Nothing's proved though. I may be wrong and he said that to get rid of me.'

'That's possible, but—'

His desk phone rang. He snatched it up but it was a routine call.

Patrick said, 'What was the outcome of the questioning this afternoon?'

'Nothing that could be described as an outcome. All he'd admit to was being on the sidelines, again, in the name of research. I don't think anyone'll get a lot of joy, to be frank. What we really need is the boss man. And of course as matters stand now there's plenty to get Hamlyn put away, probably for the rest of his life – but there'll have to be a hearing to see if he's fit to plead first, of course.'

'Do those working on Operation Captura have any idea at all where Coates might be?' Patrick enquired impatiently.

It transpired that they did not. And yes, we were all fed up with sitting around talking. We were realistic enough to know that investigations are ninety per cent talking, listening, reading, writing, watching, pounding the streets and deadly boredom. Therefore, until some useful information came to light about the possible whereabouts of Coates we decided to do a little more talking and, the following morning, endeavour to interview Claudia Barton-Jones.

The Bartons-Joneses lived in one of the penthouse flats of a modern development in Teddington, overlooking the river. Patrick told me that he had money on the woman now living there on her own, her husband having seen sense, this intelligent guess well on the way towards being proved correct when we arrived and saw that the apartment was for sale. Personally, I was delighted with the prospect of coming face to face with my old friend 'Alice' again.

'You were in France – both of you,' was her opening remark.

Patrick told her exactly who we were and her face assumed the kind of expression that made me feel all jolly inside. Despondently, she let us in and showed us into a huge room with ceiling to floor windows on the side overlooking the Thames. The furnishings were starkly minimalist: black, white, Rothko-style wall paintings in red, orange and charcoal-grey. The only living thing, other than us, was a single white-flowered orchid plant.

'You'd better sit down,' said Claudia Barton-Jones, eyeing me curiously. She looked much the same as when I had seen her before and was around forty years of age, of medium height and slightly overweight in the way that would make it difficult for her to find clothes to fit, that is, big in the bust with short, and slightly bandy, legs. Her dark brunette hair had red tints now and the crimson fingernails badly needed attention.

'This is an official interview,' Patrick began by saying. 'But we're not directly involved in the investigation into alleged irregularities with regard to your expenses.'

The woman's brow cleared a little. 'Oh.'

'I want to ask you about your connection with Clement Hamlyn.'

'He's just a friend.'

'Think carefully before you answer. What is your connection with him?'

'Look, I'm sorry I pretended to be someone else but I didn't want my husband to know I was—'

Patrick carved her up. 'I'm not remotely interested in what you didn't want your husband to know. I suggest that Hamlyn isn't just a friend as he doesn't appear to have any others. In what way are you *connected* with him?'

Crossly, the woman answered, 'I've known him for years, that's all, and we occasionally go out together. He asked me if I'd like to go to France. And I would like to point out that we did *not* share a room.'

'Why did you lie to me, and others in the bar that evening?' I asked her. 'All that rubbish about being a travel writer.'

'For the same reason that I stated just now. I have a fairly unusual name and I didn't want anyone to be in a position to know I was in France with a man who wasn't my husband.'

'Because you're divorcing him for some reason or other and don't want him to have anything he can accuse you of in order to get more of his money? I take it he's not living here.'

'No, right now he's at what I believe is referred to as a crash pad in town – it's quite near where he works. Don't you ever let your hair down?'

'Yes, but not with other *men*. And I prefer to do so without someone spiking my drinks – which you did.'

'I did not.'

'Did Hamlyn?'

'No, I fixed all the drinks myself. I was feeling generous. Why should either of us do that?'

OK, perhaps I had drunk far too much. I actually felt myself blush.

Patrick said, 'You're in the habit of accompanying Hamlyn to a house in Richmond belonging to a man called Hereward Trent.'

'He's a businessman who Clement's known for years. What of it?'

'I'm afraid we're in possession of the whole story and it's not pretty. The Trents' home was being used as an HQ for a gang of serious criminals. He's dead, murdered; his body was very recently discovered at a nature reserve in east London. Hamlyn's under arrest, not for that killing – not yet that is – but for the murder of the Trents' neighbour, Miss Rosemary Smythe.'

'I can't believe it. That can't be right.'

'There's very good evidence to support the charge. I understand you once gave this lady a two-fingered salute when you met her in the street.'

'That's not a crime. Everyone hated her – she was a spiteful old woman.'

'Everyone?'

'OK, that's what I was told.'

'Everyone being Hamlyn, Hereward Trent and his wife, Sonya, a Russian mobster by the name of Anthony Thomas, his minder and any number of vicious and boneheaded henchmen, one of whom paraded around the Trents' garden with one or more of the weapons that were kept hidden in the house.'

'I know absolutely nothing about that.'

'I think you do.'

'Did Hamlyn give you any jewellery?' I said.

'Jewellery? I don't think so.'

'It's hardly something that would have slipped your mind. Could it be a ring or a gold chain with a locket? A ring perhaps because he's asked you to marry him when you've finally dumped your husband.'

'No! I'd never marry him – he's as good as being an alcoholic. There was a time when I thought I could help him but—'

I interrupted her. 'You need a large dose of reality. He is an alcoholic and for that and other reasons he's seriously mentally ill. You must be aware of that. I'll ask you again: did he give you any jewellery?'

Barton-Jones shook her head.

'I'm quite prepared to get a search warrant,' Patrick told her.

'Then get one.'

Patrick made himself more comfortable. 'What really interests me, having talked to you, is that out of all the people we've interviewed you seem to be the only one who isn't terrified of him. Perhaps you'd be good enough to explain that to me.'

She shrugged. 'As I've just said, I've known him for years.'

'Right back to his youth, the dreadlocked yobbo who worked at a second-hand car business in London and as a hit man for one or more gang bosses in his spare time? Really?'

'Yes. I was a social worker in those days. I was involved with his family and tried to sort him and his younger half-brother out. My assignment was actually with the younger boy. Clement is around my age.'

'But you failed as far as he was concerned.'

'In some ways I suppose I did. But we've stayed . . . friends.'

'Have you ever been sexually involved with him?'

'No! I've said as much already, haven't I?'

'Perhaps you're the only person he feels he can trust.'

'That's possible.'

'And if he does have a flicker of warm feelings for you he might not have threatened to kill you as he has just about everyone else in his poisonous circle but keeps you in tow and gives you the odd present, a few days in the South of France perhaps, to ensure your silence because he knows you have a very good idea what he's doing.'

'That's a terrible thing to say.'

'Am I right? Yes?'

Again she shook her head, but her lower lip trembled.

'Mrs Barton-Jones,' Patrick murmured. 'When I worked for MI5 they used to let me loose on people who in those days were referred to as traitors. I don't want to have to upset you unnecessarily.' When she still made no response he continued, an edge to his voice: 'I know you're lying.'

'I . . . am . . . not . . . lying,' the woman ground out slowly.

'I know you're lying because I'm trained to know when people are lying and the reason you are is that you *are* frightened of Clement Hamlyn. I have an idea he forced you – a mixture of gifts and threats – to make those fraudulent expense claims to fund his drinking and gambling. He could be behind the reasons for the other criminal charges levelled against you as well. Tell the truth.'

'Then I'm surrounded on all sides!' the woman suddenly cried. 'The police, him, my husband, my employers and now *you*!' She got up from her seat and ran over to the window and my heart leapt in alarm, thinking for one awful moment that she might be about to try to throw herself out.

'No,' Patrick said quietly. 'I'm the answer to all this.'

She turned. 'The answer!'

'Please come back and sit down.'

Hesitantly, she came.

'It's over,' Patrick continued. 'Most of those involved have been arrested, or soon will be, some are dead. There's every chance that Hamlyn will be found unfit to plead and spend all, or most of, the rest of his life in a secure mental hospital. Your only chance is to tell the absolute truth – to me, and I'll try to help you.'

Perceptively, the woman was now shivering. 'Sorry, I simply can't perceive of a time when this nightmare will be over.'

'Would it be a good idea if Ingrid made us all some coffee?'

She glanced at me and waved vaguely towards a door behind where I was sitting. 'Yes . . . do.'

The kitchen was immaculately clean. I left the gleaming Italian coffee machine severely alone – it looked as though one needed a degree in computing science in order to work it – and filled a kettle. By the time I had found everything I needed, made the coffee, instant, and returned to that stark room Claudia Barton-Jones was recounting, presumably at Patrick's prompting in an effort to get her to relax, some of her early experiences as a social worker.

'Clement and his half-brother were brought up by their grand-mother,' she was saying. 'I'd been told – in confidence obviously but it hardly matters now – that his father was a French merchant seaman, his mother a prostitute with a drug habit who was the daughter of the woman who took the two children on. Further contact with their parents was impossible, Clement's father having predictably disappeared back to sea, the mother left home and eventually died of an overdose. The father of the other boy was unknown.'

'And you've kept in touch with Hamlyn ever since you were assigned to his family,' Patrick said, putting a spoonful of sugar in his coffee.

'Oh, no. There was a break of quite a few years after he first got into trouble with the law and then went to prison. I didn't meet him again until after he'd had a couple of books published and he looked me up. I was thrilled, of course, that he seemed to have turned his life around but . . .' She stopped speaking for a moment and then said, 'And now . . .'

'You might go to prison if it can be proved that you're an accessory to murder.'

'That's your job, I suppose,' Claudia said dully.

'The gangland killings of mobsters murdered because either they did not pay up having been threatened with death if they didn't or as a result of old grudges is the responsibility of the Metropolitan Police – and we're talking about hired hit men under investigation here. *Eventually* that will lead to the mobsters at the top. SOCA's not prepared to wait. My original brief was to catch Miss Smythe's killer. We have: Hamlyn. He killed her because, although no one's admitting anything, it was thought she'd gone off with a sub-machine gun that had been left lying around. She had, took it as evidence and hid it in her loft. We've found it. But he's not the brains behind everything, someone else is.'

'You must believe me when I say that I'm not involved.'

'How many times did you go to the Trents' home?'

'Three altogether, I think.'

'What happened?'

'Nothing much. The men usually went off into Hereward's study – for some of the time, that is – while I had a glass of wine or two with Sonya. Once it was during the summer and we sat in the garden. She said that the woman next door used to peer at them from her tree house.'

'It was sabotaged and collapsed while the eighty-year-old-plus lady was in it, causing her to break her leg and suffer cuts and contusions. Go on.'

This news, or reminder, did not appear to penetrate, a sign perhaps of how worried this woman now was.

'Did Hamlyn not discuss with you the purpose of the meetings?'

'No, and I didn't like to pry. I have to say I did wonder what was going on but never met people you've just described as henchmen.'

'And Sonya Trent made no comment?'

'Yes, she did actually. She whispered to me once that she didn't like these people in her house, didn't like the look of them at all. All Hereward would say was that it was business.'

'I'm not quite sure why Hamlyn took you along.'

'Perhaps to keep Sonya company.'

'She's disappeared, by the way.'

'Oh, that's awful. We became quite good friends.'

'Did she ever mention a friend who she might go to in an emergency?'

'I can't remember her mentioning anyone. I have an idea she didn't make friends easily.'

'What about these local authority contracts that it's alleged you were involved in placing in iffy circumstances?'

'You said you weren't involved in investigating that.'

'Not *directly* involved, I said. Insofar as it involves this bunch of mobsters it's relevant.'

She sighed.

'Let me guess. This was Trent's side of things. Vehicles supplied for official use on a leased basis? The mayor's limo? Staff permitted to buys cars at reduced rates?'

'It involved a van for the dog warden and cars for social services and wasn't iffy,' Burton-Jones said defiantly. 'It was actually a good deal. And I'm sure Hereward isn't – sorry, wasn't – a crook.'

'Did you tell the police who interviewed you about this?'

'Er – no.'

'So what did you get out of the deal?'

'Nothing. But—'

'Hamlyn got a backhander from Trent for introducing you and you then made sure Trent got the contract.'

'Yes.'

'In exchange for what?'

'What d'you mean?'

'What did Hamlyn give you? The trip to France?'

'Yes.' This very quietly.

'Jewellery?'

There was a long silence which Patrick broke by saying. 'It has blood on it.'

'Blood!' Claudia almost shrieked.

'Ingrid mentioned it just now. A diamond ring, two gold chains, one with a locket on it, disappeared from Miss Smythe's bedroom when she was murdered. Hamlyn tried to sell the chains to a fence but failed.'

This time she fled right out of the room. We sat tight. I glanced at Patrick but he was doing his inscrutable thing. The seconds ticked by.

Claudia Barton-Jones then came back into the room almost as quickly as she had left it and thrust a small box into Patrick's hands. Then she threw herself back into her seat and burst into tears.

The solitaire diamond surrounded by smaller ones glittered in the sun streaming through the huge windows.

'Rosemary Smythe's mother's engagement ring?' I wondered.

Claudia Barton-Jones scrubbed at her eyes with a screwed-up tissue and said huskily, 'That does make me an accessory to murder, doesn't it?'

'Only if you knew where it had come from.'

'He told me that he'd *bought* it for me in the West End.' Her voice choked.

'Just this? No gold chains?'

'No. God, I couldn't keep anything like that now, knowing . . .'

'What else did he want you to do? Hand over some of your fraudulently claimed expenses?'

'Once or twice he did. What you must understand that Clement was perfectly all right when he was sober, quite a gentleman. It was when he'd been drinking that he'd . . .'

'Just once or twice? Are you sure?'

'I feel so stupid, weak and awful.' Claudia said in a low voice after another long pause.

'Did he grab all the money off you that he could, especially when he was drunk?'

She nodded.

'And he was getting drunk more and more often and you've been feeling completely trapped – surrounded as you yourself said just now – which is one of the reasons this apartment is up for sale as you need to get right away from him, escape.'

Another nod.

'Good,' Patrick said briskly.

'Good!' She stared at him, horrified.

'You have the perfect defence. It's the answer. I didn't mention this before but as well as being as mad as a box of frogs Hamlyn's actually responsible, directly and indirectly, for several murders. You've tried to help this man for years and ended up by being completely dominated by him. You're probably lucky to be alive. Be as frank with the investigating officers as you have with me – I suggest you go and see them today – and get yourself a very good brief.'

We were going out of the front door, Claudia Burton-Jones appearing to be totally bemused, when she suddenly said, 'I've just thought of someone who Sonya might have gone to. She swore me to secrecy and told me that one of the men who came to the meetings now and again was an old flame. So *he* can't be a crook. I only know his first name's Danny. That's not much help though, is it?'

'Daniel Coates?' Patrick asked, turning to face her.

'Sorry, I've no idea. Apparently Clement hated him.'

'He does.'

'Oh, you know of him. Sonya said he'd bought a semi-derelict

farm, in Sussex, a sort of estate, as an investment with some business associates and was going to turn it into a country house spa
hotel and conference centre. It sounded lovely.' She smiled brightly.
'I expect she's safe and well there.'

'Any idea where this place is?' I enquired, Patrick momentarily
lost for words.

'She just said somewhere near the South Downs.'

SEVENTEEN

'It's not inconceivable,' I observed when we were sitting in
the car. 'Daniel Coates, east end of London mobster, could
have been one of those involved in buying the Keys Estate
near Steyning with Brad Northwood, nicknamed Uncle, another
east end of London mobster. They could easily have been in it
together. As we ourselves know all too well, Northwood, together
with his sidekick cum minder Joy Murphy were arrested several
months ago and—'

'Five months, three weeks and five days ago actually,' Patrick
broke in with.

'Thank you,' I said, deliberately ignoring the deeper implications. 'If they really were, or are, going to turn the place into a
country house hotel and whatever else they will have to get
planning permission and, before that, form a proper business, a
company. The whole project will all cost a great deal of money,
millions, more probably than these crooks would have possessed
individually.'

'Money laundering in a big way,' Patrick said under his breath
and reached for his mobile. The signal was poor so he got out
of the car and walked a short distance away towards the river.
Our vehicle was attracting the attention of a traffic warden so I
lowered my window and showed him our official parking pass.
He shook his head sadly and went on his way.

Patrick returned, looking thoughtful. 'I've just contacted Sussex
Police, who still appear to be digging into what happened at the
Keys Estate that night. According to a local solicitor who handled

the sale for the Woodley family's heirs, who as you know owned the property, it was bought by a London consortium calling itself Jones Enterprises. This outfit still seems to be in possession of it.'

'Which is listed as owning Coates' catamaran!' I exclaimed. 'But surely, Coates wouldn't have the brass neck to hide out there. He's a wanted man.'

Patrick shrugged. 'I agree that it's unlikely. But a stolen identity or two, a change of appearance . . . Not only that . . .'

'What?'

'Some DI wants me to be interviewed again. Soon. Quote, "to tie up a few loose ends".'

'It was always a possibility.'

'I know. It will look very bad if I refuse.'

'You were completely cleared of blame.'

'I know that too.'

'Did you mention Coates?'

'No, he's SOCA business.'

'I'm well within my rights to forbid you to attend,' Michael Greenway said, frowning. He hates what he regards as outside interference. 'That affair is over and done with.'

'Perhaps I need to lay a few ghosts to rest,' Patrick said. 'Revisit the place.'

'I respect that. OK, see what you can sniff out about anything else that might be of interest us while you're there.'

'We may as well find out if Coates is indeed lurking there disguised by three wigs and a beard. Grab him right under the Sussex force's noses.'

I was not taken in by this outward joviality and nor, possibly, was Greenway. Neither had I ever seen a spark of fear in Patrick's eyes before.

We drove to Sussex the following morning slightly cheered by the news that Claudia Barton-Jones had presented herself to the relevant police station prepared to make a full statement. In due course she would be sent to prison for twelve months in connection with the expenses fraud and the local authority contract offences, the sentence a light one due to the mitigating circumstances.

Jane Grant had been permitted to return home. Sonya Trent's description had been circulated to airports and bus and railway stations but so far there had been no sightings of her. The latest information on Clement Hamlyn was that he was unwell, it was thought as a result of alcohol withdrawal, and might have to see a doctor. Otherwise the various and exhaustive investigations were progressing, mostly, one got the impression, at a snail's pace.

I guessed Detective Inspector Jessica Sturrock to be in her early fifties. She had short grey hair quite stylishly cut, small blue eyes that were gazing at us steadily through gold-framed glasses and was clearly nobody's fool. She had apologized for keeping us waiting for a few minutes, a courtesy as we ourselves had been a little late for our appointment because of having been held up by an accident in the Horsham area. I would have preferred to have had a quick look at the old farm first, hoping that if Patrick were to see it now, in bright sunshine, after several months had elapsed it would slay some of his gremlins. But there had not been time.

'I regret that I'm new to the job and was not here when all this took place,' the DI was saying. 'And I've found myself in the position of now being expected to write the report which my predecessor did not because, sadly, he died. I've read all the CID case notes here, your own report, the findings of the inquiry and the conclusions of Complaints. I have to say that it took me rather a long time but I think I've built up an accurate picture. I've also tried to find out as much about you personally as I can, not easy as having worked for MI5 you appear to be an Official Secret. By the way, do you regard yourself as some kind of James Bond?'

Patrick smiled and shook his head. 'No, I regard myself as an army officer who, having resigned his commission, works as an adviser for SOCA as that is *exactly* what I am. Previous training I've undergone has had the effect of sometimes saving my life in dangerous situations, and without wishing to brag, those of other people.'

'Would you prefer me to call you Lieutenant Colonel?'

'No, Patrick's absolutely fine.'

'There's a deafening silence from the hierarchy at SOCA as well.'

'His name's Richard Daws – that used to be an Official Secret but is no longer.'

Now he had completely retired from MI5, that is.

'And according to your boss Michael Greenway your wife acts as some kind of adviser to *you*. Isn't that a bit unconventional?'

Patrick looked at me, reminding the woman that I, too, had a tongue in my head. 'Is it?'

'I worked with Patrick in his MI5 days,' I said. 'SOCA seemed to think we came as a package.'

'I see.'

She didn't but carried on talking. 'Despite all the various findings I'm going to find it very difficult to explain why this police force didn't arrest you for the murders of the three men who supposedly had been sent out, one at a time, to watch you in the event of your escaping from that barn where they had you trapped.'

'I wasn't trapped. I chose to stay there. I said that in my report.'

She appeared to ignore his reply. 'I've read your report three times and have to say that it's very clear and concise, exactly what one might expect from a one-time soldier but you simply don't touch on the reasons why you weren't charged with murder.'

'Perhaps I didn't think police reasons for doing or not doing something were my business.'

'But it *was* murder. Unlike the two indoors who had been ordered to kill you, these men weren't actually attacking you at the time you killed them, were they?'

'No, although I think two of them had tried to assail the barn previously – it was very hard to tell in the dark.'

'How dark was it?'

'There was a faint intermittent quarter moon. But mostly, very dark.'

'And you killed them – in the dark.'

Patrick stirred restlessly in his chair. 'Yes.'

'Did that worry you at all?'

'Yes, afterwards. But at the time I felt it was them or me.'

'Does it still?'

'Yes.'

'Really?'

'Yes, really,' I said.

She ignored me too. 'But this wasn't war, was it?'

'Congratulations, you've succeeded in getting right at the heart of my problem,' Patrick whispered.

'A man like you then,' Sturrock went on quietly, 'would be capable of – what shall I say? – perhaps persuading a mere DI who had the job of sorting out that God-awful mess into not sending him straight off to the custody suite. Or did you threaten him with more of the same?'

Patrick turned a wide-eyed stare to me for a moment, his incredulity boundless. Then he said, 'You've read all the conclusions but not built up anything like an accurate picture of what happened. I'll remind you. When, as it says in the report, Mick the Kick's gang turned up with revenge in mind there was a shoot-out that Ingrid and I were not involved in. They were all terrible shots, hardly anyone suffered further injuries and the original lot threw down their weapons and were then locked up in a garage. Ingrid, using our emergency number on her mobile – mine had been taken from me – was responsible for your lot being alerted when this started to happen. If the police had arrived before the other gang there would have been a bloodbath as there were sufficient weapons in the farmhouse to have started a small war.'

'I understand it was the original gang who had also been involved in gang warfare in Bath.'

'That's right, a gun battle when several members of the public were killed or injured. That was why I had stayed, to wear them down and try to reduce the odds; that was why we had fired no shots so the neighbours had not dialled 999, all the while hoping that they would either drink themselves into a stupor or start killing each other. Your predecessor, whose name I distinctly remember was Bob, and I'm really sorry he's dead, wrung my hand for saving his lads from being slaughtered. Perhaps I should have put that in my report. I was completely open with him about everything at the time – I told him I'd killed them – but if he subsequently came to the conclusion that the three bodies in a ditch had been despatched under less than a hundred per cent self-defence circumstances then he kept quiet about it.'

I said, 'Patrick made an immediate report to this officer, giving him a lot of background information about the case as well, someone gave him a temporary dressing for the knife wound in his arm and then I drove him to Worthing hospital as he had lost quite a lot of blood.'

There was rather a long silence broken by Jessica Sturrock saying, 'I have no choice but to accept your explanation but am nevertheless deeply unhappy about it. When I write my report I shall have to state that due to his illness – he had been suffering from throat cancer for some time and was undergoing very unpleasant treatment – Bob acted in a way that did not promote and reflect the best principles that this force ought to offer. Are you content with that?'

'Let me ask you a couple of questions,' Patrick said.

'Go ahead.'

'Do you expect me to be content with it?'

'Yes, I think so. Why on earth shouldn't you be?'

'Then having read all this stuff you not only haven't got the right picture, you have no idea of the sort of bloke I really am. Did this man have a family?'

'Yes, a wife and two teenage children.'

'So you're quite happy to publicly blacken this man's character and life's work just to get your report out of the door and make everything all right for you and the force.'

'Look, I'm sure he thought he was acting in everything and everyone's best interests at the time. And no doubt he was . . . well . . . grateful to you. But you can't expect me to be.'

'No, and I'd prefer you to write down your first inkling, that I threatened him.'

'But you said you didn't.'

'No, of course I didn't. But I'd rather you went for that option than have him blamed for dereliction of duty. I'd survive that, possibly, but his family will have a husband's and father's name blackened for ever.'

'I can hardly say that if it's not true.'

'I'm glad to hear it.'

'You've put me in an impossible position.'

'I suggest you've put yourself in it. All you have to do is reiterate the official findings. You weren't here; no one will expect you to do anything else.'

'I can't do that, it's slipshod.' The DI got to her feet. 'Nor can I come to any definite conclusions until I've seen this place for myself – later when I'm off duty as there's no justification for using my time now. And I'm afraid I shall have to insist that you take me through exactly what occurred right from the beginning.'

'As you wish,' Patrick said tautly. 'But I feel I must caution you that the property still belongs to an outfit known to have criminal connections. There's every chance that—'

Sturrock interrupted him. 'We are keeping an eye on the place.' She swept on with, 'Can you pick me up outside here at six thirty as you know exactly where we're going? Sorry, but there's a late meeting that I have to attend.'

We rose to leave.

'I do understand that it's the last place on earth you want to be,' the DI said to Patrick with a thin smile.

'You're very quiet,' Patrick said some time later when we had found somewhere to have a light lunch.

'There's nothing useful that I can say,' I replied. 'Really, really nothing useful.'

'Me neither.'

All the talking about it had been done.

We toured the district to give us something to do in the time available, driving to Bramber where we wandered hand in hand among the tumbled rocks, grassy ditches and mounds of the ruins of the castle. Then we had lunch at a pub in the village: I hardly noticed what I ate. Afterwards we headed for the coast and walked along the beach at Lancing, again hand in hand, the tide right out but on the turn, a muddy-looking English channel creeping in little rivulets ever closer to our feet across the rippled sand and stranded pieces of seaweed. I picked up a few shells and then tossed them aside.

Why did I have this strange feeling? We were only going to talk a Detective Inspector through events when a gang of London mobsters had been apprehended. While it was true that my husband might experience a few bad moments what else could happen?

'I have to say something purely from the oracle point of view,' I said into the silence.

'That your cat's whiskers are giving you hell?' Patrick hazarded with a squeeze of my hand.

'Yes, they are.'

'I didn't think I had any but mine are too. Must be nerves.'

As if setting the scene for us Nature had erased the early bright sunshine with heavy cloud moving in from the south west. It would get dark early.

'With your permission we're going to carry this out initially from Ingrid's point of view and that's why we asked you to dress in rough walking gear,' Patrick said. 'You've read all the reports, you must know mine almost by heart by now but that only mentions her from the moment of her arrival, bringing her mobile, the short-barrelled Smith and Wesson that she carries with all due permissions, plus our other usual emergency bits and pieces including refreshments in the form of chocolate bars and water purification tablets.'

Sturrock, who was in one of the Range Rover's back seats and we gathered had had to go home in order to change – apparently she had a flat just around the corner – looked at me. 'Do you have it, the gun, with you now?'

'It's in the locked cubby box between the front seats together with Patrick's Glock 17,' I told her, wondering if Patrick's fingers had been crossed during the 'all due permissions' bit. 'Sometimes it's in my bag – all my bags smell of gun oil.'

We were still parked at the front of the police HQ, in Sturrock's own designated space which she presumably did not normally use.

'Do you intend taking the weapons into this property?' the DI then wanted to know.

'You said you wanted to see everything exactly as it happened,' Patrick replied, turning the key in the ignition. 'Besides, I carry it for a very good reason – there's a price on both our heads from the criminal and terrorist fraternities.'

The woman made no further comment about that, saying instead, 'Water purification tablets? Were they necessary?'

'Yes, I was half dead with thirst,' Patrick answered. 'There was only a stinking water butt and a few drips of rain leaking through the barn roof.'

'I don't remember reading that.'

'Soldiers tend to stick to the details of an engagement, not about themselves,' Patrick told her absently, coping with the rush-hour traffic. He then said, 'From the point of view of convenience and authenticity we've checked into the hotel in Steyning where Ingrid did first time around. It's very handy as we can leave the car there.'

It took around another twenty minutes to reach it. I had dressed in almost the same clothing as I had on the first occasion, a short-sleeved dark blue top and matching trousers, over these a lightweight, showerproof jacket made in Wisconsin that has an amazing number of pockets and is intended for the use of those who go game shooting. Along with the other garments it is mostly kept in the Range Rover and, as always, I had replenished all the contents of the pockets. The only difference was that I now put the Smith and Wesson in one of them instead of the shoulder harness I had worn before.

We had just parked the car and got out of it when Patrick's mobile rang. He apologized to Sturrock and answered it, and I immediately realized that the call was from Greenway.

'Good or bad news?' I asked when the call was over.

'Two things. Sonya Trent's been arrested at her parents' house where she'd arrived last night with a female friend she'd fled to. Her mother persuaded her to contact the police, mostly on account of her saying that Hamlyn had raped her. Because of that and the other circumstances, that her husband's been murdered, she's being interviewed briefly and will be released on police bail to be with her children.'

'Thank God she's safe.'

'And there's been a long overdue response from Cannes harbour authority about the stealth boat we saw. Apparently it had been confiscated from someone they did not care to mention but not connected with this case and now belonged to a boat yard, having been in their words, "disposed of".'

We started walking south and soon came to a crossroads. If we turned right we would have to pass the little cottage where my aunt used to live, the reason I knew the area quite well, having visited her several times in my late teens. But we carried straight on and soon the road began to climb: we were at the northern foot of the South Downs here. A quarter of a mile farther on the road forked, the right one would narrow into little more than a country lane with passing places that crossed the downs and finished up in Sompting, not far from Lancing and Worthing. If we wanted to enter our destination by the main entrance we would go this way. But we did not and took the left hand road.

'Just to set the scene,' the DI said. 'You, Patrick, had somehow got yourself in a car when this gang had abandoned the house where they'd gathered in Bath for a party when their leader realized that the place was being watched by the police from the house across the road.'

'That's right. Even the people driving were too drunk to notice a strange passenger.'

'But when you all arrived here Joy Murphy, the mobster's girlfriend, recognized you and you were grabbed. She took your Glock and mobile phone away from you and invited two of the gang to help her beat you to death.'

'Correct. But she didn't know about my knife.'

'Do you have that with you now too?'

'I always have it with me.'

'I see. You killed these two men with it and then made for the barn.'

'Yes. She tried to grab me again but only succeeded in pulling out a chunk of my hair. Which she sent, Guaranteed Next Day Delivery, to Ingrid. She wrapped it in a sheet of a local free newspaper, which was her undoing.'

'You didn't put that in the report either.'

'It wasn't relevant at the time.'

'Go on.'

'That's it really. The rest you know.'

We walked on.

'A little running commentary would be helpful,' Patrick said to me.

'Sorry.' I gathered my thoughts for a few moments and then

began. 'Patrick had been missing, right out of touch, for over forty-eight hours when I decided to look for him myself,' I began. 'By the time I had tracked this place down following receipt of the piece of the local newspaper and other info it was much later in the day than it is now and getting dark. I can remember a lot of white flowers in these hedgerows – it was late summer – which sort of lit my way for a short while. This helped but I had to be very careful of passing traffic as, as you can see, there's no pavement or verge.'

'Did you have a map?' Sturrock asked.

'No, there had been no time to buy one.'

'So how did you know this was the right way to go?'

'I didn't. I intended to go across country. I had been given rough directions and had worked out that any farm worth its name, that is, with sufficient land, had to be at the foot of the downs with higher pastures on the slopes. It is, as you'll see.'

After a short while the whole of a shallow, almost secret, valley, a fold in the downs, opened up before us as the ground fell away over to our right. We paused in a gateway for a better view. I knew that all this land, mostly down to pasture and just about as far as the eye could see, belonged to the estate, presumably now rented to local farmers. The farmhouse could just be glimpsed set in the trees at the head of the fold, the barns and other buildings set slightly apart from it.

I continued: 'It was almost dark by the time I reached this spot and as I stood here a couple of lights came on in the house. I was really worried that someone might be keeping watch with binoculars in case the police raided the place so I decided to walk along this road sheltered from view by the hedges as far as possible. The field with the big clump of trees growing in it which you can see over there to your left seemed to be the best low-risk route to use in order to be unobserved.'

We carried on walking at a good pace, a few spots of rain beginning to fall, the road curving gently around to the right. Occasionally a car went past and once a lorry travelling at a stupid speed, forcing us to flatten ourselves into the brambles. Sturrock got her anorak caught up and we had to help release her.

'I was running,' I continued. 'I had a sense of urgency that I can't really explain now. I just wanted to get there.'

'You people must be very fit . . . train all the time,' the DI commented, slightly out of breath.

'I'd had a baby not all that long before and wasn't that fit,' I told her, vividly recollecting blowing like a horse.

She stopped dead. '*Really?*'

'We've three children of our own and two adopted.'

Sturrock frowned. Obviously people like us were not supposed to be distracted by having a family.

EIGHTEEN

After what seemed to be a much longer walk, in increasingly heavy rain, than I remembered we climbed over the gate into the field that had the clump of trees in it. These beeches had been planted in an almost perfect circle and even with just the light cover of newly budding leaves would successfully block the view of our progress from the house.

'I paused here,' I said when we had reached the centre of the ring. 'And tried to make a plan but couldn't think of one.'

'I have to say I'm a little surprised by that,' said, or rather puffed, the DI a little sharply. Perhaps her new-looking walking boots were giving her blisters.

'So I looked up at the stars and prayed,' I added and carried on walking, heading for the outbuildings over to the left, just as I had done the last time. The house – there were hardly any windows visible from here – was sideways on to me and still slightly uphill now. The boundary hedge was as straggly as ever. I bore left as I had done before when I had thought the hedge might be thinner in that direction. It was but there was also a gate. When I reached it, the others a couple of paces behind me, I stopped. Such was the state of the hedge that we had to force aside the vegetation in order to see clearly.

In an undertone I said, 'The whole place is on a much bigger scale than I had imagined. It was fairly dark then but I could just make out the roofs of the buildings.'

The yard was huge and remained cluttered with derelict farm machinery. The range of cowsheds and similar buildings plus one large barn and a smaller one were even more dilapidated by this time, the bare roof beams of the latter silhouetted against the sky reminding me again of the broken ribs of some large animal carcass. The large barn's roof had an even bigger and more ominous sag in it now.

'Someone was smoking,' I said. 'Outside here. I could smell cigarette smoke. Then I saw the tiny red glow as he inhaled. The glow moved jerkily, as if he was nervous. Then he suddenly bolted for the house. I heard shouting in the distance and very shortly afterwards he returned – at least I thought it was the same man – and he had a bottle with him this time. I climbed over the gate.'

The three of us climbed over the gate, very warily as it was wooden and rotting and then walked a short distance into the farmyard, the house not visible from here. Patrick had gone very pale.

I went on: 'There was deep shadow here on the other side of the hedge which, as you can see, has a ditch at its base and I sensed, rather than saw, that there was something in it, almost at my feet.'

'It was one of the bodies, wasn't it?' Sturrock said. 'I don't understand how you could have known it was there if it was as dark as you say.'

'I can't explain it either but it might have been because it was still warm.'

Patrick walked quickly in the opposite direction for a few yards and vomited under the hedge. Then remained where he was, his back to us. I wanted to go to him but did not.

'My first thought was that it was Patrick,' I continued. 'And when I discovered that the corpse was that of a bald man I could only think for a moment that Murphy had pulled out all his hair. Then I found that it couldn't possibly be him as the body had a real right foot.'

'I beg your pardon?' said the DI.

'Patrick was blown up on Special Operations and eventually

lost the lower part of his right leg.' When, understandably, the
DI remained silent I resumed with: 'Then I found another body
and that wasn't Patrick either. The man who was smoking took
a drink from his bottle and belched and from that I knew I was
very close to him now. I think there must have been a glimmer
of moonlight then as I noticed for the first time the stairs on the
barn that gave access to the loft. Someone was coming down
them, very slowly. Then whoever it was disappeared, or seemed
to, but the water barrel at the bottom of the stairs might have
been a little wider. Sometimes when you're trying to see something in the dark your eyes play tricks with you.'

Patrick was still throwing up.

'The man with the bottle now seemed to be facing me. He put
it on the ground and reached into his pocket. My eyes must have
become more used to the dark as I could easily make him out
now. He must have seen me. Then Patrick knifed him and the
gun the man had been holding fell to the ground. He was put
into the ditch with the other two. It was then that I spoke to him.'

'How did you know it was him?'

'I know my husband in the dark.'

Sturrock gazed at me disbelievingly. I left her where she was
and went over to the barrel.

'It still stinks to high heaven,' I called across to her.

She came over.

I said, 'We went up into the loft – I took some of the water
up with me in a fold-up drinking container I had with me and
gave it to Patrick in small amounts plus some Kendal Mint Cake
and chocolate and he quite quickly started to revive. You know
the rest of what happened, before I arrived and afterwards.'

Sturrock wrinkled her nose and moved away a little. 'Do the
tablets take away the smell?'

'Oh, no, just prevent the stuff from making you ill,
probably.'

'He said these men were attacking this building in twos, threes
and even fours.'

'They were. Come up. Be careful, the handrail's missing where
he chucked a couple of them through it.'

This was the first time I had seen the interior of the loft properly
as before I had only risked using the torch for a couple of seconds

at a time to conserve the batteries. The mental picture I had created matched almost exactly what was before me now; the low beam towards the far end that one of the mobsters had practically brained himself on, the trap door in the floor that would once have been used to throw fodder down to the animals below and through which a couple of invaders had succeeded in climbing, the pile of logs and larger chunks of wood to one side of the doorway. The door itself was still missing.

'What are you looking at?' the DI asked as I peered over the pile of wood.

'The bloodstains from where he was knifed in the arm. You can still see them. We hid down here when the gun battle started and I phoned for help.'

I then saw that were drips and smears of blood all over this area of the dusty and straw covered floor. The oil drum with which we had weighted down the trap door was still up here, the pickaxe handle I had helped to drive off the mobsters by the side of it. Rain dripped and trickled though the roof in a far corner where an attempt had been made to gain entry by ripping off the tiles.

'Then,' the DI was saying, 'After hospital treatment for him, you drove home as you feared the gang leader and his girlfriend—'

'Minder,' I corrected. 'She killed for fun.'

'—had gone to Hinton Littlemoor, where you live, to hide in a closed-down pub one of the gang had run as manager. Which they had and you arrested them.'

'Detective Chief Inspector James Carrick officially arrested them. Patrick was at the point of collapse by then.' He had delivered a haymaker to Northwood and dragged him into the pub's office, locking the door. Murphy had fainted when he had sprung the blade of his Italian throwing knife right under her nose, the same knife with which he had killed her two henchmen in the house.

'I see. I think I have it all straight in my mind now.' Sturrock added wryly, 'It must have been the crime scene to end all crime scenes. But the deaths of the three men out there in the yard was still murder. He could have simply rendered them unconscious.'

'And he also stole a pint of milk and a packet of biscuits for us from the house when he went in to look for his Glock before the police arrived,' I said stonily.

We stared at one another and Sturrock dropped her gaze, murmuring, 'I assure you, there's nothing personal in this.'

There were footsteps and Patrick came into view at the top of the stairs. I was instantly brought to mind of the way he had stood exactly in that place at the end of it all; bloodied, almost out on his feet, and yet still exuding the kind of authority that had caused Mick the Kick to accord him a grudging respect and then leave, taking his followers with him.

'I'm going to have a look at the house,' he said and went away again.

We followed, the rain pattering on the hoods of our anoraks.

There was another gate on the far side of the farmyard, newly erected – it had not been there before – fitted with a chain and padlock. It had a large sign affixed to it that intimated that the Keys Estate was private property and trespassers would be prosecuted. Guard dogs were loose, it warned. As a final deterrent barbed wire had been wound around the top bar of the gate, twice.

'That's that then,' Sturrock said.

Patrick said nothing but went back into the yard and, in the dusk, rummaged. He went behind an ancient tractor and I think was sick again. Returning a few minutes later with half a dozen filthy old plastic feed sacks, he slammed them on to the top of the gate and, with all due care, then pushed them on to the front barbs of the wire, stuffing the ends between the wooden bars. Rinsing his hands in a nearby drinking trough he wiped them on his handkerchief.

'If you climb over carefully without dislodging it on the other side you won't get hurt,' he said, gesturing towards his handiwork.

'No,' Sturrock said. 'We need a search warrant.'

'I've no intention of searching the house,' Patrick informed her. 'And bear in mind that this is only a gate to the yard. If you want to leave and not have to go back over the field you'll have to come this way – the main drive's just over there.'

'But the dogs!'

'There aren't any. If there were they would have found us by now.'

Still Sturrock stood there. 'Sorry, I don't like dogs. I've been bitten before.'

Patrick got really impatient with her. 'Look, if there *are* any I'll shoot them for you!'

She threw up her hands in a gesture of despair and success-fully managed the gate. Patrick and I followed and he was the only one to encounter the wire, spiking a finger. He swore, sucking it.

'Tetanus jabs up to date?' I asked, giving him a tissue to wrap around it.

'Too right.'

'Are you OK now?'

'I don't know.'

He wasn't but I desisted with the wifely concerns stuff.

We walked along an overgrown path, a wide strip of rough grass that had probably once been a lawn on either side of it, dense shrubs and trees encircling them. Rubbish lay everywhere, bits of which Patrick and I had stumbled on as we had blundered our way towards the house those months ago. A matter of twenty yards farther on we emerged through a thicket of wild willows and self-sown ash trees into a wider area, once a garden, the house now in full view. It looked smaller than I recollected but my memories of it were vague, just a darker shape against the night sky. Those windows I could see were boarded up.

Patrick manoeuvred the pair of us back into the vegetation and we all paused for a moment as we heard the whoosh of tyres on the nearby wet road as several cars went by.

'That's just an ordinary farm house,' I said. 'To be called an estate the property must have originally been much larger with a big house, a mansion. I'm guessing that it was sold off separately.'

'And the mobsters must have been, or are, hoping to demolish everything here for their hotel complex,' Patrick muttered. 'It must cover at least twenty acres.' And to Sturrock, 'It goes without saying that this place was sealed off as a crime scene for quite a while. What actually was removed, other than obvious things like weapons?'

'Class A and Class B drugs plus bloodstained clothing and other similar potential evidence items,' she answered. 'That's all.'

'No computers or mobile phones?'

'They found one mobile phone, smashed, probably by having been trodden on. I can only guess that the few gang members who got away took any laptops with them. There was a lot of drink but that's not illegal so we couldn't touch it.'

'There were only personal possessions and two hands guns in Northwood and Murphy's car at Hinton Littlemoor.'

I said, 'Could Clement Hamlyn have been here that night or beforehand or even in Bath at the party?'

Patrick stared at me. 'God, what a thought. I didn't see him.'

'If he was, is, part of this empire he could have rolled up here at some stage, drunk himself senseless and was comatose that night somewhere in the house.'

'It's perfectly possible as I was only in a large room at the front for a matter of minutes.' Patrick brooded for a moment and then said, 'Stay right where you are for a moment.' Cautiously, he disappeared into the thicket.

From where I was standing it was possible to peep through the branches to see that no vehicles were parked at the front of the building. Some work appeared to have been begun as a large stack of tree trunks and foliage was just visible in the dim light beyond one corner of the house. Nearer, there were also piles of rubble, timber, and sheets of rusting corrugated iron that suggested outbuildings had been demolished. Perhaps it was those I remembered. The overall effect was of utter desolation.

'I think I should go back,' Sturrock said. 'It'll be quite a long walk down that other road in the dark. I might phone and ask a friend to pick me up.'

'Just wait here until Patrick comes back,' I said.

'There's no need, surely. The drive must start from just over there.'

'Please wait. Now we're here you're our responsibility.'

'As you wish,' she responded stonily.

We stood there for what seemed to be quite a long time and the DI became more restless. Finally, when she appeared to be on the point of leaving, Patrick reappeared and spoke quietly.

'There's a very interesting development on the far side of the house.'

He was still a pale shade of grey.

'Does this concern me at all?' the DI enquired tartly.

'It might. When were the windows boarded up?'

'I believe it was around a month ago.'

'In view of who still appears to own this place I think you ought to remain with us for your own safety. You interrupted me before when I was about to remind you that this house is a criminal bolt-hole. Daniel Coates, wanted by the Met and in connection with Operation Captura, has a boat registered as being owned by the same company, Jones Enterprises. Is that enough evidence to keep you here?'

Sturrock nodded. 'All right.'

He turned. 'Move as quietly as possible.'

'Why, is someone here?'

'There's a car parked at the back.'

'Perhaps I ought to call up help.'

'No, this is going to be done properly.'

Thunderstuck, she turned to look at me. I shrugged. She wouldn't understand.

It was comparatively easy to reach the other side of the house as, after getting through the various thickets of self-sown trees and long grass we were able to drop down into a sunken lane. It was inches deep in a mixture of mud and ancient manure in places but even in the gloom we made quick progress and soon arrived, having climbed a bank, at the entrance to the drive. With all due care, we crossed it, finding ourselves in what was quite likely a continuation of the same historic way but it was not so deep and muddy here. It met another track rutted by vehicles which both petered out at a farm gate, this a sturdy metal one clearly in fairly constant use. Patrick opened it and led the way. The farm's boundary, an old brick wall here, was on our left. At a section that was broken down we climbed over it at the rear of a very large new-looking wooden shed. From my limited view – there was very little room to move here – it appeared to be at least three-and-a-half times longer than it was wide. There were no windows on this side.

Making our way through tussocks of coarse grass and thistles we reached the end of the shed that turned out to be the rear. There were no windows here either. It was a very cheaply-made building, staple-gunned together, the wood full of knots, the sawn edges of the overlapping thin slats rough and splintery. One of these had been levered up at a join until the staples lifted. Patrick now got hold of it again and bent it up and back, muffling the sound with his body, until it snapped. There was now a hole roughly a foot long by three inches wide.

'Take a look,' he invited Sturrock in a whisper.

'I hope you can put that back,' she muttered and peered through. 'It's a boat.'

'How many outboard motors?'

'Eight. *Eight?*'

'It's a RIB, a rigid inflatable boat. This one's a stealth boat. They can do around eighty knots and outrun everything else on the water. As you can see it's painted black or dark grey and is a rather unusual shape. That makes it practically invisible to radar. You must know what these have been used for.'

'Drugs running.'

'That's right, from North Africa to Spain. It was rumoured a while back that one had been glimpsed in the English Channel but I don't think it was this one as it appears to be brand new, smaller that the one Ingrid and I saw in Cannes. This is only around thirty feet long.'

Sturrock moved aside for me to have a look. There was just sufficient light within, what there was coming through three small windows in the other long side, to make out the boat, the stern of which was facing me. The smell of petrol wafted through the hole, no doubt emanating from a row of jerry cans along the wall beneath them. What looked like a very large tarpaulin was dumped in a large heap at this end, the top of it just beneath our spyhole.

'The next move is up to you,' Patrick told Sturrock.

'I will need to consult with the DCI,' she responded, sounding surprised.

'Will he ask you what the hell you're doing here and anyway see him about it in the morning?'

'Probably.'

'If you'd rather forget about that I'm happy to escort you to the road if you want to leave now.'

'What are you going to do?'

'Find out who's in the house.'

'But . . . I can't just walk away and leave you here. I mean, you wouldn't actually need me but . . .' She petered out a little sadly.

'So you're willing to accompany the Serious Organised Crime Agency in a surveillance operation.'

'Oh, yes.'

I kept a very straight face. She would be able to write that in her report, no bother.

Sturrock and I stayed out of sight while Patrick looked around the corner of the shed. The rain had eased off, a gap in the clouds making the sky a little lighter. Patrick stayed where he was and I could hear the strange way he was breathing: he was still suffering from nausea.

'Sorry,' he mumbled. Then quickly came back into hiding as the sound of another vehicle approached. The gears crashed as it swung into the drive, too fast, the tyres squealing and then the engine roared as though the wheels on one side had gone on to the grass and skidded. The headlights swung away over towards the house and as it did so there was brighter illumination, as if security lights had come on. After a brief silence following the car coming to a halt a car door slammed.

Patrick took another look and swore softly. 'It's Hamlyn!' he exclaimed.

'*What?*' I simply could not believe what he had said.

'There's no mistaking him. God, he must have escaped somehow.' In an undertone he explained to the DI who Hamlyn was.

'We ought to arrest him,' she said.

'That might be difficult.' He turned to me as another door slammed, this one of those on the house by the sound of it. 'I'm going to make for that tree over there before I do anything else. Watch from here and cover me if you can, don't move away from here. I mean it! Don't move from here!'

Then he had gone and, whoever was over by the house and whatever they were doing, they did not notice him.

I peered around the corner of the shed. Already aware that some kind of security lighting had been activated by the arrival of the car I was unprepared for how bright it was, the yard to the rear of the house lit in a circle of light, like a stage. Clement Hamlyn was standing facing the building talking to another man who must have emerged from it, the latter carrying a firearm that looked like a sub-machine gun. They were talking in low voices, not loud enough for me to hear what was being said.

I could see Patrick by the tree, this a mature specimen with a usefully wide trunk. Then he moved again, bent low, obviously endeavouring to get himself into a more favourable position and went from my sight. The actual choreography of this kind of thing is a mystery to me, I simply do not understand the tactics of warfare. His one huge advantage was that those by the house would be virtually blinded by the blazing security lights, unable to see anything in the near darkness beyond.

'You bloody animal, you can't deny it, you raped her!' the man with the gun suddenly yelled. I was fairly sure it was Daniel Coates.

'How was I to know she was your trollop?' Hamlyn's voice boomed back.

'This is Sonya we're talking about, not some tart I picked up in the street! She rang me and told me you'd not only raped her but pushed her out of the car in some God-awful slum.'

'Look, all I want is somewhere to stay for a couple of days.'

'Not only that, you took it into your thick head to act alone and blackmail the Trents, forcing them to let you use their house to hide stuff in. What the hell for? You know damned well I have plenty of storage. And you killed Hereward, didn't you?'

'He was bloody useless!'

'Get out of my sight! This is where you and I part company – for good.'

'At least let me have a drink!'

'You're still not listening. I wish to God I'd shot you on the boat instead of just making you grovel for your money. Clear out or you'll end up in that nice little hole in the ground over there.' The weapon jerked, presumably pointing at where it was for a second or so.

'Shall I call up help?' Sturrock hissed from behind me.

'There's no time,' I said. 'Shut up.'

'Just give me a bottle and I'll go away,' Hamlyn pleaded hoarsely. 'We used to be chums, Danny. You know that.'

'You used to do as you were told but now you're a complete shit!' Coates bawled.

Patrick's voice cut through Hamlyn starting to reply.

'Armed police! You're under arrest!' he shouted. 'Put that weapon down and lie face down on the ground or we open fire!'

The weapon made a quiet but rapid coughing sound and Clement Hamlyn was flung backwards as though a rag doll. It carried on firing, Coates spraying the entire area before him in a large parabola with hundreds of shots scything through the greenery. I flung myself down, succeeding in thumping Sturrock on the head with the palm of my hand as I did so, the pair of us ending up more or less flat on the ground. Bullets tore and smashed into the woodwork above our heads, showering us with splinters. Seconds later I crawled to the end of the shed to look out but was forced to stand upright again in order to see as long grass blocked my view.

Gingerly – he probably could not see anything as it was almost dark – Coates was walking over to the spot roughly where I had last spotted Patrick, only a matter of fifty yards from me. I heard him say something; he then quickly aimed the weapon as he appeared to detect a sudden movement and fired a short burst.

Two further shots rang out.

I ran to the spot where Coates had fallen. He was moving, trying to reach out to where the weapon lay on the grass near him. A matter of yards away, I put another shot into the ground near him and he froze.

There was a rustling sound and Patrick appeared close by. 'No, you couldn't see me,' he said to Coates. 'That was just my jacket.'

'Are you hurt?' I asked him.

'No, he fired too high.'

Sturrock arrived, out of breath for at least two reasons.

'I've broken all my own rules,' Patrick told her, flashing his little torch over the man on the ground. 'I normally shoot to kill a man armed with a weapon like this as they can cause untold carnage even when dying and it's a huge risk to try to knock the thing out of their hands. Get up, Danny boy, you fell over on impact and it's only your hands that hurt.'

Coates scrambled to his feet, muttering and nursing his right hand.

'Nice boat in that shed over there,' Patrick drawled.

'I like power boats,' Coates mumbled.

'For a new project running drugs from Northern France to somewhere not too far from here?'

No answer.

'I have news for you. The cops and navies are using choppers to catch them now. Well, here you are, Detective Inspector,' Patrick went on. 'Daniel Coates – far too valuable as a source of info about serious international crime than to be in a body bag right now.'

'He's SOCA's suspect, surely,' she said.

'But you're the senior officer present. Strictly speaking, I'm only a constable.'

'Then please take charge of that weapon.'

'It's wrecked and, as I'm sure you're aware, is a Heckler and Koch MP5 SD, the last letters meaning that it's silenced.'

'It occurs to me that if I'd called up help he could have shot them all to pieces with it as they arrived.'

Oh, yes.

NINETEEN

'I missed,' I said. 'It could have resulted in your death.'

'Did you fire from by the shed?'

'Yes, my husband told me to stay there and for once I did as I was told.'

Patrick was stretched out luxuriously on one of the sofas in the hotel bar – we virtually had the place to ourselves – a tot of his favourite single malt at his elbow. 'It was a long shot in next to no light for a hand gun. I'm glad you didn't hit him.'

Not surprisingly, Hamlyn was dead, having been shot several

times from point-blank range. Only within the past hour had we been informed what had happened. The man's health having apparently taken a turn for the worse, he had collapsed and been taken to hospital with two of the remand staff to keep an eye on him. But it had all been pretence and as soon as the ambulance doors had been opened on arrival he had made a run for it, knocking the heads together of his escort. Exactly what followed had not yet been established but at some stage he had stolen a car and, presumably, driven it straight to Sussex where he knew there was shelter and hopefully, at the top of his list, alcohol.

We had left DI Sturrock to deal with the aftermath as soon as her reinforcements had arrived. She had been in reflective mood but I guessed relieved at not having a loose cannon around any longer and had arranged for us to be given a lift back into Steyning. A hot shower and fresh clothing had never felt so good.

'How long have you had that dress?' Patrick asked, emerging from a reverie.

'About five years. Why?'

'I can't remember seeing it before, that's all.'

'I wore it around a week ago.'

'Oh.'

'Are you hungry?'

'Absolutely starving.'

We went in to dinner.

The following morning Patrick received a phone call from Jessica Sturrock. She had been contacted by Greenway – 'So pleasant for a commander!' – who had congratulated her on her arrest of Coates and gone on to say that he would be in touch with her senior officers. Sturrock had reported that the suspect had received hospital treatment for two broken fingers and that she would await orders. She then told Patrick that she had pointed out that she would not have been able to achieve what she had without the support of one of the commander's own teams. Greenway had brushed aside her thanks, saying it was his personnel's job: support. All Patrick had to do now was attend the police station and arrest Coates on behalf of SOCA, each police authority dealing with their own specific crimes.

Eventually the DI would write her report on the Keys Estate

Case. In her summing up she would state that she could only reiterate the conclusions of previous findings having visited the site herself, and with the help of the two officers of SOCA who had originally been present, reconstructed what had happened. To them she was particularly grateful.